# WILLOW
# BORN

### BY
## SHANNA MILES

RochelleandReed.com

ISBN (ebook) 978-0-9986380-03
ISBN (print) 978-0-9986380-2-7

# PART ONE
## I'm Beginning to See The Light

*Lake Murray, South Carolina One Summer Night*

The imp prowls anxiously behind the ancient Willow tree, his muscles rippling under his too-tight feline skin. He knows the old witch isn't as skilled as he needs her to be, but the pickings these days are slim. She's the best of what's left.

Warm breeze scatters scorched sections of the day's newspaper, creating tiny cyclones around the bonfire. A photograph of a young girl with thin dreadlocks floats on dusty air before lighting and turning to ash.

Miss Collins picks up her bottle of hooch. She drinks quickly, spitting the rest into the flames. The cat,who is anything but a cat, chases the darkness to keep hidden. Shielding his emerald eyes from the flares.

"They call them 'Dolls', Lord! 'Dolls'! It is the coven who hears their cries." The old witch wails into the darkness as starlight dribbles like sweat through the boughs of the tree.

Herb perfumed smoke rises thickly to the heavens. This is what he's been waiting over half a century for. This night. This spell.

"Lord, fourteen precious girls have gone missing, then dead. My task is great, but your mercy is greater. I come to you, a daughter of Odion, the first of our kind!"

At this, she pulls the tree-shaped dagger from her waistband. Without taking her eyes from the sky, she slices open her palm and flings the first drops of blood into the flames. Glittering blue flares erupt where blood meets ash.

"Yes!" he hisses to himself as the fire stills and ceases to flicker, freezing as time slows and the wall between heaven and earth burns away. She recites the names of her mother, and her mother's mother, and her mother's mother going back nearly 300 years to the first Willow born witch, Odion.

The good sister sways, and her movements slow as her heels slide on their own accord in the sand. The right movements and words come out sleepily and soaked with liquor.

"I am the daughter of Odion. I make my claim and bid the angels hear me!"

She mumbles in a monotone, falling into a trance that lasts for hours, lasts until the final embers of the fire die out, lasts until the moon drifts into slumber and the sun wakes, lasts until she finally, finally gives up, and she is sure that she has failed.

# CHAPTER ONE

I died. I am sure of this. There was a fire. I can still feel life, my soul, slipping away like a large fish in my too small hands.

How long has it been?

Blood rushes past my ears to the beat of my racing heart and the urge to breathe grips me. I connect brain to lungs, lungs to mouth and open it only to swallow a mouthful of water. I try again and get another gush of water, ice cold and dirty. My brain makes the final connections from arms to toes, and I am thrashing. I am drowning.

Electricity rages inside my chest, and it licks at my throat to scrape at my brain. I fight harder and will myself to see. My arms reach in every direction, and with the farthest tip of my right hand, I graze the surface of the water.

The air blows in cool gusts across my face, and the water smells of earth and sand and growing things.

Home.

Echoes of people ride on the wind along with music playing and lots of laughter. It tinkles like jingle bells across the water still warm from the summer sun. If it were a food it would be powdered sugar, landing like snowflakes on my eyelids, on my tongue and in my ears. *God, I'm hungry.*

In my exhaustion, I can't even attempt to put up my shields.. Even if I did, I'd still be able to see the swirling cloud of pink and sunset orange emotions hovering over the lake house on the faraway shore like a selective storm atop the gates of Oz. I can see this because I'm an empath. All my life I've been able to see emotions. I can also feel them, so much so that if I'm not careful they overwhelm me. Make me do things I don't want to do. Say things I don't want to say. The sight of that roiling tempest of joy and anxiety is the last thing I want to swim into.

I won't make it anyway. I'm going to run out of time, my burning muscles are telling me so. Soon my puppy paddle crumples into little more than a sad half-dead dog splashing.

About the time when my arms decide to give up, I feel a pang of nervousness pull at my stomach and then knot. Someone is close.

"Hold on!"

It's a man's voice, but I can't tell where it's coming from. I'm tired. Really tired and I need to keep paddling.

The faraway sound of splashing paddles fills my ears and then closer, right before a life preserver knocks me in the face. Hard.

"Ah, man. I'm sorry. Grab the doughnut, and I'll pull you in!"

My lip is bleeding, but all I can think about is how grateful I am to stop paddling. The doughnut is sweet relief. The blood, icing.

### 

"You think she's an angel?" whispers the other boy, excitedly.

"What? That is literally the dumbest thing you've ever said to me. I think angels can save themselves from drowning. Besides, she doesn't have wings," he says flatly. "She must've been at the party," the familiar voice speculates.

"Naw, I would've noticed her. And you don't know that they all have wings. They can look just like us," he hisses. "You think she's one of the missing girls?"

I can only catch snippets of their conversation. It's taking me awhile to wake up, and the anxiety in the room is pressing down on me as heavy as a boulder. A sickly yellow pallor appears behind my eyes.

Someone pulls the blanket tighter around my middle and picks something prickly off my face. The brush of skin is electrified ice, so cold it burns and radiates so that even my shoulders know I've been touched. He is gentle though, as if he doesn't want to wake me.

"What are you gonna do with her?" the voice spits. Anger, long simmering and oddly powerful scratches at my mind like a wool sweater, prickly and cloying, I cut it off quickly with my shield, but I'm only able to shut one of them down. I'm still getting soft waves of concern from Mr. Familiar. It sits lightly on my skin and sinks down. It's calming and I'm better for it. Otherwise, I might be a nervous wreck.

If I had sense, I would be a nervous wreck. I shouldn't be here, right? This is dangerous, isn't it?

As I come to, I can feel Mr. Familiar's emotions move from concern to anger and frustration and it rolls over me in a multi-colored fog behind my eyelids, all with that unfamiliar electricity tickling my spine. It's too much too soon. I try to shield myself, but it's not working with him.

"She's opening her eyes," says Mr. Familiar softly.

I sit up slowly, pressing my body firmly into the cushions of a white leather couch, creating as much distance as I can muster between me and this stranger.

He's handsome. Almost too handsome, and the first thing I notice is honey. Dark, wildflower honey colored skin, thick sandy-brown hair shaved to an odd curly peak, and hazel eyes that sparkle like amber. Shocks of blonde shoot through his curls and look so yellow as to be fake, but the calluses on his hand tell me he'd never waste time on such a thing. That and the jaw so sharp it could chop wood.

I've been quiet too long. I never know what to say at the best of times. My tongue doesn't tie; it just sits like a dead fish. Now is no different. Amber eyes rest on me and brim with a relief that seems too personal for a stranger. Tiny dew-like beads of charcoal-colored worry collect on my boat captain's upper lip. He hands me a mug from the coffee table behind him.

"Hey. Drink this," he says softly.

It is full of something sweet and warm. Black Tea with lemon. I blink hard and try to seem grateful even though I don't have the words. The muscles in my face twitch, and I hope I'm smiling sweetly.

I inadvertently graze his arm when I try to tip the mug back, and a shock of electricity shoots through my arm. I yelp and a bit of the tea spills on his shirt. Twice. That feeling. This has never happened before.

He winces. "It's cool. It's alright. I got it."

He stands up to his full height and slips off his tank top. He's not short, but not really what I would call tall, but good Lord, he is muscular. He looks like a jungle cat when he goes to pick up a replacement from a hamper nearby. He's still wearing the damp khaki shorts he must have carried me in. Dark water spots color the space where thigh meets hip. Sculpted boy hips. I should stop staring.

He has to nudge past the other boy who has been staring from the stairwell the entire time.

"Get out and do what I told you to do," he says firmly, but lowly to the other boy.

The other boy, the white boy, looks to be too big and too old to let someone push him around. His eyes are red, the same as his cheeks, and his short brown hair has been mussed a bit. He's 280 if he is a pound, but from the way he walks I can tell he doesn't have much heart. He's weak; the kind of guy who walks away from a good fight and lies about it. Without a word, he trudges up the stairs quickly never really meeting my eyes. If it's his house, why would he let him talk to him like that?

"You can't talk to him like that." I murmur hoarsely as familiar boy makes his way over and fixes me with a brotherly stare. I'm the little sister who's gotten the flu.

"Oh, I can't? Why's that?" he asks, not unkindly.

"It's his house. H-he could call the law," I stammer nervously.

"Well if he does, I'm sure they'd be confused, because this is my house," he answers. "Why did you think it was his?"

"I-I just… well, he's w-white." As soon as I say it, the words sound stupid, old and ridiculous in my mouth. I don't know why.

He chuckles softly. "Wow, you must have hit your head pretty hard."

"I'm sorry. I don't mean to offend. I'm s-s-orry," I stutter.

"Don't worry about it. I'm Matt." He presents his hand for me to shake. I cough into my free hand as a cover and nod my head instead. I never touch people. Ever. Emotions are the most powerful when passed skin-to-skin.

"I'm Colette. Th-thank you for helping me."

"Thanks for letting me see you naked. Most girls don't really let me get that far on the first date."

I gasp, drawing in each molecule of breath as I quickly look under my blanket and flames erupt in my cheeks.

*Sweet Jesus, where are my panties?*

He's dressed me in a wrinkled cotton shirt and some flannel pajama bottoms that are three or four-sizes too big.

"S-sorry. Just kidding. I say stupid things when I'm nervous. I mean, full disclosure, I did look, but I knew you'd be embarrassed so I dressed you."

I want to be mad, and if my shields were working I would be, but he is so calm that I can't fight it. I feel what he's feeling. His calming breath calms me. That irritating mosquito bite on his leg irritates me. But that burning, why is it getting stronger? Why aren't my shields working?

I was nearly eight years old before I learned how to create a mental block that shielded me from people's emotions. Avoidance is the best defense. At least that's what Mama used to say. I don't think she anticipated situations like this.

"You okay? You passed out earlier," he says, concerned. I do feel a bit woozy, and my head is swimming. I feel a knot on my head, and my fingertips snag on burs in my hair. Not only do I feel horrible, but now I know I look it.

He notices the change in my face. "It's not so bad," he murmurs affectionately. "You just need a shower… and your own clothes and …a comb." And then he bursts out laughing. Again, I want to be angry. I actually try, but my shields are useless, so I start laughing too.

Just then I hear a door open and slam abruptly so that the pictures on the wall jangle. Chairs slide against the floor, and the sound of the screeching assaults us. Matt springs up, staring into nothing as he listens. I listen too.

His brow is furrowed, and soon I see the ghost of a decision being made flit across his face. He walks quickly to the dresser pressed against the wall. As he opens it, I realize it's the gun closet. He loads quickly.

"Stay here," he whispers. "No matter what you hear, don't come up stairs. Might be Thumpers."

I don't have time to nod before he flicks the switch on the wall, covering me in darkness.

A minute passes, and I think about slipping out of the glass patio door. I could disappear into the darkness and escape. But I don't know where I am. How will I find my way home? I've never even been to the post office by myself.

Indecision and fear bloom at the base of my neck, making my ears feel clogged. A few minutes go by, and Matt doesn't return. Finally, I decide.

I'm going to run.

I fling off my blanket and tip toe to the sliding door. The door handle is ice in my grip. I glance back at the stairwell and listen intently. Still nothing. I unlock the door and take a deep breath. I give myself until the count of three.

One. Two. I pull the door open with a strong jerk and a high pitched beeping fills the room. A woman's voice calls out from nowhere, "Basement door open. Basement door open."

I slam the door back and the beeping stops. I look around for the woman quickly, but hear footsteps slowly descending down the stairs. I'm still searching when the light flicks on and I hear a familiar voice in my head.

*Dear One!*

# CHAPTER TWO

*Tell the boy you have a cousin. It is only a half-lie, so it is a half-truth.*

Raphael.

Light spills into the room as Matt flicks on the light.

"I think I almost shot your cousin," he says as he sets the shotgun down on the right side of the stairs, but his movements are jerky and his words come out slow like he's got cotton in his mouth.

Raphael's voice, as clear as it has always been, rings familiarly inside my head. Telepathy or insanity, I don't know. I am sure that Matt hears nothing as Raphael appears behind him on the stairs.

"You can see him?" I ask cautiously. In human form Raphael has chosen to look about 5'5" with a jet-black Bob dyed electric blue at the ends. Most of the time, he appears to me as a shifty-eyed tabby cat. All of the time, I'm the only one who can see him.

"Him?" Matt asks, crinkling his brow.

"Hi!" Raphael says out loud and perkily through super shiny glossed lips. "You must just be all tore up, girl. Daddy knows you were in his special liquor cabinet after bible study."

His t-shirt reads "Flirt", and he looks like the kind of girl I was raised to never be. Matt is clearly confused…as he should be. I am confused.

Raphael is my imaginary friend. At least I thought he was imaginary.

At first, Matt keeps looking from me to Raphael. His head rocks from me to him like he's watching a tennis match, but soon his motions slow to a crawl. He stares out into the room with an unfocused glare, his eyes seeing nothing. Jaw slack, his eyes glaze over.

I wave a hand in front of his face. It's like he's in a trance or maybe time has stopped. Maybe this is some weird version of purgatory or Hell. I don't think I've done anything so bad as to go to Hell.

"Is he going to be all right?" I ask and take a long hard disbelieving look at Raphael. "He can see you."

"He'll be fine. As an added bonus, I'll even let him remember you were here," he says in the flirty girl voice he's affected.

He walks over to me, side stepping red plastic cups on the way, and gives me a big hug. He smells of sugar and bread flour.

"I've missed you," he says in his regular voice. "Good to have you back."

He picks up a coil of my ratty hair and clucks his tongue.

I'm stunned for a second and then recover. "Are we really going to talk about my hair?"

"Of course not, clearly you must know what it looks like. If it feels half as bad as it looks then, well, you know…"

"What am I doing here Raphael? What's happened to me?"

If I ever had a grip on reality it's unraveling. I died I know this and yet I'm standing in this basement dressed in a strange boys clothes. I'm dreaming. That's what this is.

He shakes his head as if I've asked a question that irritates him and bounds up the stairs. We've left Matt staring into the darkness. My feet hesitate in mid-air for the slightest of seconds. He did help me. He didn't have to. My hesitation doesn't last long. I follow like a good girl. I always do as I'm bid.

"Let's go," Raphael says brightly as we burst into a room covered in stuffed ducks, deer and other woodland animals.

"Where?" I ask.

"You are going to your new home," he chirps. We quickly make our way upstairs and past more slack-jawed teenagers. I don't see the boy from earlier, though I could have missed him, we're moving so fast. We walk out of the house and into the night air.

A boy is sitting on the porch with a cup in his hand, frozen, but not asleep. Raphael whispers into his ear, and he moves. Raphael follows so I follow too, all the way to the boy's car where we strap ourselves in. Another whispered instruction, and we're on our way.

"I'm dreaming aren't I?" I ask.

"No, Dear one," he replies.

"But I died."

"You did," he replies matter-of-factly. The boy drives on like a servant, blinking slowly every few seconds.

"You're imaginary," I remind him. I say it as if by saying it, all of this will fall away, and I'll wake up, like telling yourself you're dreaming inside the dream cancels out the crazy.

Raphael leans over the front seat and looks at me with his teenage girl's face. "Oh, Darling."

Doesn't he know that bass timbre out of that glossy mouth is frightening?

"You are going to your *new* home. Your mother is dead. She has been dead for a very long time. It is my job to help you get settled again."

My breath catches in my throat, and I clench my fists digging my nails into my palms as the tears quickly fall. I knew this. I don't know how I knew. But I knew as soon as I took my first breath in the lake. The air smelled different, wrong somehow.

I am not dead, but my mother is. I am not going back to my old life. These are facts. I need to keep track of what is real.

"What are you?" I ask calmly, ready to accept whatever may spill from his mouth.

"I've always been. Some call me a familiar, but your Mama just called me friend," he replies.

I sit for a long time and think about that. Mama never chastised me for playing with Raphael, even when I got far too old for an imaginary friend.

"Am I immortal?" I ask. I stare into Raphael's foreign eyes and wait to fall apart when he answers. I want to be strong, but I'm tired.

"No," he says seriously.

"What's wrong with me then?"

*You have been apart from the body for some time. One with the universal consciousness. Here and not here. There will be things you know, but have no memory of learning and others that will be completely new to you. Your mother's death is not news to you. In a way, you mourned her long ago.*

"What on earth are you talking about?" I snap. You're a cat! Universal consciousness? I'm sure I'm dreaming. I just need to figure out how to wake up.

"Mortals," he hisses as he rolls his teenage eyes and turns to the hypnotized boy. "I don't know why I even try."

We come to a stop at a grand house on a quiet street with brick walkways, rippled and broken by roots from the ancient magnolia trees that line the street. The closed shutters make the house look like its sleeping with peeling paint for eyelashes.

"Here," he replies.

We get out of the car, leaving the boy drooling and staring in the front seat as we walk through the filigreed wrought iron fence. There's a bird fashioned at the top of it that looks like it was frozen in place just before it was to fly away. It squeaks when I swing it open. The sound stops my momentum but Raphael nudges me. Dry leaves crunch under my bare feet and acorns dig into the arches. I pause again. I'm noticing too much. Dread is here, lurking behind the twin crepe myrtle trees in the yard. This is not a dream.

"What am I doing here?"

"Standing in the dark about to catch your death."

"That's just it, Raphael. I *was* dead. Now, I'm not. I've been waiting to wake up this entire time. I'm not, am I?" I'm whispering fiercely and the irritation that floats over Raphael's head like a ghostly halo softens to pity. He waves a hand towards the porch steps.

"Sit down."

The porch is solid and wide like Mama had always dreamed of having with big cement flower pots full of dead leaves and twigs flanking the steps. Raphael takes a seat on the first one. I sit next to him as a breeze rustles my hair. I feel as if I can hear a whisper or a groan but I can't tell which.

"You've always known you were special. Your mother knew it, and it scared her. She never let you walk ten feet out of her sight."

"She was just protecting me," I protest.

"She stifled you."

"She loved me."

"She was afraid of you!" he argues.

I bite my lip in anger at what I know is true.

"Don't misunderstand. She was mostly afraid for you. It was the beginning of a dark time. She had good reason," he offers.

"Did…" I pause, afraid to say the words, and afraid at the answer. "Did… Am I the reason she's dead?"

Raphael wraps me in his arms and squeezes hard. Love pulses through me, and it makes my heart race and head spin. He whispers in my ear.

"Your mother loved you so much that she would do more than kill for you, more than die for you. She would give up her soul for you. You are not responsible for her death."

I open my mouth to speak, and then close it again.

Raphael's face is blank, and he goes inhumanly still. The pupils of his eyes bleed out into the area around them so they're just shining black orbs in that pretty girlish face. He's frozen for almost a minute before he blinks and smiles as if nothing's happened.

"Let's go in!" he says brightly and stands up.

"What?"

Dust escapes into the air as his feet settle on the second step.

"We were just talking about Mama, about how I died. Aren't you—"

He cuts me off.

"Plenty of time for that later. I want to give you a tour before I go."

"Go? Where are you going?" I know I must sound hysterical.

*I cannot stay. You know the rules.*

I remember with ever more rising dread that Raphael was never in human form very long. He always changed back into a cat after a few hours. He'd slink around the house now and then, but he may be gone for days or even weeks without word.

"Who's going to take care of me? What am I supposed to do here? I don't know why I'm here. I don't know who or even what I am?"

Raphael laughs without humor and unlocks the door. He flicks the switch and light spills out from the inside, falling on me like a stage lamp.

"Collette."

All he's said is my name, but the implication is very much, "Get in this house or else."

I don't move.

Again his eyes go black, and a knot builds in my stomach, but I stand my ground. What is the worst that he could do? I've already died once.

"You can't leave," I whimper.

His voice rumbles with otherworldly authority as he speaks; his features looking ever more feline as the minutes tick by.

"It is not my place to tell you who you are. There are those who are better equipped for it. Here."

He reaches into his pocket and hands me a folded and yellowed envelope in my mother's handwriting.

"She gave that to me before...well, you know."

I want to say that I don't have a choice, that there is nowhere else for me to go, and Mama taught me that we always have a choice. Even if the situation is life or death, we have a choice. I finger the envelope in my hand, afraid of what it might say. She knew this was going to happen or she wouldn't have written it. She knew Raphael was real.

I look up and see the sky, dark as ink, a liquid blanket of impenetrable blackness that covers everything, but the stars who refuse to be snuffed out. They are laughing at me, at how I know so very little.

I close my eyes and ask Mama for strength and a whistling fills my ears. When I open them, Raphael is gone, well, not really. He is no longer the flirty girl; instead, he slithers around a pair of glittered snow boots. He cocks his furry head toward the open door of the house. I sigh.

He leads me inside, and I close the door, sliding under the weight of sleep to the floor.

Mama wrote this.

I slide open the envelope weathered by I don't even know how many years. It's a page from Mama's bible. Isaiah, Chapter 34. She's written on it like it was stationery. The instruction is simple.

*Get thee to a church.*

-Mama

# CHAPTER THREE

Get thee to a church? Mama doesn't even talk like that. What does that even mean?

I turn it over and over in my head and finally decide it means she just wants me to be a good girl. Prayer, right? That's what I need.

When I woke up yesterday, it was nearly noon and too late for church anyway. I told myself that this is a second chance, a gift and a new adventure. I almost believed it. But, the space in my mind between uncertainty and excitement is wide as an ocean. There is the possibility of something I've never really had.

Friends.

True to form, Raphael, even in cat form was gone. I'm sure I'll see him soon enough, and this time he will have time for more questions. He left a note on the kitchen table and a few things for me, including a trunk full of completely inappropriate clothes. To his credit, he did make preparations like he said.

Summer, the niece of my lawyer (I have a lawyer now), came to pick me up and introduced me to her uncle, apparently council to the supernatural. We spent almost the entire day in his office which just happened to be a stifling trailer outside Blythewood. That was…interesting, but today? Today is downright scary. It's my first day of school.

"Those gloves are super cute by the way," Summer shouts over some god-awful noise she says is called hip-hop.

I pick at my gloves with my fingernails. They're one of the few things Raphael left for me, my armor. Skin to skin contact is too intense. I get the full brunt of the emotions from whoever I'm touching is feeling, and not just the most prominent ones, but the buried depression and simmering anger people learn how to hide, even from themselves.

I entertain the idea of shaking hands with girls from all over the city, smiling and talking about books, but let the dream thin and blow away in the wind whipping in from the car window.

"Thanks," I reply nervously.

She thinks I'm nervous because I'm a former home-schooled student who is new to town. This is my back story. Uncle Silas spoon fed it to me yesterday in his office while Summer sat outside, well after he broke the news that I've been dead for over half a century. At this little bit of news, I couldn't even cry. I'm still holding out a mustard seed of hope that I'll wake up from this nightmare.

We pull up to a sprawling campus that emerges like a great ant colony as we crest a hill. A few adults are congregated at the gates with picket signs that read: *Repent!* in bold thick letters. One of them points a weird flickering box in our direction. A few of them eye me with crazed expressions as we cruise to the parking lot.

"What's that all about?" I ask.

She shakes her head. "Don't mind them. *Thumpers.* They can't come onto official school grounds. Resource officers keep 'em out."

I nod as if I know what she's talking about as we drive around to the back of the campus. The clouds of emotion are so thick over the building that I imagine it as a battleground in the midst of a great paint war. I nervously twist my tree-shaped cross pendant between my thumb and forefinger, an old habit. Uncle Silas also returned my necklace, my birthday necklace to me. Only God knows how he got his hands on it. It is the only thing, outside of my own body, that remains of my old life.

"Don't be too nervous, okay. It looks worse than it actually is," she says as she eases the wheezing clunker into a space in the underclassmen parking lot. Can you imagine it? Teenagers with cars. So many that there have to be different parking lots!

She's trying to be reassuring, but I can tell that she's nervous too. A toad green pallor seeps out of her pores and covers her skin as slick as the film on the back of a frog. We're early so that we can avoid the crowds.

I hate crowds.

"Okay, I'm going to take care of a little business and then walk you to the front office to check in. Uncle Silas said you were registered last week."

Last week? Irritation and tension battle in my chest and burn. Raphael knew I'd reappear as far back as last week?

Summer opens the door, and I follow suit. A quick count to four and a deep breath later I'm standing beside her as she opens the trunk of her car and pulls a broomstick out to hold up the hatch. Brown paper lunch bags are all arranged neatly in cardboard boxes.

"What's this?"

She smiles down at me. Summer's what some people call willowy. Her strawberry blonde hair is incredibly long and fantastically curly, almost as curly as mine. She tucks a strand behind her ear and whispers.

"I think I told you my Mom was an herbalist, so I'm kinda into the same thing. I sell lotions and face cream and stuff on the side."

A girl in a pair of overalls walks up and gives her a hug, slipping a twenty dollar bill in Summer's pocket in the process.

When they part the girl starts talking robotically and a little too loud.

"Those cupcakes you made last month were delicious. I'm sure my sister will love these cookies. You should sell them at lunch."

Summer winks and replies, "This batch is so much better than the last. Tell your sister I said, Hi."

The girl turns to leave, and I'm sure the confusion is made plain on my face.

Summer giggles. "I know. It's like a drug deal. I can't technically sell on campus because the pimple creams are like prescription grade. I gotta work in code. See it's like this…"

She's about to go on when a football flies between us and crashes into the trunk.

"What the hell!?" she yells.

"Sorry!" A boy's voice calls from off in the distance. Summer tosses the ball on the ground, and I help her check the bags for broken merchandise.

We're opening and closing bags furiously when a burning sensation starts to build in my spine. It's an odd feeling, just like the one I had on Saturday night. It gets hotter, and my hand instinctively goes to my back to rub it out of existence. I'm still bent over when I hear his voice.

"Hey, Summer, aren't you going to introduce me to your new friend?"

My breath catches. Mr. Familiar.

"Introduction my ass. You almost killed all my product with your stupid ball."

I turn and lock eyes with my rescuer. I don't remember him being this tall, but I have to tilt my head to look into his eyes. His lips curl in a knowing smile, but uncertainty bleeds into the whites of his eyes. He's nervous too.

Summer blows out a deep breath. "I should put you on my shit list for this."

"Aww don't be like that," he says shifting his focus from me to her.

"You and all your old teammates," she spits pointing her finger into his chest.

He doubles back as if the digit were a sword. "Ow, that hurt. Be reasonable. It was an accident."

"Fine. You gonna buy?" she barks.

"Sure, if you introduce me."

Summer doesn't take her eyes off him. "Collette, Matt. Matt, Collette. There, you're introduced."

"Oh, you can do better than that," he croons.

He gazes at me fiendishly. There's something farcical about this whole thing, like he's puttin' on a show. Whether it is for me or Summer I don't know. Please God, don't let him say anything about Saturday night.

Summer huffs again. "This is a lot to be asking from someone who ain't buyin'."

He rolls his eyes and digs in his pocket. He hands Summer a crumpled bill.

"What d'you want?" she asks.

"Whoop Ash," he announces.

She puts her hands on her hips. "Really? Got a lot of dry, ashy skin these days?"

He laughs. " S'not for me. It's for your brother."

Summer stiffens. "Don't call him that." She turns around and roots around for the bag she's looking for. She shoves it into his chest.

"C'mon. With all that repressed anger, if you're not careful you might turn into a Thumper. You guys need to squash whatever beef you got."

"And you need to stick to thera…You know what? I was about to say something mean, but *I* am better than that."

Something dark flashes in Matt's eyes and his jaw tightens. He swallows hard and turns to me.

"Collette, nice to meet you."

I nod.

"Summer," he says and then turns his back on us both, his middle finger in salute as he strides away to a group of boys hanging off the back of a pick-up truck.

"What was that about?" I ask as Summer slams the back of her Volkswagen Beetle. She calls it a Bug. Clever.

"Nothing," she says tightly as we walk towards the building. She's walking fast, and I follow, but something tells me to look back.

At just that moment he turns around too and our eyes meet. With a smile, he winks.

### 

The front office assigns me to a peer advisor. I'll have to shadow her until my schedule is finalized. She's a wisp of a girl with a head full of the tiniest braids I've ever seen falling midway down her back. Her black t-shirt reads: Qutey in glittering bubble letters.

I follow Qutey down the narrow corridor of the counselor's wing until we spill out onto the hallway.

Qutey rounds a corner and swipes her ID on a device attached to a set of double doors marked: Advanced. The doors swing open slowly, activated by some pressurized device, and we walk through. This hallway is peaceful as the others we've walked through were riotous. The air even seems cleaner here.

She stops in front of room 242 and knocks. An older man in a knit tie and a brown checkered short-sleeved shirt smiles at us and ushers us in.

"Qutey! I was worried about you," the man says in a raspy smoker's voice. He is average height and wears the telltale darkened lips of a lifetime smoker. I want to say he looks to be sixty-five years old, but he is probably a great deal younger.

"Hi Mr. Lee, this is Colette. She's shadowing me today. I got held up in the counselors' office," Qutey replies.

"Not a problem. We're just getting started."

I follow Qutey to a table in the back of the room. This truly is my first day of school. Mama kept me home and out of people's way so I wouldn't be overwhelmed by them, at least at first. Later, it just felt like a prison.

"Alright, we've talked about current events, and last week's bloodbath between the reds and the blues about the upcoming election is something that I will never repeat so I want to steer clear of politics for a few weeks. If you've already turned in your weekly podcasts, that's great. If not, you've got one more day."

"That's not fair!" shrieks a pale girl in a ratted black t-shirt and matching plastic bangles that cover her wrists to her elbows. Are those safety pins in her ears? "I worked all week to get that in on Friday. Anyone who turns it in late should lose points."

"Mary-Beth! For the tenth time, the server was down and some people were not able to upload their work. I sent an email to everyone about this," Mr. Lee moans.

"Boooo! Mr. Lee" cries Mary-Beth. Mr. Lee shoots her a look that is at once severe and playful.

"Are you done?" he asks.

"Quite."

"Good. Now on to this week's project. I'm sure you've all heard about the murder of the young girl at Wellington." Indistinguishable murmurs break out amongst the small group of students.

"While we grieve for her family, this does provide us an opportunity to flex our investigative journalism skills."

A pretty dark girl with brazenly unstraightened hair shouts from the corner, "Why aren't the murders on the main news networks? At least thirteen Black girls have gone missing."

Mr. Lee sighs, "I won't speculate. What do you think, Keisha?" he asks thoughtfully.

"I think it's racist," she replies.

A few heads nod, still a few others shake their heads in disagreement.

"Everything isn't racist," Mary-Beth adds.

"No, everything isn't racist, but if you went missing the same time that Amber went missing, whose family would the channel 2 news be interviewing?"

Amber, waves robotically from the front of the class, her blonde ponytail swinging as she nods regally as a queen.

Mary-Beth gives Amber the middle finger and nods to Keisha in the back.

"Point taken."

"I think Thumpers are doin' it. Everybody knows those crazy holy rollers are capable," Qutey pipes in.

What on earth is a Thumper?

"Now, now, girls. You know we don't use that term, and we can discuss that later. We'll save it for an open discussion day. Now, back to the assignment. A journalist has to be part truth teller and part detective and solving a mystery will not only get you the front page, it may even make you a household name. Can someone name some unsolved mysteries or famous scandals that you've heard of?" Mr. Lee inquires.

I expected hands to shoot up all around me, instead a barrage of answers shoot out from the tiny group in scattershot.

"What about the Lindbergh baby?" I whisper to Qutey.

"Shout it out," she whispers back. I shake my head. "Ok, raise your hand." She grabs my arm and thrusts it in the air, just as my cheeks start to burn from embarrassment. Thank God for knit cardigans.

"Yes, Miss …Colette?" Mr. Lee asks, pointing directly at me.

I snatch my arm out of Qutey's hand. "Th..The…What about the Lindbergh b-baby?" I reply shakily.

"Perfect! Yes, the Lindbergh baby is an oldie but a good-ie," he croons.

"Who's that?" a voice asks. I can't locate who it is because I am too busy shooting daggers at Qutey who must think the entire affair is the most hilarious thing she's seen all morning.

"The Lindbergh case was like the Jon Benet Ramsey scandal of the 30's. A famous aviator's baby was snatched from his home and no less than 12 ransom notes were sent before the baby's body was found weeks later. The tabloid coverage was unprecedented."

"Did they catch the guy?" asks a boy in a bowtie.

"Um, yes. The case was central to changing federal law too. Ok, so why are we talking about all this? We're talking about this because I want you to investigate a mystery of your own. It could be something that has been going on around school, it could be one the angel appearances or so-called appearances. The only rule is that it must be local. I want you guys to do some field work on this and gather first-hand accounts. So you know what that means?"

"We get to use the cameras!" yells Qutey, who almost jumps out of her seat to do some sort of jerky happy dance. The class giggles and claps with excitement.

Mr. Lee laughs. "Yes. Now sit back down, but thank you for the impromptu interpretive dance. I enjoyed it thoroughly."

"Ok, guys. Get in your groups and brainstorm," he says finally.

Until now, Qutey and I have been sitting alone, but now the handsome boy with the bowtie comes to join us. He has a bronze face dotted all over with tiny brown freckles and although he's hiding it well, a milky-green anxiety is buzzing around him.

26

"Hola, chica." He smiles at Qutey and slides into the empty seat across from us.

"Hola! Que tal, Carlos?" she replies.

"Nada mucho, sistren. Who's this? New group member? You gonna hang with us now?" he asks.

I don't have time to answer. Qutey beats me to it. "She's my shadow. I dunno. You think you might want to join the class? You haven't embarrassed me and you've had the opportunity to either spaz or sleep and you've done neither. You've passed my test."

"What's the question?" I ask confusedly.

They both laugh. "Do you think you might want to join the class?" Carlos asks. He inches closer to me and looks into my eyes a little too long. If I didn't know better, I'd think he was flirting with me. But, I do know better and something is off. Very off, but he does seem nice.

"Oh. Yes, it really seems like fun. I have to admit though, I don't know anything about computers," I reply.

"How can you not?" Qutey asks, an incredulous look on her face. Any ground I may have gained by impressing Mr. Lee was surely lost with that statement. A flicker of exasperation runs across her face for a second and then softens.

"Homeschool."

That will be my answer to everything. It's a catch all, and happens to be true. It's not as bad as I thought. The class is small and quiet for the most part. It's easy to keep my emotional shields up here. My biggest worry is if I have any classes with Matt. I hate to admit it, but I'm kind of disappointed that he didn't remember me. I guess it is for the best though.

"Wow. We don't get too many of those at Spring View. Don't worry about it. Carlos is the master with all things technical. He'll get you up to speed in no time."

"What's a Thumper?"

The question has been rolling around in my head, and I just can't let it go.

"Wow, you really were sheltered," Carlos says while he fumbles with some plastic contraption with a video screen. "Um, so they're like religious nut jobs who think we shouldn't have to go to school now that the 'end of days' is upon us."

End of days. Is that what's going on here?

"Watch this," he says while Qutey and I crowd around the thing and peer down at the tiny screen.

"That's the President jet skiing on vacation off the coast of the Virgin Islands. Looks like he's having fun right?"

I nod.

"See that fat guy next to him? It's the head of the American Baptist Ministers Coalition, the pastor of pastors."

I draw in a sharp breath as the pastor slips off his jet ski and flails. "He fell."

"Not just him, the President too. Something happened with the jet skis. They're too far off for the Secret Service to get to them. They both know how to swim, or reports say they did, but they're drowning. Totally weird. Now here comes the freaky part."

Suddenly the screen goes dark as if the sun was turned off, and the sky peels back like ripped paper revealing the night sky. A piercing white flash fills the screen for just under a second before a man with glossy iridescent wings descends from the opening. He glides down purposefully and plucks the President out of the sea like a fish, and then the screen goes black.

"That was the first sighting, or rather the first sighting caught on tape. There are whole websites dedicated to angel sightings. The Thumpers sprouted up a few months after the video saying that the pastor was being judged for his sins and that the apocalypse is right around the corner. They calculated that the world would end in four months. When it didn't, they just started breaking into people's houses to steal enough food and stuff to survive while they wait for Jesus to come back."

I settle in next to her, not sure what else to say.

"Crazy, right?" Qutey chimes in.

She says all this as if we're discussing the best way to baste a turkey. This can't be normal.

"Don't worry. Thumpers aren't your biggest problem. They haven't killed anybody in years."

Oddly, this doesn't make me feel better.

# CHAPTER FOUR

"Nice gloves!" Qutey calls from what I can tell is her usual spot in the far corner of the room. She looks as if she's been settled in for hours, books spread out with multi-colored page markers fluttering like confetti, not to mention a stack of notecards sitting neatly at the head of the mess.

"Thanks."

I'd gone for purity and gratefulness this morning in a long eyelet cotton dress with matching crocheted gloves. Today I get my real schedule, but I get to start with Qutey again. Consistency. I like it.

Carlos walks in right behind me. He flashes a face splitting smile and slings his messenger bag onto the back of the seat. "How are you TO-DAY?" he stresses.

"Damn it, Carlos. I guess I'm not going to get anything else done before class starts if you're here," Qutey half-jokes.

"As if you hadn't already gotten everything done."

Soon Mr. Lee materializes, and class finally gets started.

"Okay," he bellows and turns his back to write on the whiteboard. I can't help but be a little nostalgic for the smell of chalk.

"I told you all yesterday that we were going to begin a new project today. I know some of you are still anxious about yesterday, but security measures have been increased and the band plays on."

He coughs a smoker's cough that grates the walls and continues, "I was inspired by our new member's mention of the Lindbergh baby a few days ago, and it got me thinking about cold cases. Some of the most interesting research you'll ever do will be when no one else is looking. The people who no one care about. Do you think Jon Benet Ramsey was the only child to go missing that year, in that state, in that little city even? Was it her Dad? Was it angels? Aliens?"

"Who is Jon Benet?" I whisper to Carlos. He holds up a finger to silence me. I guess talking is strictly forbidden.

He rips out a piece of paper from his notebook, scribbles on it and passes it my way.

*Ha! Homeschool. I'll explain it to you later...Partner.*

"You and your partner will find and research a cold case. You'll need to do an interview with a witness, so the case must be local and it can't be too old. This will be a joint project with Ms. Laurent's Forensics class," Mr. Lee states to the class' dismay.

Groans break out across the room.

"Why?" cries a large boy in dirty jeans, work boots and a Dick's Sporting Goods t-shirt.

"Well, Brian, I'll answer that question as soon as I start answering to groaning children who break protocol."

"You'll be paired randomly with a team in the Forensics class. To get you brainstorming about where to start, we'll be watching a documentary on The Black Dahlia."

Mr. Lee stands for a beat to see if there are any questions and then dims the lights to start the film.

A few people fall asleep, and I distract myself by timing Carlos' nods to the tap of his foot to see if I can catch the beat of whatever song he's listening to while I try to tune the movie out. It brings back too many bad memories, but as I try to block the images from rising up from the past, an idea comes to me and I know exactly what cold case Carlos and I will be investigating. My own.

### ###

Qutey put in a good word for me with the counselor, and we basically have the same schedule now, but there are some caveats. I am all alone in third period.

The idea of gym makes my mouth itch. Getting sweaty in the middle of the day and making a fool of yourself in front of girls is bad enough, but the idea of co-ed sports is just too new age for my liking. Like diet soda.

"Alright girls, we're starting a new unit today," Coach says feigning excitement. "We're going to learn how to play badminton. You'll learn teamwork, and it's relatively low impact so I don't want to hear any griping about your bad knees, bad back, debilitating acne, diabetes or rickets. And for God's sake if you're on your period, keep it to yourself. So pair up and meet in the corner to get your rackets."

I groan inside. Pair up? Soon, I'm the last one standing and Brianna, a chatty girl with farm-girl charm becomes my partner. In a flutter of half-heard conversation we arrive at the edge of net 6.

"Okay!" Coach breathes out. "You two will join Miller and Taylor here."

Brianna can't contain herself. "OMGeeee! Omigod. Really?"

"Calm down, Baxter. It's just a badminton game." Coach hands us our rackets before breaking out into a sprint to go help a girl who, by some strange series of events, has gotten her ponytail knotted in one of the nets.

"Okay," she takes a deep breath and closes her eyes, "Okay this is just gym class. This is just a game."

She's talking to herself now, and I'm beginning to feel as if I'm intruding. She takes another deep breath, smoothes her hair back and smiles grotesquely at me.

"Check my teeth. Are they fine?"

"Fine."

"Okay, good." She smoothes her t-shirt, pivots on one foot and starts walking, but this time she's on her toes and bounces a bit so that her ponytail swings in an exaggerated way from one side to the other.

Miller and Taylor are on the opposite side of the net talking. Well, one of the girls' is talking; the other is just nodding quickly whenever there is a pause. Both girls wear matching oversized pearl necklaces—much too large to be real—and exaggerated white hair bows. They don't turn to greet us, even though I'm sure they see us waiting.

A minute later Coach blows her whistle hard twice, and I start walking over to the other side of the net when Brianna stops me.

"No!" she whispers fiercely through her smiling teeth. "You have to wait until she talks to us."

Just as I'm about to leave Brianna to her neuroses and introduce myself, both girls turn in unison to face us. With the same swingy walk that Brianna modeled, the smaller of the two walks around the net towards us.

"Hi, I'm Celeste, that's Lilah," she says in a slow breathy voice. She's talking to me only, even though Brianna is right next to me.

I take a step closer to Brianna hoping it doesn't seem obvious. "Thanks, I'm Colette and this is…"

Celeste cuts me off. "Yeah, so we think you should serve first. Do you play?" She flicks her ponytail to the side with a flourish.

"Uh, I've played before, but maybe I'm not the best to start. What if Brianna serves?" I lean on the girl's name so

Celeste will have to acknowledge her. She doesn't even glance in that direction.

Celeste finally lets an irritated gaze fall on Brianna, and she draws in an impatient breath. "I'll have to ask." She pivots on one foot in the opposite direction to look at Lilah, and cocks her head in Brianna's direction in a way of asking. Beside me, Brianna is a straining balloon of anticipation.

After a moment Lilah, nods serenely. "She says it's okay."

We move to positions, but Brianna stops me mid-court.

"What do I do?" she asks.

"You serve the ball. I thought you knew how to play?"

She rolls her eyes. "No. I mean, do I throw the game or dominate? My Stepdad has a house on the Jersey shore, and we go up every summer for like a month, and there is nothing to do but play badminton and eat ice cream. I mean, I guess the only things we're allowed to do are play badminton and eat ice cream."

I move my hand around to get her to get to the point. Even though my eyes haven't left Brianna's face I know that Lilah girl is staring me down.

"Oh. Yeah. I mean I'm really good. Do you think Lilah will be mad if I beat her?"

Really? Is that what this interruption in the regular programming is about? I stop myself from rolling my eyes and give her a reassuring smile. "Just do your best. That's what my Mama always says."

She seems to take that and trots back to her corner. "I'm ready."

In the next few minutes Brianna delivers a dazzlingly graceful set of serves, smashes and hits, all while I flail miserably and try not to fall on the waxed floor. She's so fantastic that the coach stops to watch and give her a few pointers. Without my help, we win both games.

The coach blows her whistle twice and hustles to the end of the court. "Alright girls, good job! Especially Baxter who showed some exceptional talent today." Everybody claps, even if some do it sarcastically. Brianna blushes and smiles.

I follow her to the other side of the net. I guess the win has imbued her with a confidence that won't let her wait to be acknowledged. She stops a few feet short of Lilah and Celeste, who've resumed their earlier talk-nod dance, and waits with a smile. I wait for a minute or two, but enough is enough. I snatch Brianna's racket, plaster a fake smile on my face and thrust them at Lilah.

"Hi! I'm Colette. I think we're supposed to give these to you." My voice is sickly sweet with honey. I even bat my eyelashes for good measure. This is the textbook version of "nice/nasty".

All Lilah has to do is blink in Celeste's direction, and she retrieves the rackets. A weird smile unfolds on Lilah's face.

I think she's going to say something when Celeste breaks in, "Lilah thinks you should ..."

Lilah waves a manicured hand to silence her and says, "I'm Lilah." She doesn't offer her hand, which I'm grateful for, but still perceive as a little rude. "You're new," she breathes in an accent I can't place and looks long at me from head to foot. Her eyes are an odd reddish brown. They look almost wolfish, hungry even. It's unnerving, especially when she says "new" as if she's saying "diseased".

"My friends and I usually do volunteer work after cheer-leading practice. We bring food to the Thumper camps. You should come."

Celeste's carefully constructed visage cracks and shock tumbles out like a kicked over bucket. Brianna's even worse, with her mouth wide open and if I'm not mistaken, eyes watering.

Volunteer work? "Maybe another time. I have to catch the bus home."

Her eyes flash for a second, not even a full second, but she shrugs nonchalantly and continues, "Maybe some other time then." She pivots gracefully as a ballerina on her foot to turn and head to the locker room. With equal polish she strolls to the end of the court with Celeste following clumsily behind her. I can see now what she and Brianna had been trying to copy, but in comparison it's like watching a half-blind kindergartener try to reproduce Rembrandt.

I turn to Brianna. "You really were fantastic. Ready to go in?"

Her mouth is still open, disbelief, a straightjacket tightening around her.

"You turned her down?!" she screeches. "You turned her down. You get a personal invitation, and I don't even get a 'Hi'. I literally killed on the court and you were awful. I should have croaked like you did. You did this." She points an accusatory finger at me.

"This was my chance, and you ruined it. Now, who knows when I'll get another opportunity like this! Never, that's when." She turns abruptly and starts marching toward the locker room, leaving me behind.

Girls.

# CHAPTER FIVE

After Brianna's blowup and the most exercise I can ever remember doing in one stretch, I decide to skip the lunchroom. I take my mashed potatoes and block of meat-like stuff out to the parking lot and find a wall to perch on.

I pick at the stuff on my tray and resolve to make lunch from now on. For a few moments, there is blessed peace and my mind sleeps until a few boys spill out from the cafeteria on the opposite side to start a pickup game.

I feel him before I see him.

Matt.

He cuts through the sea of cars in the parking lot like a shark and all I can see is the golden fin of his hair, which I learn is called a Mohawk, getting closer and closer.

I don't know if I should be excited that he's happy to see me or deathly afraid of the secrets he might still have locked away in his mind. He walks toward me and with each step it feels as if I'm sinking.

"Hey", he says.

"Hello." I squeeze my hands together in my lap as a hazy yellow-gray cloud of nervous confusion envelops us.

A barbecue scented breeze whips past, but does nothing to disturb the cloud. An awkward silence sits like a crow perched on a doorframe.

"Food for the gods I see."

I look down at my tray and grimace.

"I'll be bringing my own lunch from now on. What is this?" I pick up the loaf by a corner and let it plop back down on the Styrofoam plate.

"Hell if I know. Players don't eat that. Our lunch is catered in by some special company. I still eat with them, even though…Well, I don't play anymore."

"Oh." I pause. He's standing directly in the sunlight so that the light forms a halo around his head and images of saints flash in my memory. "Were you any good?"

He smirks and holds his arms out in an imitation of Jesus. "The best! At least…Well, one of…"

His voice trails off, and his arms fall. We're silent for a moment.

"Thank you," I say for lack of anything else to say.

"For what?"

"For helping me the other day and not saying anything to Summer. Ab-bout Saturday. For not telling my secret."

With all this talk about angels, it's Matt who always seems to be there when I need it.

"It isn't my secret to tell. Besides I'm not sure what did happen."

My back goes ramrod straight as he sits next to me, a hands breadth between us.

"I wasn't sure what I'd seen, I mean you. I didn't fully believe you were real at all until I saw you again on Monday. That'll be the last party I let Chamberlain talk me into for a while." He pauses. "Are you okay?"

I know what he means. This isn't about my bruises. He thinks I'm running from something, something mysterious and dangerous.

"I'm okay. I moved into a nice house in a place called Linwood."

"Oh yeah? My boy Chamberlain lives over there."

38

This is nice. Casual. Can I be casual with him? *Is* this safe, for *me?*

Another awkward silence swoops in and lands.

"I'll pro—"

"I'm sorry what?"

He clears his throat and sits up a little straighter. "If you need help, I'll help you."

I know he's sincere. No one can lie to me without my knowing it before they even form their lips to speak. We both stare into the distance past the rows of cars, past the boys with their football, past even the field into the hills. His hand moves slightly so our pinkies almost, almost touch, an invisible tether linking them, drawing them ever closer like magnets.

He wants to help me. Concern pulses at his temples, but his eyes are soft. Too soft.

I turn my head and jump down from the wall. I haven't figured out who I am or why I'm here. If it's something bad, I can't let him know it. To him I'm just a normal girl. I can be that with him, and I want that with him.

It's settled. He can't know.

I smile brightly. "Hey, you know, I…uh don't know what got into me that night. Must have been my Uncle's moonshine. Wild nights happen to everybody, right?"

He looks at me confused. I pull my lunch tray down and begin to walk backwards towards the cafeteria.

"It, uh, r-really was n-nice to meet you, and I can't thank you enough for b-being quiet about all this. It's so embarrassing and starting a new s-school…"

"Hey, wait."

He drops down to follow me. I turn my back and walk quickly. I'm no match for his long-legged stride.

"Don't go. I wanted to…"

He's struggling to get something out, and I won't…I can't let him. Whatever it is.

I smile again and laugh.

"Wanted to pick on me about being so clumsy? Don't be so cruel. I'll see you 'round, okay!"

I blow past him and rush into the cafeteria where a wall of emotion nearly knocks me on my bottom. I have to stand in the doorway to catch my breath, and when I do. When I finally have the composure to look over my shoulder, I see him on the other side of the glass, back turned to me with fingers running through his hair, and I know with absolute certainty that what I just did wasn't water, but fuel to the fire.

# CHAPTER SIX

Vikki Vintage is tucked away in an old house on Gregg Street between a dentist's office and a church, they too old houses. The windows are stained glass with scenes from the bible, one the story of Jonah and the whale and another Noah's Ark. Thumpers, Angels, even these windows remind me of Mama's instructions. How literal was she being? I chew this over as we walk in, and I take in the quasi-religious décor even Vikki, herself, is a work of art with an impeccably coiffed electric blue bob and horn-rimmed glasses.

I managed to make it out of lunch without incident and the rest of the day blew by. With Matt's eyes still boring into my brain and that terrible echo of gunshots still ringing, I'm glad to have a distraction. Shopping.

Raphael, who I still haven't seen, left a trunk of clothes behind for me in addition to my gloves. After looking through the haphazard jumble, Summer suggested we trade them in for stuff I can actually wear.

"Where did you find this stuff?" Vikki asks in her thick as cold grits West Indian accent. "The embroidery, ah, the stitching, by hand. Oh! How much do you want for it?" she asks tentatively as we fold each piece and lay them on the table. A nervous yellow tinge bleeds into the whites of her eyes and I can tell she's nervous, but I'm not sure why.

Summer pipes in, "We were thinking more of a barter arrangement, kind of a dress for dress exchange. Collette needs some more clothes for school and all she's got is this stuff and some old homeschool things. She has to make a good impression."

You can see the pent up anxiety seep out of her like a deflating balloon. "Oh! Oh, I'm so glad. Gul, I'm gwon hook you up!" she squeals and claps her hands before she begins scribbling on a notepad.

"Ok, girls. I did a bit of figuring, and I'll have to contact a few people to price a few things but here's what I came up with." She slides her pad across the table for both of us to look at.

"Jeezus Colette. That'll keep you in scarves and skirts for the next decade."

"So, what do you say Collette?" Vikki whispers in anticipation.

"Ow!" Summer pops my hand with a pair of lacquered chopsticks.

"Take the deal," she hisses through clenched teeth, and I get the weird sensation that I'm on stage with a whole audience watching me.

"It's a deal."

"Great!" they both chime in unison.

Soon Summer starts talking about people I've never met or have only gotten a glimpse of but we're falling fast into friendship, and it feels good. I've never had many friends.

We flutter around the store as two butterflies picking up skirts and dresses from the fifties and a few frocks from the sixties. When I go into the dressing room, I leave Summer on the floor to pick through the seventies rack for peasant blouses.

"Whadoyouwant?" she yells.

"Lots of color!" I call from behind the curtain as I contort into a pretzel-like shape trying to zip up a bright yellow wool dress that hugs from the knees on up to my chest. I'm truly in my own world and let my shields thin so I can relax. I'm still squirming when the bell rings over the door to signal someone else has come in the store. Before I can really register someone else or even try to adjust my shields an overwhelming grief rains on me from above and swirls around my heart before it pools inside thick as spilled blood. In seconds I'm crumpled on the floor in tears.

"I can't stay inside another minute Vikki and I've kept these suits for her appearances long enough. I...I know.." she sniffles in husky timber, surely the result of hours of intense crying.

"Linda I'm so sorry. Is there anything I can do?" Vikki manages to squeak out in a cracked voice.

"Yes. The church is organizing a search of the woods. I don't want to think she's out there. It's been weeks. I just..." And then she breaks down into a painful sobbing that makes the walls pulse in anguish. It sprays out, fast and full, ploughing into me from the top down with liquid hot misery and all I want to do is cry out, but God is merciful and sends something, something small and invisible to snatch my voice from me as quick as a thief and run off into nothingness.

Vikki whispers and continues to console the woman with words I can't hear and then a rapid knock on the dressing room partition, like a woodpecker or shots from a machine gun shock me.

"Colette!" Summer calls in a forceful whisper. "Which one are you in? "

I am still crumpled on the floor and grief still has my voice so I just stick my hand out from under the curtain so she'll know which stall and pray she won't open it.

"Oh, my God! Do you know who is here? It's Tressa Lancaster's Mom."

I don't respond. I am still trying to catch some sort of neutral thought, a life preserver, to save me from drowning in Mrs. Lancaster's burning sorrow. Summer takes my silence as an admission of confusion and keeps talking in the loudest whisper I've ever heard.

"Oh! You don't know what I'm talking about do you? Ok, so, about a few months ago the reigning Miss Teen South Carolina US and Miss Dutch Square High left to go out on a date and never came home, which isn't too out of the ordinary from what I've heard about her. She's been on the news nearly every night trying to get tips on where she went."

I don't really hear her. She's muffled. I'm not here in this skin, in this body so attuned to other souls, constantly outside myself. I'm not here. I smell my Mama's neck as she hugs me, pressing her palm against my forehead. I've got the flu and she's taking care of me. I'm not here, crumpled on the floor like a wad of tissue. I'm on the couch in Matt's lake house. His hand brushes my earlobe, and I'm vibrating. It's enough for me to tune Summer out and pull myself out of Mrs. Lancaster's lake of fiery despair. I let the feeling last just long enough to pull my shield back up like a lead blanket.

"Colette? Collette, are you ok?

"Hmm. Yeah, uh…yeah"

"You don't sound so good." She pulls back the curtain. "Oh, I'm sorry. I didn't mean to upset you with the story."

"I'm fine, really."

"I can really be stupid sometimes. I didn't know…Man, I'm sorry."

"It's ok, really. I, uh…just let me get some of this stuff together. I think I want to just head home." I sniffle.

I curse myself. I'm so weak. Whatever task I'm supposed to be here for I can't possibly complete.

Mama, I hear you. I hear you.

# CHAPTER SEVEN

"So why is Matt blowing up my cell phone trying to find out where you live?"

Busted.

Summer and I pull into a space in the far end of the parking lot in front of the school and the hum of the car dies as she pulls the keys out of the ignition. She stares at me dead on with a wicked smile on her face.

"What did he say?" I ask nervously.

"Oh no! I ask the questions. You, ma'am, are full of mystery, but we are not walking through those doors until I get some info. He was all nervous and desperate. What did you do to him?"

I frown. I still feel weird about the whole situation. On one hand there is this irresistible attraction and on the other there is self-preservation. What if I slip and say something and he hates me? I don't want that look that people get around me, fear, or worse, pity.

I *should* stay away. I should just cut my losses and enjoy being alive again; but isn't living dealing with stuff that hurts and stuff that scares you and makes your heart beat faster and your pulse quicken and then turn cold with goose bumps? It's a rollercoaster, or what I imagine what one would feel like. I think about that for a second.

"Have you ever been on a rollercoaster?" I ask her.

"What!? Don't change the subject. We are talking about Matt, and his crazy nine phone calls to me trying to find out where you were or if I could get in touch with you and finally some very unseemly pleading and bargaining for your phone number. I'll have you know I turned down some very nice things to guard your privacy."

"Nine times?"

"Nine, and that doesn't even include the text messages."

The wicked smile is still there, and she's waiting. I'm not sure what to say. Nine. I've never had anyone be that interested in me. Everyone thought I was so weird. Well, I guess I am in retrospect, but in those days I wasn't very good at it.

"I saw him at lunch."

"Stop." She holds up her hand. "You *saw* him at lunch or you went to *see* him at lunch."

"I went out to the parking lot and…"

"You went to the jock lot?" Her voice is high pitched and suspicious.

"I just went outside."

My voice gets drowned out by the shrill squeal of drills and hammers. Qutey was right. A barbed wire fence as tall as two men is slowly rising around the school.

"Yeah, that's the jock lot. Only jocks are allowed out there without invitation. So did he invite you?"

"He talked to me. It was innocent."

At this admission she squeals, "Ooooh, and how innocent was it Mademoiselle Collette?" She's faking a French accent now and I giggle. Even though I'm not spilling my guts I feel better about the whole situation. I must have given her enough information because she finally opens the car door and grabs her bag from the back. I do the same, and we make our way to the building.

"Okay, you don't have to answer that. The last thing I want to do is pry," she sings in a conciliatory tone.

"What kind of guy is he?"

"Oh, total superstar jock. He was like the big man on campus last fall. Captain of the football team. Debate team champion. And he wasn't all whorish either, well not too whorish. He had a girlfriend. A class act."

"What happened?" I ask.

"Came down with some weird brain thing. Seizures. They said he could stay on the sidelines, but he finally quit out right after his girlfriend went missing. Police stopped looking for her ages ago. At least that's what I heard. Not that we're like the best of friends or anything. I mean we're friendly; we went to elementary school together. I remember this one time..."

She's rambling, but, wow, she is in a good mood. I can't help but feel better. I try to catch everything she says about the boy who saved me, the golden god who's keeping my secret.

"Here," she hands me a small plastic contraption. "It's a cell phone. Uncle Silas told me to give it to you. I've already programmed my number *and* Matt's number inside. Call him or don't. Choice is yours."

I take the phone and put it in my suede purse and soon we say our goodbyes until later.

Later comes sooner than expected when the whole school is called into the gym for an emergency assembly. In the crush of classes I'm able to find Summer, and we both warm a bleacher on the Home side of the court.

The room is buzzing with 2,000 vessels of math formulas, hormones and stupid jokes. Apparently, this really is impromptu because Coach Rinkard is piercing our eardrums with the high-pitched squeal of a hastily put together sound system. Principal Lewis looks sober and in control, but even with my shields firmly in place I can tell she's fighting a hornet's nest of nerves in her chest. She's wearing too much makeup and beads of beige sweat are piling up on her forehead.

"Can I have your attention?" Principal Lewis booms over the mic, far too loudly. Some adjustments are made and she continues, "Can I have your attention?"

"I know that you are unhappy about missing the latter half of first period." A kid on the opposite of our section boos loudly. I scan the crowd for Matt and come up empty. I'm disappointed that he's not there and that I didn't fight the urge to look.

"I hope that you will take this time to be as attentive and serious in this assembly as you would be in class. I have asked Officer John to join me at the podium, as well as Ms. Crowley, some of you know her already. She is our school social worker."

A hush falls over the crowd as they both walk to the podium and flank the principal; Ms. Crowley, a little slower than the officer in a pair of impossibly high heeled boots. They look like generals about to go to battle.

"As many of you know there have been a number of disappearances in the metropolitan area. A volleyball player in Lexington, a JV cheerleader in Hopkins and most recently an AP Art student in Dutch Fork have gone missing. Unfortunately, we must add one of our own to the list." She takes a deep breath, while we hold ours.

"Brianna Baxter went missing last night."

Shock crackles through the crowd and erupts here and there with a "No!" or undecipherable curse.

"And this morning the JV cheerleader who went missing from Carol High was found in Lake Murray."

Fear rises up in a yellow-green ash as if a bomb has been dropped. Summer covers her mouth and I can see the collective incantation of 'Oh My God' ripple and bubble through every row. A few people make the sign of the cross and others sit sullen or angry.

Officer John moves the mic closer to his mouth and takes a deep breath. "The best offense is defense, and I can't express to you enough how important being aware of your surroundings is…"

He goes on about checking under your car and keeping your keys in your hands at all times. "And ladies, never be afraid to look someone in the eye. Ask them the time or where the nearest Bojangles is. Someone is less likely to murd…Um, attack you if you can identify them."

He has a list of things he wants to cover, and I can see him make his way through each item. I wonder if I'd have died like I did if I had been given this speech, and then I think that it wouldn't have done any good. He's thinking that a stranger is targeting these girls at random, but even though I can't remember it, I know my death was on purpose. These girls are lucky they have a chance.

Officer John is finished now, and Ms. Crowley steps up to speak. In a tiny voice she tells us that it's okay to feel whatever we're feeling. A few girls in the crowd sob audibly. Are the tears for Brianna and the other girls or for themselves?

"We know that many of you love and care for Brianna, so if you would like to join the search party you may line up outside the attendance office so that we can get verbal permission from your parents. A school bus will join other volunteers at 1PM today, immediately after lunch."

Summer is sobbing next to me, and I'm glad I decided to bring a scarf today because I'm able to rub her back a bit without getting too much transference. She's more afraid than broken up by what's happened to Brianna. I guess most of the girls are.

Principal Lewis takes the mic again, "Thank you Officer John. Ms. Crowley. Students, I hope you've taken the time to really absorb what has been said here today. And I also want to add that this life is short, and we must be kind to each other;

49

we must look out for each other. Please be careful, watchful and wise. Please stand for a moment of silence, and then we'll dismiss for the remainder of 2nd period."

The somber crowd stands and I find him, seventh row and fifth kid in. He doesn't look sad, he looks fierce, determined. At the same moment, he finds me and we lock eyes, and it's as if the sun has come out, and I'm warm all over and glowing like a light bulb. I don't smile though. I'm not happy; I'm just certain of myself... of him. While everyone bows their heads, we stand in the moment together and light up the room.

# CHAPTER EIGHT

Brianna is dead. I know this. I think the adults know this, but what none of us is doing is admitting this. We're pretending. The student council is organizing search parties in the woods behind the school as if she got lost on the way home like Hansel and Gretel.

I wonder if the community rallied around the tragedy of my death, or did it just seem like an accident? On the way to school, I toss the thoughts around in my mind and hope that when they fall I'll have acceptable answers, but that's me pretending too.

Summer isn't very chatty this morning, but she's got a happy secret. I can tell, and not just by the fact that she decided to wear a skirt today. Why everyone insists on dressing like a hobo to school is beyond me. Everyone is in jeans and sweatpants, and if anything gets ironed, it must be a special event.

After the metal detectors, Summer and I split and I make my way to first period through nearly vacant halls.

"Nice dress."

Like always, I feel him before I see him, that twitching in my spine, wild and sharp as a downed electrical wire. I know it is my imagination, but he feels large, like if I turned around he'd block out the sight of reality.

"Thank you," I whisper without turning around. I peer out of the corners of my eyes to get a glimpse of him, the anticipation of seeing him is almost too much to bear. He had to have been waiting for me. No one but Qutey and I come in this early. The halls are always deserted at this hour.

"There's something in your hair," he says as I feel fingers float of over my head. I can't breathe. I'm waiting, waiting for him to touch me. It's feather soft when it finally comes and is gone so quickly. "Got it. Perfect, now."

I see Qutey round the corner and then duck back behind a column when she meets my eyes. I don't think Matt sees because he comes to face me. His eyes roam over my face as if he's looking for something and then he smiles.

"What?" I ask.

"You're just…beautiful."

I try to look anywhere but in his eyes. I can't look there, because if I do I might do anything. Flashes of orange lightning spark in front of my eyes like pixies in a bug zapper. Nervously, I twiddle my necklace between my fingers.

"You're here early." Casual. That's good, right?

"I came to see you."

"Oh. Why?" I breathe.

"Because I had to, because I needed to?" There is a question in his voice and confusion ripples across his face for a second. "There was another angel sighting."

"Oh?" I'm staring at that scar in his eyebrow. I'm thinking of a word for it, but the only thing that makes sense is sexy. Sexy. Sexy as in sex, as in so close that skin seldom seen touch. I shudder slightly at the thought that at once repulses me and excites me. I think of riotously blooming bougainvillea. Violet. Grapes so full they split down the middle and the juice spills out. Juice running down his chin.

"Huh?"

"I said did you see the sighting on the news?"

I shake my head.

"Brazil again. There was a gang shootout in a Favela. The girl was in the middle of the street. She should have died, but an angel appeared out of thin air. Her wings deflected the bullets."

"Her?" I ask while I tear my hungry eyes away to focus on the loose tape on the "Find Brianna" poster looking over us. I don't want my eyes to say things I would never speak aloud.

"There can't be female angels? Not very feminist of you?" he jokes. I don't know why, but I always think of angels being men. In my mind they look like him.

"What do you need from m-me?" I stammer, suddenly hot and needing an escape.

"I don't know yet. I've been here since six. I didn't know where you lived, and I didn't have your phone number to call even if I did. I had a speech. I mean I knew what I was gonna say, but...I can't seem to remember any of it now. I never have trouble talking to girls." He looks sheepish, as if he's embarrassed to have to tell me this. A locker slams somewhere on a distant hall and makes me jump.

"I had to see you. I think...no, I know I need to help you."

"I don't need any help," I say reflexively. I probably do need help, but he can't possibly give me what I need. What I need is unnamable, unknowable.

"Bullshit." He says it softly, pleadingly. "You needed help that night. You needed help Monday, and you need it now. There's something...someone out there."

Someone laughs giddily and more voices float into our corridor.

"I want you to go somewhere with me."

"Where?"

"Somewhere we can talk. Somewhere you can let go and tell me what you're running from." He tucks a tendril of my hair back into its bun and a vibration unlike anything I've ever felt nearly blinds me with its force. My bones sing with it, and it's a second before my mind clears.

No. I want to say yes, but I have to say no.

"I can't." I'm not new. He is not my savior. Some things you just can't have.

"You can."

"Really, I can't. I. . ."

I'm searching for something and coming up empty. Isn't this what I wanted? A new adventure? Why can't I just say yes?

"I have t-to g-go," I stutter and brush past him, setting my skin on fire in the process, making a bee line to where Qutey is hiding.

I brush past her so fast that the breeze rustles my hair. She follows behind me, tight on my heels.

"What the hell was that about?" she asks excitedly.

"Nothing." I manage.

"Whatever. Where are you walking so fast for *nothing*?"

"Library. We're going to the library."

It is the only place I know that will be quiet, where I can think, where I can sulk and kick myself for being a coward.

### 

All day I replay the morning in my mind and every time I hate myself a little more, so I'm more than a little eager to see Carlos for our after school research date.

In a staggeringly short amount of time and something called Google, Carlos found out that some of his church members lived in the neighborhood where I died. It's step one of several for our project that he's already outlined. A folder full of clippings and instructions greet me after school when he picks me up for Bible Study. Get thee to a church, right?

We get to the church early enough to get a prime seat in the third pew. As we sit, a stillness, unique to churches, slips over me. Soon, an old church mother in a blue-feathered pill hat with a sequined bird pinned to the side begins testifying at the altar.

"If it hadn't been for Jesus," she says in a quivering tone, "I would have surely perished!"

Everybody claps. She goes on about how God healed her from breast cancer ten years ago and how she was being tested again.

It doesn't take me any longer than five minutes before I settle into the groove of the service, wrapping it around me like a beloved family quilt on a cold night. Carlos and I hold hands (I've got on my heavy duty gloves today), we pray, we sing. We sing our hearts out and when the Reverend reaches the pulpit to deliver the word I'm on cloud nine.

"I've received a word family!" he bellows in his musical baritone cadence. " An evil has come to rest here in our city. Another girl has gone missing. We all know who is responsible!"

The crowd murmurs an agreement, and I look around me at the nodding heads. I wait for this revelation. Did I miss something? Was there an arrest?

"This evil isn't new. It isn't quiet. It isn't even that smart, but he's sly. Sly enough to know who to come for and how. Smart enough to recognize the hate that allows our mysteries to go unsolved and our children unfound. He's come for the best of us. He's come to cut off our future before it blossoms. He has come like a thief in the night," the Preacher calls out, ending 'night' as a whisper.

Something strikes in me like a guitar string being plucked. The reverend's roving eye settles on me for not even a half second, but I know this message is for me.

"This message is for you!" he shouts to no one in particular. "C'mon down if you need prayer. The prayer warriors are in attendance."

After the service, a woman hands out flyers for a candle-light vigil as we walk to the basement. The old woman in the blue hat, Mother Johnson, sits waiting for us, spooning heaps of sugar into a coffee cup.

"Good evening Mother Johnson!" Carlos yells slowly and smiles broadly. "This is my friend Collette."

"Lord, Carlos, I'm hard of hearing not slow. You don't have to talk to me like that. Sit down!"

She slurps her coffee,"Oooowee! Too hot."

She smiles at me. "Evenin' sweetie," she says to me as I sit down, never letting her eyes fall from my face. Her brow furrows. "Collette is it?"

"Yes, ma'am."

She's thinking. "What's your family name? Who're your people?"

"Uh, Hognose."

"Hognose!" she spits. "I ain't never heard a no black people named Hognose. What's your Mama's maiden name?"

"Uh…"

"Mother Johnson," Carlos thankfully interrupts, "do you remember why we wanted to talk with you?"

"'Course I do," she says and laughs. It's a skittering, rattling thing that picks at my memory like a mosquito bite you can't reach to scratch. "You want to ask me about that horrible murder."

"Yes ma'am," we both say in unison again.

Carlos produces the slimmest notebook I've ever seen from his blazer pocket. "Umm, how did you know the victim?" he asks in his best detective voice.

"I was about six or seven when it happened. She went to my church. She was my babysitter."

I gasp.

"Used to call me 'little squirrel' on account of my laugh and I called her…." She trails off tapping her collarbone in thought.

"Little Fillie," I finish for her. A flood of memories appear behind my eyes as vivid as spilled ink, a child Mother Johnson with me brushing her hair, cleaning a scrape on her knee and playing games, each memory punctuated with that same skittering laugh. She laughs again, in real time.

"Yes! Little Fillie. How did you know that?" Mother Johnson asks me. Carlos is surprised.

"It was…", I stumble, "It was in some files, maybe a newspaper clipping about the murder."

They both nod, accepting my lie as gospel. I lied in church. Surely, I'm going to burn now. For a second, I wonder if hell is real.

"Well, she was a beautiful girl. Had that good hair, like you sweetie. It's where the nickname came from. Beautiful and thick and shiny, just like yours. She was weird though."

I shift uncomfortably in my seat.

"How so?" Carlos asks while writing notes on the back of a church program.

"Hated to be touched. Even took to wearing church gloves all the time."

Carlos halts his writing for a second to look in my direction, but quickly returns to his notes. I'm grateful my hands are in my lap.

"She was also an incredibly sad girl. Saddest girl I've ever known. Made other people sad too. Could suck all the life right out of the room. Make you feel so bad you feel like you can't breathe for all the sadness."

"That's not true," I snap.

Mother Johnson looks at me incredulously. Carlos' fixes me with angry eyes and a clenched jaw.

"I..I..," I stumble again, "I meant this is uh.. all so new. You're the first person we've talked to who knew her," I recover.

"Oh!, oh." Her eyes search my face for a second. "What was your father's mother's maiden name?" she asks.

"I, uh, didn't know my grandmother. My dad was adopted," I say while pulling my gloves off under the table and stuffing them in my purse. "Whew! Mother Johnson, I know you want to get some dinner as soon as they open the kitchen. We should probably let you get to it." I stand quickly.

I didn't even meet Carlos' glare. I can see it in my peripheral vision.

"Oh, I'm fine honey," she replies.

"Good!" Carlos says too brightly. "Then Collette can sit 'cause I have a few more questions."

I lower myself down back into my chair.

"Did the detectives interview you?" Carlos asks.

"Child, no. Them white folks didn't care about her; ruled it an accident. It was the colored papers that started askin' questions. Thought it was some old boyfriend or something until that rich fella got involved. Oooweee, that was the talk of the day. I was really too young to give you any good details. Back then children weren't allowed to listen to grown folks' conversations."

"It was horrible. You know back in those days they didn't have no milk cartons and such. The little girl was just gone."

The old woman stands creakily, and Carlos helps her. I remain seated, hoping I can avoid hugging her goodbye or shaking her hand without my gloves on.

"Oh!" she jumps as if she's been stung by a yellow jacket. "I almost forgot. You know her mama was a witch."

"What?" Carlos asks. My mouth is a silent open maw.

"Yes. Got kicked out of the church for it and all. Folks like to say that's why it happened, but folks can be mean. Nobody deserves that. Nobody." She clucks her tongue.

My mouth is dry with shock. I want to rail against this old woman and yell that she is a liar, but I can tell better than anyone a lie from the truth and every word she is speaking is as good as gospel. Before I can speak, a pair of freckled twins with sandy brown hair burst through the door.

"Nana! Nana! Mama said you gotta come now," they echo right after each other. And with that, Mother Johnson is ushered out of the room, and I am left alone with a burning hot coal of revelation.

# CHAPTER NINE

After church, I could barely eat with the need to find out more of what Squirrel knew, but I had to wait until school was over the next day to get answers.

Mother Johnson lives in a scrubby neighborhood on the other side of town, and I have to switch busses three times and outrun a loose Rottweiler with a bad skin rash to get there. I go to the side door of the old house instead of the front, having stolen Mother Johnson's address from a church directory on the way out. I want her to know this is a casual visit, even though the sweat from my palms threatens to soak the bag of *Oh! Henry* bars I've brought as a present, and surely gives away my nervousness. Squirrel *loves Oh! Henry* bars.

I'm nervous. Really nervous. I think for a second, and then try to move my hips in a little dance Summer taught me, just to shake out the sillies. Is it called a twerk?

I stop as soon as I catch an old man walking his dog staring. I stare back and shame him into walking on.

I knock once, but forget how old this woman is now. The next time, I knock three good times in rapid succession—hard.

"Hold on now!" I hear a raspy voice say from far inside the house. "I'm gone tell you now I'm too old for insurance, and we already know Jesus."

It takes her a minute to make it to the door, but when she opens it isn't Mother Johnson.

"Oh, I'm sorry. I was looking for Mother Johnson. I...I must have the wrong address."

The woman, nearly as old as Mother Johnson is in a blue house dress, and she looks thoughtful behind horn-rimmed glasses. "No, sweetie, you're in the right place. She's just in the den watching her stories. Come on in. You can call me Miss Collins."

I make sure to latch the screen door once I make it into the dimly lit house and make my way to the den where the woman gestures for me to sit down on an armchair. I sink in so far on the thing that my knees brush my breasts, thank God I wore a jumpsuit, or I'd be giving the whole room a show.

I try to interrupt, "Mother Johnson, I..."

"Sssssh, Sweetie. Wait till the commercial break," she chides waving me towards a chair.

Miss Collins and Mother Johnson add their commentary to the last soap opera of the day, and it's like watching tennis. Tit-for-tat between the both of them.

A detergent commercial with a talking bear offers me reprieve. "Mother Johnson, I brought you a gift. I wanted to say thank you for helping us yesterday."

"Oh, aren't you sweet. Whatdya bring me?" She smiles and turns towards me for the first time.

"*Oh! Henry* bars." I place the crumpled bag in front of her.

She laughs. "I haven't been able to eat candy since I got these dentures twenty years ago, but it's a thoughtful gift. I can suck on 'em. *Oh! Henry* bars are my favorite. How did you know?"

"Just a guess."

"Miss Collins you want some of these?"

She shakes her head and makes her way to the kitchen.

"Mother Johnson, I was hoping I could ask you a few more questions... about the victim?" I flinch inside, hating to refer to myself like that.

"Well, it was a long time ago. I told you most of what I remembered."

"Oh, I know, I was just thinking about what you said about her mother being a witch."

"Oh, that! That was me being cute. She didn't cast spells or none of that nonsense. It was just a thing people said back in those days especially about ladies with babies and no husband. People make up all kinds of stories."

Miss Collins makes it back with glasses of lemonade and a tray of butter cookies.

"But…"

"Ssssh, the stories are back on."

Of all the reasons I'd thought my family could have been murdered, the supernatural never crossed my mind. Was it me that doomed them? Maybe there was something else. There are so many missing pieces, and Mother Johnson has them locked away in her mind, and it feels as if she's doing it on purpose, like when she'd hide puzzle pieces around the house so that, days later, she could be the hero and finally complete it.

Miss Collins' eyes twinkle with something mischievous, and I begin to get the feeling that Mother Johnson isn't the only one keeping secrets.

I turn my attention towards her. "Miss Collins, did you live in the area too? Did you know the victim's mother?"

Mother Johnson's back stiffens. "Don't ask her anything. She don't know. She was only two when it happened. I'm the older sister. I am the authority," she says with a huff. A tinge of emerald green starts to seep out of her pores as slick as sweat. Jealousy.

Mother Johnson heaves herself up. "I'm tired. I need to lay down," she announces. "Coco, is it?"

I nod just to save myself trouble.

"Thank you for the candy. Tell Carlos, I'm glad he finally got himself a girlfriend, and I hope I'll be seeing y'all at church again," she says as she makes her way down the hallway and then closes her door softly, leaving me frustrated and awkward looking in front of Miss Collins.

"Well, I guess I should go," I murmur.

"Oh no, sweetie, sit. I'd like the company," Miss Collins says.

She knows I'm bound by proper etiquette and can't refuse her. There's a cunning behind her soft brown eyes that hasn't been diminished by age.

"Watch *Family Feud* with me. You don't have to get home do you?"

"No ma'am," I reply.

"Good. Dinner will be done soon anyway."

"I don't think…" I protest.

She interrupts me, "Ssssh, it's starting."

At the commercial break, she crosses the room to sit next to me and offers me another cookie.

"That's a beautiful necklace," she pointed out waving a hand towards my neck.

I finger the pendant at my throat, the branch-like arms that form into a cross. I take for granted that it's always there. It always has been.

"Thank you. It was a gift," I confess.

"Oh? Who gave it to you?" she asks.

"It belonged to my…mother," I say hesitatingly. "She passed a long time ago."

She nods. "Do you know what it is?"

"Oh. Well, it's a cross. I got it for my birthday," I explain.

She smiles ruefully as if she's turning something over in her mind, and then sits back to focus on the game show again. At the next commercial break, she pries open a tin on the coffee table, and offers me a powdered cookie. I have to take my gloves off to eat them.

"Can I see it?"

I look at her quizzically.

"Come here and lean into the light, honey."

I pull myself out of the chair awkwardly and kneel in front of the couch so she can get a better look. She stares at my throat with a burning intensity. At first, I study her with the same attention she studies me, but I lose interest and begin counting the moles on her cheeks instead. Fifty-one.

This is a mistake.

I'm completely caught off guard when she grabs both my wrists with the strength of a grown man and presses her thumbs into my palms. I have the presence of mind to struggle, but I can't move. My mind tells me to scream, but I can't talk. The heavy weight of my will to survive sits in my abdomen solid as a cement medicine ball.

"Who are you?" she asks firmly.

Where I couldn't speak before, now I'm compelled to, as if my tongue has a mind of its own.

"A girl."

"Is Coco your name?" she demands. Her eyes are unwavering and rake over every inch of my skin.

"No." My voice is flat and even, as emotionless as a robot.

"What is your name?"

"Collette."

"Hmm. Heifer probably just got it wrong," she says to herself.

"Why are you here?" she barks.

"I want to find out about my mother," I say smoothly, without even a trace of the hesitance I really feel.

"Is she truly dead?"

"Yes," I answer.

"Is your grandmother dead?"

"Yes."

"Do you have any sisters, aunts?"

"No."

She pauses, breaking eye contact with me. Indecision prickles at the base of my neck as light as a feather. I should be looking for an exit strategy. I should be afraid, trying to escape, something, but I don't. I can't feel anything but her and her burning need to know more.

She takes a deep breath. "What does 'The Order of Willows' mean to you?"

"Nothing," I say mechanically, still unable to choose my own speech.

Her shoulders slump and pity, murky as seawater rises into her eyes. "Okay," she says with finality and the feather feeling disappears. A second later she releases her thumbs and lets me go.

"Don't run!" she commands as she sinks back into the couch. She's winded, and I wonder how much energy she had to use to subdue me.

I sink back onto my heels. I'm in control of myself now, but the need to know is overriding my need for self-preservation.

"That necklace," she huffs. "It's rare."

She takes a deep breath and pulls a handkerchief from her pocket and dabs the sweat from her forehead that I'm just noticing.

"I have one just like it." She pulls out an identical pendant from the folds of her collared dress.

I finger the twin charm around my neck as she talks. I'd never thought much about it, other than a family heirloom.

She looks at me fiercely. "You *cannot* buy this necklace. It is only passed down from mother to daughter."

I look at her dumbly.

"It is the sign of the 'The Order of Willows'."

I blink and remain silent.

"Lord! I probably shouldn't even be telling you this. Why did you choose that murder for your project?"

"It was assigned," I lie.

"God works in mysterious ways," she says quietly with a frightening smile. "That charm and that murder are linked in a most extraordinary way."

"It must be a coincidence," I protest.

"There are no coincidences!" she hisses. "Not like that."

She turns off the television and beckons me to follow her to the kitchen. Despite the alarm bells in my head, I follow. She opens the door and practically pushes me out.

"Come back first thing tomorrow. Eight o'clock."

"B-but I have school."

"This is more important!" And then she closes the door, leaving me, gloves in hand and mind completely blown.

# PART TWO
## It's Magic

*Somewhere Dark and Hidden.*

At first, Brianna thought this was all a big joke, some sort of initiation. She'd heard Lilah's voice outside the door once. At least she thought she heard it. She had no way to know for sure. She couldn't see past the end of her nose once she rounded the corner of her little room. He said it was the perfect place for a party, for her rites. And it was. For nearly a day and a half, just the two of them sat laughing and drinking and doing well, other stuff. She didn't think of her parents once, or the snotty way that her older sister treated her, or the fool that she'd made of herself at gym. He actually liked the pooch in her belly. What did he say, "soft in all the right places"? Something like that. He was going to right everything that went wrong. Freshmen don't get chances like this all the time. She had to take it.

"Hey!" she yelled, no warbled, in case someone might be near enough to hear her.

No one heard her. No one could hear anything this far down. She heard a rumble overhead, and the exposed roots loosened and rained dirt on her head. Another car.

How long was he going to be gone this time?

She had long since grown tired of finding out "who's the father" and as the drugs wore off the reasoning behind "trusting her new sisters" and leaving her parents rules behind seemed sillier and sillier. She was almost mad enough to ruin her chances of getting in when the lock rattled on the door. The rules were that she had to stay seated on the cot. No peeking, no breaches of trust.

His familiar heavy footsteps made their way around the corner and that nervousness that never seemed to go away when he was around kicked into high gear.

"Um, I thought it might be time for me to go home. I mean, how much longer did Lilah say I had to be down here?"

He didn't reply. There was that look in his eye. The one he said meant that he was just mesmerized by her beauty. She had never been called beautiful before. Cute, once or twice, but never beautiful.

He bent down and kissed her—softly. She melted into it and even let her hand wander to touch his face. He caught it in a vice grip and returned it to her side. A hand reached up and turned off the side lamp.

A protest caught in her throat and was wrestled away by lips, teeth, tongue, a whisper ,"...so beautiful."

The same roving hand that shrouded them in darkness gripped her waist, but nibbles on her chin mercilessly thwarted the good Sunday school training she'd received, and the feeling of a tongue on her neck nearly sent her into convulsions. All the better, because without them she would have noticed just how weak she was getting by the second, and when their tongues met again and teeth clicked, she thought to herself, *this is what passion feels like.* Unfortunately, it wasn't passion that held her like a lover never would. And it wasn't passion that kissed her finally, so deep that all the breath in her body, rich with virgin life, was sucked out.

After her body dropped lifelessly on the cot, he wiped his mouth with his sleeve.

Poor girl, she never saw death coming.

# CHAPTER TEN

Today, I'll be prepared. I'll be the one asking questions. I'm psyching myself up, turning up encouraging phrases over and over in my mind as I walk up to the Mother's house. A migraine slices across my vision and makes everything cloudy, and I'm looking through a smoke stack.

If I'm ever going to figure out why I was brought back, I'm going to have to figure out why I died in the first place. Miss Collins knows more about my old life than I do at this point, and I'll walk through fire to get what I need.

"Back again, huh?" Mother Johnson sighs as she answers the door. She slides past me as I walk in.

"Don't burn the house down, while I'm gone," she yells behind her as the screen door bangs on the way out, and I'm left in the kitchen alone.

"You are a comedian Mother Johnson! A real Red Foxx," Miss Collins replies wryly from deep within the house.

A moment later she appears and smiles widely at me.

"Good morning," she sings.

"Good morning," I repeat.

She slides on an apron and stirs a pot of what smells like oxtails. I'd forgotten how early folks begin to cook dinner when they get old.

"Sit down. I won't bite," she tells me and I'm forced to sit awkwardly in one of the wobbly mismatched chairs pushed in at the Formica kitchen table. The space is immaculate with showroom sparkling floors. I mean so sparkling they seem to twinkle, though it's probably a trick of the light or some new age floor wax I don't know about.

"You know how to slice greens the right way?" she asks.

I nod, and she hands me a knife. I'm not sure why she trusts me with what could be a weapon. With what I need from her, with what she did to me yesterday, I could put this knife to her throat and make her talk. The tips of my fingers itch at the thought, but even I'm not that far gone.

"Good." She sits across from me and starts cubing butter into a bowl of steaming diced potatoes. We sit like that, me slicing, her cutting for a long while; the silence sliding around us like an irritated house pet. She studies me, and I try not to stare.

She's old, but looks stronger than her sister, fewer lines in her face. Her voice doesn't hold a trace of the quavering warble some women get with age. I can tell that she had been beautiful once, before the years turned her skin to paper and her joints to rusted steel.

After the greens, she gives me peas to snap and turns on the kitchen radio to the gospel station, an AM channel blessedly absent of any of the hip-hop inspired musical candy that's so popular now. We sip tea and hum along as we work. Something about the tea smells familiar, but I can't put my finger on it.

"Oh, you know the spirituals?"

"Yes, ma'am," I say with a smile.

"Not too many young people do. Too much hippity hop."

I laugh. After she sets her dish aside, she looks into my eyes intently and begins.

"The Order of Willows is a secret society, honey. That necklace is given to all of the initiates." She points at my neck with a well-sharpened paring knife. "I have one. My mother had one, and her mother had one."

She unclasps her watch and shows me a tree shaped scar on her wrist. I gasp. "I thought it was just a cooking scar," I breathe.

"Your mother had one too I gather. Umhmm." She puts the watch back on. "It's a brand, given when you become a full initiate." She leans back and her chair groans a bit. "We are an aid organization founded by slave women to protect themselves from their masters. The first Willow was just 14, but she had a knowledge of herbs and magic she'd learned from her village shaman. It is this knowledge and this magic that we pass down to our chosen daughters."

I'm barely breathing.

"The order has always been a threat to those who prey on women, but the Thigpen murder was the beginning of the most effective and bloodiest effort to eliminate the sisters. We call it the Great Purge."

The chopping sound echoes around the room, and the space suddenly feels like a cave, even though sunlight is dancing through the windows fractured and freeform.

"Evelyn Thigpen was the first in a series of mysterious deaths of women and girls in the order. For nearly ten years almost half of the order was eliminated. Most died in fires, like Evelyn, others just disappeared."

"The police?" I ask, disbelieving her and knowing in my heart that every word is true.

"Secret organizations don't stay secret long if we start revealing who our members are. Most people, including the police thought it was the Klan. To them, the only connection was that the women were colored. One day it just stopped. By then over half of us were dead or gone and the damage was done. Our numbers are so low now we risk extinction," she laments gripping her bony hands around her teacup.

"Is that why you're telling me this?"

"Well, that's partly true. I wouldn't have told you one word if you hadn't drunk every drop of that Forgetting tea."

I shrink back and spit what's left of the tea back into my cup. Miss Collins swiftly retrieves it and dumps the contents in a pot on the stove.

"Don't worry child. It won't hurt you. If my feeling about you remains the same then you'll drink a little lemon water spiced with Night Blossom oil. If I change my mind, you'll be on your way, and you'll forget we ever met this morning, and I'll never see you again."

"What are you doing with my spit?"

She pulls the boiling pot off the stove and pours it into a travel mug.

"We're going on a little trip. I need to know who you really are, and I'm not entirely sure you *can* tell me the truth, even if you wanted to."

I take a deep breath and try to process everything. "You say that you're trying to decide if you can trust me, but how can I trust you? You hypnotized me or whatever you want to call it yesterday and poison me the next. If anybody should be skeptical, it should be me."

She looks at me incredulously and then laughs out loud.

"Oh, I like you. Yes, ma'am." She continues to laugh as she gathers my snapped peas and places them in the sink. A second later she's got her purse and keys and she's waiting for me to walk out of the door.

"C'mon. I don't wanna be late."

### 

Miss Collins drives a boat on wheels. With enough space to fit two more people in the front seats, it makes Summer's Bug seem positively claustrophobic.

It doesn't take long before we turn down a tree-lined street. Towering three and four-story turn-of-the-century

Victorian homes press together on the narrow road, a throwback from the days when people didn't have cars. Manicured lawns lead up to wraparound porches where more often than not there is a gentleman bent by time pruning the bushes.

I remember this neighborhood. Mama used to work for a lady who lived here. All that I can remember is that she was not kind.

Soon she pulls into a driveway in a cul-de-sac. The grass is nearly a foot high with bright yellow black-eyed susans, golden marigolds and purple-red zinnias peeking through the brush. The white wooden siding is gray with dirt. It looks like it hasn't been washed in years. But the porch is well swept and dotted with multicolored chairs of all kinds: plush, wooden, rocking, stools, and couches crowd into a furniture party waiting to be crashed.

"And this is it. I don't know if you're trying to punish me by not speaking, but it's better if you keep it up when we meet Miss Miller. What we've come to see she doesn't let anyone even know she has."

I nod and get out of the car, throwing furtive glances around me for whatever surprises this old witch has up her sleeve. To my surprise we walk up creaking steps and right into the house without knocking.

"Miss Miller, I'm back from the store!" she shouts.

"Alright, Jeannie," a quivering, but laughing voice replies.

I close the door behind us. "Is that your name? Jeannie?" I ask.

Miss Collins shakes her head. "No, it is not."

Still confused I follow her into the kitchen, just as spotless as hers, with that same twinkling on the floors. I've got to get some of that wax. I whisper, " Miss Collins, what are you cleaning the floors with?" I ask.

A sly smile blooms across her face as she faces me for just a second.

"I'm not cleaning the floors at all," she replies. She places herself behind me and grips my shoulders softly. "Look closer. See the shine, the sparkle? Look there and don't blink."

A jolt of curious excitement makes my ears tingle. I do as she tells me and find a spot that's so bright the light dances. As I stare I notice that it's not the light that's dancing it's something else. At first it, looks as if it's moving and then it is so still. I look closer, focusing so closely until I see it. My breath catches, and I blink and it's gone. I straighten my back and rub my eyes. It couldn't have been.

"Try again," she urges.

This time I'm dedicated and it doesn't take as long. That light is in the same place and under it, only visible for a second, if you stare just long enough, are tiny silver legs, a glittering dress, and so grey it's white, hair. "It's a girl!" I whisper without blinking.

"No, it's a kitchen elf. Miss Miller ordered some antique Chinese pottery and she…" she points, "was the gift with purchase. Needless to say, I made sure to order from the same dealer until I lucked up on the same deal."

She releases my shoulders and walks swiftly through the kitchen, past the furiously cleaning elf and on to a staircase on the other end.

"C'mon. Don't dawdle," she chides as I remain frozen watching the elf, afraid if I blink she'll disappear. Finally, I gather myself enough to tip toe across the linoleum to the stairwell.

Kitchen elves? I didn't know such a thing existed. Then again, until yesterday, I didn't think that witches were real.

The house is old and creaky, telling secrets hidden in the old wood each time we take a step higher. We climb to the second floor and then the third and with each floor, I expect

Miss Miller to materialize but she never does. Is there some violent and horrible death awaiting me in the attic? Because I realize that is exactly where we're going when another door appears before us. I hesitate at the darkened entrance, but Miss Collins snaps her fingers and I fall in close to her heels. At the top of the stairs, she flips a switch and hands me a flashlight that's been left on the top of the banister.

Weak light casts sickly shadows around the massive room. Chairs, pots, statues and all manner of strange pieces of furniture and art are displayed, covered or propped up in every corner.

"What is this place?" I ask.

"Miss Miller is as crazy as old people get, but in her day she was the foremost collector of antique Christian antiquities in the South. This is her treasure chest."

She finds a lamp somewhere hidden in the clutter, and the place is illuminated.

"Ah, that's better," she sighs. "Okay. We are looking for a standing mirror, polished brass, about your height."

I look around not sure where to start or even if I should touch anything. The items that don't look so fragile they'll crumble look too valuable to lay a finger on.

"Don't be shy. We don't have too much time."

I wonder if Miss Collins really worked for the old woman or if we were trespassing. With each creaky step I take, guilt creeps up my spine. This feels wrong. "Do you work for Miss Miller?" I ask, "I mean, are you, were you her housekeeper," I ask as I peer behind a statue of weathered and dusty stone.

Miss Collins huffs loudly. "Was I her maid? No. I'll have you know I hold two Bachelor's degrees from Spelman College and another in seminary. My sister worked for Miss Miller. I met her in my...travels. She's an interesting woman, made more so by her collection." She says something else but it's cut off by the angles of the room.

"Now this is interesting," she murmurs and opens a small box set atop a chest of drawers.

I look over my shoulder at her and strain to see what's inside. She turns to me and tosses me something from inside.

"Catch."

I reach out my hand, but I miss and the thing rolls under a table nearby. Once I'm on my knees I retrieve what looks like a copper coin, larger than a penny and much thinner. It's green with age, but you can still make out the leaf embossed on one side.

"What is it?" I ask as I run my thumb across the surface and rise from my corner of the room.

She closes the box and continues her search. "It's a troll coin."

There are trolls? Nonsense.

"You bury it in your garden as payment. Legend says a troll will come and enchant it for you. Perpetual bloom and protection. Plants are better protectors than guard dogs you know."

She says something else, but it gets cut off.

"Do you mean like magic?" I ask incredulously.

"So after all that you know and see, you don't believe in magic?"

I don't respond, afraid I'll say the wrong thing.

"Well, you're right. There is no such thing as magic, there is only energy. And if you remember from your science lessons, energy is neither created nor destroyed, it just changes form. That coin isn't special. It doesn't do anything really, but please garden trolls. But the troll, however, is gifted. He will know what nutrients, and ancient life giving properties your plants will need to thrive. They're an ancient race with ancient knowledge."

She goes back to her rummaging while I stand there thinking.

"Trolls?" I ask again, just because it still seems ridiculous.

" They're one of God's creatures just like you and me," she replies without looking up.

I think about that. If a unicycling monkey can exist (I saw one at a traveling fair once), then why can't God create trolls? I don't have a good answer.

"Ha! Found it," she laughs happily. "Come on over."

I pocket the coin, still wavering between whether to believe her or run away.

She pulls a blanket off the artifact, sending dust whirling in every direction. We both sneeze and when the cloud clears, I can see myself clearly in a gleaming oval brass mirror that reaches from the top of my head to the floor. It rests in a polished wood base that's set in a dark marble.

"What is it?"

"It's what's going to tell me who you are. It's Jezebel's mirror."

# CHAPTER ELEVEN

"Jezebel? Like from the bible?" I ask Miss Collins.

She nods.

"Yes. Like most strong women of her time she is misunderstood, but some things are true. She knew the hour of her death and like a queen, she met it with grace and beauty. This mirror revealed to her when the prophet Jehu would come for her. It can see the future."

I stare at my reflection, and the tiniest ripple flows across the surface like an animal flexing.

"It can also see the past," she murmurs as she walks over to the banister and retrieves the thermos we brought from her house.

"You aren't going to drink that are you?"

The grimace on my face must be funny to her because she laughs.

"Of course not."

Out of her pocket, she pulls a small cloth and dips it in the still warm liquid and hands it to me. On creaking limbs she stands again and hands me a folded slip of paper from her other pocket.

"Read it out loud as you wash the surface of the mirror counter clockwise."

I look at her dumbly.

Exasperated she sighs. "Remember what I told you. There is no magic, only science. This mirror is a machine just like a

78

cell phone, created with knowledge of energy systems that you can scarcely comprehend. It's simply a conduit. Think of it like a large battery. Can you read?"

"Yes, ma'am. I read Latin and Greek."

She cocks her head to one side and smiles. I look at the paper in my hand. It's three lines of simple script, all in Greek.

"Your mother taught you?" she asks.

I nod.

"Ummhmm. Collette, the order does not recruit. Even if we dwindle to only one member, we keep the traditions. But we also know that we have lost initiates to the murders, and the city needs us now as much as ever with the disappearances this year."

Brianna's face flashes behind my eyes and my shoulders tighten with pity. I barely knew her, but we both met an evil in the night and I escaped while her journey on this earth ended.

I stare at the surface as another ripple moves across the brass. It's like the mirror is shivering, as if it knows what's coming. I bite my lip and think. Maybe nothing will happen. Miss Miller could be a crazy church lady with wild notions. She wouldn't be the first that I've come across and what could it hurt. I'm just, just cleaning a mirror.

I take a deep breath and begin to wipe slowly and recite the words.

> "Αποκαλύψτε το μυστήριό σας
> Αποκαλύψτε το πεπρωμένο μου
> Το παρελθόν είναι τώρα παρόν
> Το βλέπω σαφώς"

> "Reveal your mystery
> Reveal my destiny
> The past is now present
> I see it clearly"

On the first swipe nothing happens, but on the second the surface gleams and shivers, the brass giving way like the skin on pudding, and then on the third pass, I don't notice until it's too late and I fall headfirst and completely through.

### 

The grass is wet under my fingers, and the summer heat is warm on my skin. A tiny frog jumps over my right hand, and I jump back, hitting Miss Collins like a wall.

"Where are we?" I ask. She looks hazy, like a ghost, but when she grabs my hand to lift me up she's as solid as ever. She's also silent. She's got no aura or emotional signature. It feels weird, like trying to hear when one ear is clogged. I feel cutoff.

"I don't know where we are. This is your story. You tell me?"

I look around and the attic is nowhere to be seen. The moon is heavy and pregnant above us and it must be late summer 'cause the day's heat is still lingering. Ahead of us. a house is lit from the inside and the back door is open.

"It's my house!" I cry, suddenly outrageously happy.

The screen door opens and my Uncle steps out of house and down the stairs.

"Uncle Elias!" I shout and break out into a run to greet him, but Miss Collins grabs my arm.

"Quiet girl. You're not really here. This is a time memory. He can't hear you."

I snatch my arm back and run up to him anyway.

"Uncle Elias! It's me. I'm back. Look, I'm fine."

He doesn't break his stride. I trot in front of him and wave my arms. He walks straight ahead, pecan shells cracking and crunching under his feet.

"Uncle Elias?"

"I told you, he can't hear you. This has already happened. It's like an echo of an event. You aren't really here. He isn't really here."

I look at this woman and feel hate burning in my belly. I step out of Uncle Elias' way and watch him walk through the yard and out the back fence.

Miss Collins makes her way to the back door of the house and peers in. I follow suit.

"You look very much like your mother."

It's a compliment, but I don't thank her. I climb the steps and position myself in front of her so I can get a better look inside. Mama is pouring something blue and noxious into a glass vial at the kitchen sink. She looks beautiful in a white dress and makeup. She looks like she's going out, or just coming in. Her hair is still done, and she's still wearing her heels, something she never let me do. Raphael is whispering something to someone wrapped in a blanket lying on the couch.

Without any aura wafting off of them, I know that the person must be dead. A cold feeling slips over me despite the heat of the night. Frogs creak loudly in my ears as I strain to try and hear everything and anything going on inside the house.

"Ready, Evelyn?"

Miss Collins makes a noise behind, but I ignore it and focus on Mama. She's crying and a tear falls into the vial she's holding, making the liquid seize and steam.

She sniffles a bit and turns to Raphael nodding her head. "Ready."

As her heels click across the floor my eyes are fixed on her and it takes me a second to notice that she's not holding the vial any longer. It's suspended in air above the sink.

My eyes dart from her to the sink to Raphael in rapid succession until I catch Raphael's eye and I'm sure he sees me. I am sure of it, and I'm about to speak when he sets his eyes on

Mama and hugs her. Her back is to me and it could be a trick of the light but it seems like Raphael is shaking his head, telling me not to speak. When he lets her go, he whispers something into her ear.

I strain, but I can't catch it. I go to grab the screen door and open it, but my hand won't grip.

I want to hug Mama too. I can feel the time slipping away, the memory crumbling. A moment later, Mama laughs and wipes her eyes.

She shouts, "You tell her her mother loved her more than her own life."

A second later she waves her hand above her head and the vial floats from the sink to hover above them.

"I'm scared, Raphael," she says and fear wafts through the room like cooking smoke, but as soon as she says the words, courage crowds it out.

"Willow it out?" she shouts and Raphael laughs. Before she can return the laugh, her hand drops and down goes the vial exploding in a fire that knocks me and Miss Collins off the steps.

"Mama!"

I scramble to my feet but in the time it takes me to get up, the house is in smokeless blue flame. Even in my ghostly state I can feel the heat.

"C'mon child. We have to go." Miss Collins urges, dragging me backward.

"But we have to help her!" I cry pulling away and screaming.

I'm about to knock Miss Collins down and finally race in when I see a winged figure move through the flaming carcass of the house. The weird fire has devastated the house in seconds to the point where we can see through the frame in some spots. One of those spots is my room, and it's there that the figure stops. He lifts something encased in light, a body. I try, but I can't make it out. And then,

"Don't touch me!" I yell just before the blackness takes me.

### 

When I open my eyes I'm in the attic again on my hands and knees. It feels like I've been sucked through a tube, and the lights are brighter in my eyes. Night must have fallen because there isn't any sun leaking through the cracks in the roof and my skin is cold from the night air seeping in.

I hear Miss Collins cough, still catching her breath behind me.

"She did it," she wheezes. "She called and they came. She did it," she coughs again.

I'm crying. Hot wet tears are streaming down my face, and I don't want to move despite the cold seeping into my muscles.

I just watched my mother die. I just watched my mother kill herself. And, then lower on my list of soul shaking revelations, my mother was unequivocally, a witch.

"Bold she was. Regal in death! Hot damn she did it!"

She claps her hands and without looking I can tell she's smiling. I can barely make her out through my tears, but her elation is rolling off her in big gusts.

I want to throw up, but there's nothing in my belly. I want to cry here alone and then sleep, but I have to move. I have to sit in a car with this woman I suddenly hate.

"Sweetheart?" Miss Collins asked softly. I guess she realized she's been the only one speaking.

I flinch at her oncoming nearness. I can feel the warmth of her body coming to hug me, but I don't want her to. I want to think about what just happened, and I don't want to be touched.

"Okay. Okay."

I hear her rise and make her way to the stairs.

"It's night time. You just sit there as long as you need. I'll be waiting in the kitchen."

I hear her creak down the stairs slowly, and when I'm sure she's gone I sit up and stare at myself in the mirror. I stare until my nose bleeds into my eyes, and my cheeks into my chin, until I disappear, until I'm numb.

# CHAPTER TWELVE

We ride to Miss Collins' house in silence. When we get there, Mother Johnson sets a plate of cornbread, collards and baked chicken in front of me. My manners take over when my brain doesn't, and I manage to whisper a thanks, the first words I've said since we made it back. I force myself to eat.

"I want to show you something." Miss Collins says to me softly from across the table. I refuse to look into her eyes.

She leaves the room and comes back with an old book and a stick of incense. It rattles the wooden table with its weight when she plunks it down in front of me.

"Mama's bible," I sniffle.

"No," she breathes, "it probably just looks like it."

She lights the incense on the stove and visibly relaxes. "This is a Fountain book. It's a bible as well, but it is also a journal, a reference and a spell book. Only a clairvoyant Willow is allowed to write in the journal."

I finger the worn leather and onion skin-thin paper. I can see its identical twin resting on a podium in the hallway, Mama hunched over it, a wrinkle of confusion deep in her brow. How did I miss all this growing up? Was I blind? Mama could move things with her mind. How did that go unnoticed? I lose myself in guilt for long, sad moments before I notice Miss Collins staring at me.

"What?" I ask.

"I prayed. I prayed, day and night for a girl. I called every Willow in three states, and they all had sons or their daughters were too young or too old."

What does she mean? She doesn't mean that I'm the answer to her prayers? A pot rumbles on the stove, and she jumps up to take care of it just as Mother Johnson peeks in.

"Those collards warm you up?" Mother Johnson croaks.

I nod and give her a weak smile.

Miss Collins waits until her sister makes her way back into the bowels of the house.

"You're Evelyn Thigpen's daughter aren't you?"

I don't want to answer this woman's questions. "Why are you asking me questions you already know the answer to?" I whisper fiercely, staring down at my half-eaten food.

"That angel saved you that night. Your mother called him," she says as if she's answering the winning question on a game show. Her voice is high and excited and her eyes twinkle with new secrets.

"I don't know what she did. I don't know what I saw. Maybe it was a dream."

Miss Collins shakes her head. "No dream, girl. That was God's honest truth replayed. You are lucky. No, blessed. Yes, blessed. Only a most powerful Willow could have done what she did. The concentration involved had to be staggering. The sacrifice. Umm, umm."

"Stop talking about Mama like she's a prized cow. It's time for me to go home."

Miss Collins excitement deflates like a balloon.

"You're upset. I understand…"

I cut her off. "No, you don't understand. You didn't just watch your mother die. You didn't see the angel pass over her and come to you. You didn't wake up alive and alone, so you don't understand anything."

I stand up quickly, making the chair squeak across the linoleum. Out of the corner of my eye, I see the kitchen elf dart from the corner to attend to the scratches immediately. She's so clear now it seems ridiculous that I could have missed her before.

"I'm sorry, sweetheart," Miss Collins apologizes," but you have to understand that this is all a revelation to me too. I'm looking at this through the eyes of a sister Willow, and I should be looking at them through a daughter Willow's eyes."

"I'm not a Willow. I'm not..."

I cut myself short this time, because I don't know what to say. Am I a Willow? What does that mean? I need to get out of here, and before Miss Collins can offer anything else, I'm out the door and into the night.

### 

I once was blind and now I see.

With all that I now know, maybe it was better when I didn't know what was real and what wasn't. Witches? Real. Elves? Real. Resurrection? Real, too, but to what end I still don't know. I know that I didn't die by accident, not that it does me any good. I know how I died, but I don't know why.

Right now, I don't want to.

According to Summer, Wingtastic is the place to be for Spring View alumni and students alike. It's only a mile from the school, and you can smell the smoke from the barbecue pit at least two miles in every direction. Not helpful for me, seeing as how Miss Collins' revelations keep playing over and over in my head giving me a migraine. Sleep came fitfully, when it finally did come, and grief tinged with weary is making my feet drag.

Because I couldn't sleep and because I needed to talk to someone who could really sort this out for me, I searched around the yard in the dark looking for Raphael. He was never really a house cat, but he didn't tend to go far for long. Maybe he's changed. Everything else has.

"You don't look so good," Summer notices.

"Headache. No, a massive headache."

"Got just the thing," she says as she pulls out a small pill bottle from her bag and hands it to me.

"What's this?" I ask and pull out one of the pills.

"It is a magical elixir that will solve all of your problems. It is..." she pauses. "Valium."

She shakes the pill bottle before dropping it back in her bag.

"What's that?"

"Drugs. Plain and simple. Best on the market and free of charge, courtesy of Uncle Silas' less than legal clientele."

She hands me a water bottle from her comically oversized bag, and I wash the pill down just as we make it to the front.

The girl at the desk is our age, waifish and beady eyed with too-bright artificially whitened teeth. She smiles so big it's easy to tell this is her first job and she's happy to have it. I've never seen her before, but I know she's a Spring View student by her "Save Brianna" t-shirt. They do work quickly around here, I see.

"Welcome to Wingtastic! Our wings are so cluckin' good! Hold please."

The girl nods us closer while she balances the phone between her shoulder and her ear. "Dine-In or To-Go?" she asks cheerily.

"We're actually meeting someone. Can I look inside to see?" Summer asks.

She nods. Summer mouths "Nice shirt," and the girl gives her a thumbs up as we walk away.

Thankfully, I don't have to worry about sitting in the claustrophobic dining room because the open air sweeps away my concern as Carlos waves us over from a table under an awning on the rooftop deck.

"Wow, shade! Who did you bribe to get this table?" Summer gushes as we settle ourselves onto the counter height stools.

"I'm just lucky I guess," he chuckles.

As soon as we sit his eyes dart suspiciously from side to side as he whispers, "You got the stuff?"

Summer laughs and jerks her head up. "Ha, ha," she replies sarcastically. "Don't do that. People will think that I'm a drug dealer."

"You kind of are," he shoots back with a big smile on his face, obviously proud of himself for his joke. I don't have the heart to tell him that it is a joke that nearly all of Summer's customers make at one time or another. Wait, am I a customer?

When Summer called to say that we were meeting Carlos, I was surprised. Apparently, they had gone to elementary school together and just happened to be in the line for the volunteer search party for Brianna together.

I'd missed all this while I was with Miss Collins, not that I would have been caught dead there anyway. The grief would have been too much for me to handle, even with my shields. I've lost track of the conversation. I've been quiet too long.

Carlos opens his mouth to say something when a hush falls as gently as snow over the patio as the double doors swing open.

Lilah.

She breezes onto the patio on the balls of her toes in that dance walk she does and a mixture of cold and a feeling I can't quite identify makes me shiver. Have we been waiting for her? It seems like we have, though that doesn't make any sense at all. I shake the thought from my head.

Seemingly oblivious to the distraction she's causing or possibly completely aware, she strolls over to the only open table in the opposite corner of the floor leading a beautiful dark boy with almond eyes quietly behind her with his one massive index finger encircled by all five of her tiny manicured ones. Every head on the deck is turned in her direction.

Carlos breaks the silence. "She can make an entrance, but she can't write an introductory paragraph for shit."

"Language!" I chide and the letters feel jumbled in my mouth as if my teeth aren't in the right place.

"Sorry," he apologizes.

Even with my shields up I can tell Carlos has the same unidentifiable feeling slinking over his skin that I do. It's mottled and brownish green. On everyone else it's shimmering and pink.

"She's an 'It' girl." Summer says breathily, shaking her head as if she's shaking dust out of her hair. An almost imperceptible frown is flickering at the corners of her mouth.

The mood is changed and we order in flat voices while the waiter refills our glasses. I don't take my eyes off the boy and Lilah. I wonder if the feeling I have is fear. Am I afraid for him?

He's dark, dark as a starless night and as pretty as the sound of wedding bells as he sits stiffly in the seat next to the pale girl. I glance for signs of unrest. I remember the days when a black boy could be murdered, freely for what he's doing right now, sitting next to her. To me, it was just yesterday.

All eyes are on them and God bless her, Lilah picked the exact spot where the sun would fall over her so that the light frames her face creating a halo. She laughs and it rings out like wind chimes, though I'm not sure at what because the boy hasn't said a word since he sat down.

"Uh, you tryin' to read her mind or something?" Carlos snaps me out of my reverie.

I realize now that I've been staring because I've been hoping to catch the boy's eye. The feeling is niggling in my brain. It's not fear, but something, something else. Maybe if we lock eyes?

"Didn't your mother ever tell you it was rude to stare? Besides, I don't want you turning into one of her creepy acolytes."

Brianna's face appears behind my eyes as she tries to will Celeste to speak to her. Is she cold wherever she is? I imagine her cold face half-covered in dirt. My stomach turns.

"Ever since she arrived a little after the Valentine's Day dance, so it must have been March, she's had the teen queen thing on lock. At first it was just one or two girls, and the next thing you know it was the entire cheerleading squad. They call themselves 'Bells'."

Summer's staring at her fingers, flexing and unflexing as if they've got the answer to all of her problems. The frown still flickers at the corners of her mouth ,and the tips of her curly hair are blazing a wildfire in the wind. I think at that moment she's more beautiful than Lilah, but she'd never accept that.

"Ah, the walk," I comment.

He nods.

"You know I was surprised the kidnapper went for Brianna. If he's keeping true to his pattern you'd think he'd go for Lilah."

"Pattern?"

"All the girls he kidnapped before were beauty queens or really popular. Student council presidents and ice skating champions."

"Those are two different people," Summer says sadly.

"That's what the police want you to think so they don't have to find those black girls or admit that they didn't run away. C'mon Summer, you know it's true. You just don't want to admit it."

"Can we talk about something else?" she says in a small voice.

The table is silent and a deep sadness flares on her chest and shoulders like a bruise. I don't ask if she knew Brianna that well. It doesn't matter. The pain she's feeling is beginning to bloom in her cheeks in tiny purple spider veins. I know she's about to cry and embarrassment would only make things worse. I know this sad feeling. I know the color of it. I've had it.

I want to do something. I want to make things better, if not for myself, for someone else. I want to help, to not feel helpless in the face of fear, and I'm glad and both loathe to do it. I take a deep breath and slip my hand over the table and grip hers. At first she's just surprised at the touch and we both gasp and then the flood begins, first her insecurities and my heart begins to beat faster, then her fear of rejection boils hot in my belly and my mouth goes dry. Tears prick my eyes and one rolls fat and hot down my cheek. I pull back.

She looks at me, a tiny smile on her face, and draws in a deep breath. "Collette, are you alright?"

I swallow hard and nod. "Are you?"

She looks around the patio and stretches her arms wide over her head as a giggle titters out of her throat. "Why wouldn't I be?" she laughs and then pauses with a confused look on her face. "What were we talking about?"

# CHAPTER THIRTEEN

Carlos is confused, a grey film of the emotion collects around his ears. "What just happened?"

"Nothing." I croak. "Girl stuff."

He shrugs. "We still on for this afternoon, right?" Carlos asks.

"This afternoon?" I ask.

"Yes! We have an appointment with that Miller lady over at the Garden Club. Didn't you get my message?"

I shake my head. I probably did get it, but it will take me a good long while to recover from Summer's pain and my head is muddled. I don't know if it is normal for someone like me or not, but I can take pain away, if I choose to.

The waiter brings our food and Carlos digs into his plate of ribs. "I did some more research and found out that it was a Miller that bought the tombstones for the murdered family. And remember how I said I wanted to canvas the neighborhood?"

I nod once, lightning fast and with a blank face.

"So yeah, the last living Miller, who is supposed to be like some president emeritus or some shit. I don't know." He trails off at the end and takes another sloppy bite of his ribs. His eyes roll to the back of his head, and he's in pork heaven while I realize I'm in a hell of my own creation.

###

"You okay?" Carlos asks.

I nod slowly.

I took the other half of Valium after I touched Summer and my muscles feel warm and jellylike. My headache is just a memory, if the sting of willingly accepting Summer's pain hasn't. If someone is in pain you help them. It's that simple. Mama taught me that. I think of her face inside the house just before she dropped the vial. She was so scared. I can see her so clearly and then I can't. It just slips away.

"I've never been in this neighborhood. I had to print out directions this morning. I didn't even know all this was back here," Carlos announces.

Dread mixed with a hope that coincidence isn't married to cruelty roils under my skin as the houses become familiar.

We ride for a minute or two before he pulls into that same driveway in the cul-de-sac. Everything is the same, save the arrangement of the chairs on the porch. Today, they're grouped by color. He turns off the engine and gets out. I hesitate and then follow him up the steps.

Coincidence. This is all just a coincidence and besides Miss Miller never saw me yesterday. This is fine. Fine.

Dear God, why did it have to be the same woman?

He takes a step closer to the door while I take one back. He presses an ear to the stained glass and closes his eyes. The window depicts a swan in a meadow nestling its beak into its wing. It's beautiful.

We hear a shuffle and then floorboards creaking.

"Ms. Miller?" Carlos shouts, blasting his dill pickle breath in my face and nearly splitting my eardrums.

"Hey!"

"Oh, sorry." He shrugs his shoulders but keeps stock still while he listens.

"Coming!" we hear faintly. "Coming up soon, sweetie!" the voice says a little louder.

I'm still trying to gather myself when Ms. Miller opens the door dressed in a midnight blue muumuu with persimmon colored flowers wrapped around it. Shockingly long white and grey braids are pulled on top of her head and arranged so that she resembles a pineapple.

"Good afternoon, Ms. Miller."

The woman waves a boney hand at us. "Call me Jeannie; everyone else does." The barking menace turns out to be a shih tzu that looks almost as old as she is. Jeannie? I thought that was the name of the maid. Was she talking to herself yesterday?

"Ms...I mean Jeannie. I called you yesterday about the tombstone. I'm Carlos and this is Collette."

"Mmm, Collette. I like that name. Maybe I'll be a Collette in my next life." She smiles at me and then turns quickly to walk back into the house leaving the door wide open. She doesn't know who I am. Thank God for small favors.

It reeks of expensive perfume and rancid pond water inside. The sheers are drawn over the windows to block out direct sunlight so that only a few rays peek through the lace giving off a feeling like we're in a funhouse or falling down the rabbit hole. Was it like this yesterday? I keep an eye out for the kitchen elf or other hidden house help.

"You know I was a prostitute in my former life," the woman says to no one in particular without breaking stride. I turn to Carlos and flash him a wicked smile. With the danger of discovery averted, I seem to be doing alright, but Carlos is beginning to look downright afraid. I don't know if it's the Valium, but I am all too willing to go down the rabbit hole with this crazy old biddy, just as long as we stay far away from the attic.

"It's why I've never been married. Oh, I've been asked. Countless times, yes, but I would never commit. My blood is wild, even now when my tits reach down to my ankles."

"Jesus!" Carlos breathes almost imperceptibly.

We follow the old woman further into the house and down a flight of steps. The light fades and we're covered in almost total darkness for a short moment before we go through another door and see a cobblestone path appear at the end of the steps.

"I went to a fortune teller when I was sixteen and she told me the exact moment, day and time I would die." She stops short and I almost crash into her when she spins quickly to face me her sagging skin molded in a crooked smile.

"So I'm not afraid of anything," she whispers, and then turns to continue down the stairs.

I want to throw my head back in a cackle. Miss Collins was right. I didn't think they made this kind of crazy anymore. One day, when I was six, my Mama was away for some reason, I don't remember why, but I had to go with Gran to work. She used to care for an old woman named Mrs. Kaney. I don't remember much of that day except that we spent an hour playing a reluctant game of hide-and-go-seek with a naked Mrs. Kaney who claimed that an imaginary friend who looked suspiciously like Teddy Roosevelt had stolen all her clothes and burned them.

We emerge out of darkness to what must be the first floor terrace and then into a garden of dreams. I am Alice and have just walked into Wonderland.

"Wow," Carlos whispers behind me, astonished.

It's almost October, but you wouldn't know it by the still blooming hordes of Echinacea, Wild Iris, Shooting Star, English Tea Roses and bush upon bush of almost golf-ball sized blueberries. I remember the coin Miss Collins gave me yesterday that's still in the pocket of my skirt at home.

For the next half hour she proceeds to prance and tell us about her days as a Vegas showgirl and as the world's oldest hippie (her words). I especially enjoy the side bar about the pros and cons of free love. For a second, I think Carlos is going to retch right there on the patio.

"Now," she huffs breathlessly before collapsing back into her seat, "tell me what you came here for."

Neither of us speaks, waiting for her to continue her story, but after a beat I realize this is our turn to speak. "I, uh, we, ahem, wanted to know about a tombstone."

"Tombstone!" she coughs through sips of tea.

Carlos breaks in again, "A family tombstone. We're doing a school project about the Thigpen murders. Do you remember them? It was in the late 40's and a newspaper article said that your family paid for the services and tombstone."

The old woman regains her composure and sits up straight. "My, my, you are an interesting pair of visitors. Escandalo," she says evenly and winks at us both.

"The family didn't pay for that tombstone. My uncle did. The family was quite scandalized by the whole thing. Quite scandalized." She takes another sip of her tea and shakes off the crazy for a moment to tell us more. "My uncle…, "she trails off for a second, searching her brain for the name. "Peter, yes, Peter."

The name rings with an unforgiving accent so that it sounds like Pee-tah. "He was the oddest of us all. Small and quiet, none of us knew what he was up to. When that colored family got murdered, of course we all thought it was the Klan. Who else? They were always runnin' 'round in those silly sheets screamin' about protectin' the race before they decided to string some poor colored boy up or rape some little girl. So when Peter started calling in family favors to investigate the murders people started asking questions."

"What kind of favors?" Carlos asks. I am frozen with my cement smile, a bandage soaking up every blood-soaked word. Was it the Klan she was running from? Was it better to kill herself than to let them get to her, us? Were they witch hunters? A thousand possibilities run through my head.

"Oh, honey he called the Chief of Police and demanded that the perpetrators be found, and when that didn't work, he hired a private investigator from Charlotte to come down. The pièce de résistance was the tombstone he bought for the murdered woman. Lord, it was the largest and most expensive piece in the cemetery at the time. If it wasn't clear before, everyone knew from then on that she was his mistress, and most folks assume the missing child was his." She pauses to whistle.

"Ooooh, my Granny was livid! Even more livid than when I ran away that first time with a bandleader from New Jersey."

She stops to cackle at the memory for a moment. I can't look at Carlos. I just stare at the woman's wrinkled hands and chipped nail polish. I want desperately for her to fill in the gaping holes to the story of my family. Was it better to think Mama was murdered?

"He was distraught. He lost what little weight he had on him. The whole thing was highly embarrassing for Granny. She could barely show her face at the garden club meetings. He died, himself, not long after.

"Secrets, dearies, are the worst kind of addiction. They'll take you to heaven before you realize you had to die to get there."

She laughs and then yawns.

I've been wondering how long she was going to be able to go, given how old she is.

"Hmmm, Peter. I haven't thought about him in eons," she says sleepily through closed eyes.

Carlos kicks me under the table. "Ow!" I hiss. He jerks his head to one side and mouths "Let's go" exaggeratedly. I reply, "No" in the same fashion. He mouths a "Yes" and slides silently out of his chair and starts backing away from the table towards the stairs.

"Ms. Miller!" I shout.

"Yes, yes, dear. I'm just resting my eyes."

"Yes, ma'am. It's getting late in the afternoon, We should probably go and let you get some rest."

"Really? So, soon. I haven't even shown you my garden."

The garden beckons in the afternoon light. It is Technicolor and wild and beautiful. She definitely has to be a talented gardener. I wonder how she is able to manage it in her old age and then chuckle at my own stupidity. Of course I know how she maintains it.

"Maybe another time. We'll talk about something happy. You can tell us about all your travels."

"Oh, honey," she says condescendingly. "My life's a tragedy. That's not a happy story at all. I'll be sure to make up something fabulous for you. Next time?" she asks sweetly.

I nod. "Next time," I lie.

My father's name was Peter.

# CHAPTER FOURTEEN

I get up early everyday. Earlier than most, but today, when I do I can't get his name out of my mind.

Peter?

Peter. It's such an everyday name. Not grand, not unique. How many times have I heard someone talk about a man named Peter? Did Mama say his name? Did she mention him, and I've just forgotten like I've forgotten everything else? I turn the thought over in my head a dozen times while I sit on the porch the next morning. Suddenly a giggle bursts out of my lips from nowhere and then I hear them. Dogs.

I didn't see them round the corner, but at the end of my walkway stands the boy with the almond eyes from yesterday in a USC sweatshirt, shorts and two of the cutest little bull dogs wrapping quickly around his legs.

"Need a little help," I call down.

"With these guys?" he replies. "Nah, they're just pups." He says it with a little good natured sarcasm. He smiles at me in the fog and rising sunlight. He looks divine in the biblical sense, fallen from grace. I take a sip of my coffee and set it on the banister. If he talks with me, maybe I can convince him to come back later when Summer's here. Yes, that's a good reason.

"Hey, let me help you." I skip down the stairs in robe and kneel down. I'm careful not to touch him as I pull the leather leashes away so he can step out of the tangles. Even through the fabric you can see the muscles move on his, uh…backside. *His legs are totally hairless.* How is that possible? I wonder if he has chest hair.

"Thanks. I'm Chamberlain."

Oh that Chamberlain, and for the first time in a long time I really take a good long moment to think about Matt. It wasn't long ago that he'd been number one on my problems list. Now… not so much.

"No problem," I say as I give one of the dogs a scratch around his ears. It's a welcome excuse not to shake hands. I like dogs. They're genuinely happy most of the time, so I don't have to worry about their emotional signatures at all.

"The good reverend 'don't walk dogs' as he says, so I charge him a little extra for his yard work. Speaking of…" He nods behind me to my overgrown grass and untended bushes. I'm a little embarrassed.

An awkward silence fills the space between us.

"Uh, welcome to the neighborhood."

"Thanks! You're the first person to welcome me."

" Really? You've been here awhile. I saw Matt chattin' you up at school, and I saw you yesterday at Wingtastic. I meant to come and talk to you, but …" His serious eyes are locked with mine. Even with my shields up I can feel the warmth of his smile. I smile back stupidly in return.

"But?"

"I'm sorry, what?" He laughs dryly. "I lost my train of thought."

He laughs. "Oh, yeah. I know what I wanted to ask. Are you some sort of teenage millionaire?"

"'Scuse me?"

He waves a hand at the house. "You're in this house by yourself. Up at the crack of dawn drinking coffee like an old lady."

"I'm not in this house by myself," I say a little too defensively. "How do you? Have you..?" As soon as I say it I feel ridiculous. Of course he hasn't been watching me, and here I am accusing him of being some kind of weirdo. He did mention that he knew I'd been in the neighborhood.

"Well, to be honest I did notice you." He's not so cool anymore. He has the good manners to look sheepish. "I walk the dogs this way every day and this house used to be empty, but now… There's never a car in the drive way, but…" he lifts his nose to the air, imitating a bloodhound and closes his eyes. "Is that? What is that smell?"

Shoot. I'd forgotten about breakfast just that quick. "Oh! Well, yes. I have to… Can you wait a little…ah, come on up?"

He looks down at the dogs and hesitates.

"They can come too. I don't have much furniture. It's not like they can hurt anything." I'm speaking quickly and walking away. I don't want to be rude, but I don't want my ham to burn either.

"Um. Ah, hell. Alright," he concedes.

He follows me up the stairs and onto the porch. He hesitates at the door. It's cute. It's nice to have people drop by, nicer to have the dogs, sorry to say. Maybe I should think about getting one.

I pull the cinnamon buns out of the oven and set them on the stove. I've caught them just in time.

"Jesus, that smells good."

"I've got enough if you've got time. You're welcome to stay. Ham is done and the red-eye gravy will be ready in a jiff. By the way my Daddy works late and is away on business most of the time." I spit the lie out so fast I think he doesn't even catch the statement. I hear a rumble, but it's his stomach not the dogs.

"I think your stomach knows what to do, even if you don't, "I laugh. He looks away in fake shame and shrugs.

"You got me. What's for breakfast Mom?" he jokes.

"Ha, ha. Cinnamon buns, grits, smoked ham and red-eye gravy. I would've made eggs, but I ran out yesterday."

"Wow. Did you cook all that yourself?"

I give him an incredulous and then insulted look. "Of course I did. Cinnamon Buns are one of my specialties. I'm sending a box to all the parents of the missing girls."

"Wow, that's really cool." The dogs bark again at something I don't see. "Uh, I really should go. Thanks for the invite though." The dogs pull on their leashes again and half drag him down the porch steps.

"Oh, well. Wait a minute." I run inside and pull one of the sticky buns off the pan and put it in a paper towel. "Here you go. For the road."

His eyes light up, and he tears into it. It's got to be burning the roof of his mouth, but he doesn't seem to care. A sugar crusted smile erupts onto his face as the dogs continue to drag him down the walkway.

"Thanks!" he says while chewing. He seems nice enough. I wonder what Matt's said about me?

"Hey, what did..." I call out, but I hear a whistle ring out from somewhere far down the street, and the dogs take off in a full sprint snatching my question with them. I don't even have a good minute to consider the fact that my hair is still tied up in a sleeping scarf when a large black sedan with tinted windows rounds the corner.

My heart skips a beat once and then twice as it stops in front of my house, and I can't help but take a few steps back.

"Good morning!" the disembodied voice croons, riding on a cloud of cigar smoke.

Uncle Silas.

###

"You..(smack!)..should...(smack!) sell these. Mmmm!" Uncle Silas says with a mouthful of cinnamon bun.

I smile at the comment, even as I bristle at his presence at my kitchen table. Uncle Silas has an air of danger. My Gran would call it the stain of sin. His head is shiny and his teeth seem too big for his mouth. I want him to leave.

"What can I do for you Mr. Bluefern?" I ask.

"Nothing. I thank you for the breakfast. I remembered how you didn't really care for the office so I thought I'd drop by some paperwork and a bit of news for you."

"News?" I'm curious. Uncle Silas doesn't strike me as the kind of man to make house calls so I know this must be important.

He wipes his mouth with a napkin and slurps his coffee, even though I know it's scalding hot.

"Brianna Baxter is dead."

I gasp.

"How do you? Where did they?"

He waves his swollen hand in front of me. This is where I silently acknowledge that he knows things that most men don't, does things that most men won't.

"They'll announce it later this afternoon. Tomorrow morning at the latest. The only reason why I'm telling you personally is because there is something wrong with this case. The girl didn't die like she should have," he confesses.

I look at him dumbly. How *should* a girl die? I think about the darkness the reverend talked about and the disappearances that have Miss Collins on edge.

"This isn't a simple abduction and as much as they hate to admit it, the police are going to have to take a second look at that string of missing Black girls. Though, I'm sure they won't be announcing *that* anytime soon." He laughs hard and loud at himself. I don't get the joke.

"They've had a few high profile mistakes in the last year, and I don't think they're too eager to work cases that don't add up," he chuckles.

"Can I ask you a question?"

He cocks his head to listen, still licking glaze from his lips. "Alright."

"How much do you know about me?"

His eyes twinkle and a smirk develops. "I'm not sure if I could say the words if I wanted to." He shrugs. "It's the deal I've made to be in my position."

I think about that. We're dealing with the supernatural. I can't imagine what kind of deal he's made to keep quiet about it, or who he's made the deal with.

He pushes himself away from the table and points to a manila envelope he's placed there. "This is your insurance policy. If things start to feel...*wrong* in any way, there is enough cash in there to get you far away for a while."

"Why would they feel wrong?" I ask him.

He waves his hand again, like the question is silly, even though he just posed it.

"They shouldn't. This is just insurance. Don't worry about it. Everything should be fine. But I do want you to steer clear of any new friends, especially boys." He goes to pat me on my shoulder and then remembers himself.

I don't know what to say, but I remember my manners.

"Thank...th-thank you for telling me and for c-coming by personally." I lead him to the door when a piercing wail rips through the air like an alarm. Uncle Silas blocks the door with his body and walks backwards to the kitchen, motioning for me to shuffle backwards as well. A second later something explodes against the door way, then again, and then once more against the front window and the room goes dark as something red and thick dribbles down the screen, looking very much like blood.

My heart pounds in my chest, and I cover my mouth so I don't scream out loud. Fear, noxious and acidic fills the room as we both stand stock still and wait. I don't know how much time goes by until another wail pierces the silence followed by a disembodied voice through a microphone, "Repent! The end is near!"

Again, louder than before, "Repent! Repent!" And then we hear screeching tires tear off down the road.

Uncle Silas curses under his breath and visibly relaxes. "Damn Thumpers."

"W-what?" I stammer.

He turns around to me and blows out a gust of exasperated air. "Thumpers. Let's go assess the damage."

I don't know what he's talking about until he stomps heavily to the front door and opens it onto the porch now covered in blood.

"Shit! I hope this ain't real blood this time."

I'm shaking I'm so scared, but Uncle Silas is more irritated than anything, which should make me feel better, or at least not so on edge, but it doesn't.

He takes a thick finger and drags it along the floorboards of the porch, which now resembles a gaping wound instead of an outdoor sitting area. It drips ominously and he sniffs it.

His shoulders sag in relief, "Pudding. Watered down pudding and food coloring."

I look around at the carnage and try to stop my shoulders from shaking despite the reassurance that someone hadn't been bled at my front door.

Uncle Silas gives me a pitying look. "Sorry, sweet girl. I know this is a lot to take in. This is a Thumper stunt. They've done it before. Albeit, not in a long while. It's a message. Meant to scare us."

"Well, it worked," I stammer.

"School board ruled that they couldn't homeschool their kids anymore. The isolation makes 'em crazy, turns them into little psychopathic terrorists. I guess now's a good time to mention that most of the school board lives in the neighborhood."

"Oh," I say flatly, finally allowing my breathing to come back to normal.

Is anything just quiet and normal anymore?

"Should we call the police?"

He shakes his head. "You, little girl, should never call the police. Low. Profile. Do you want them to start asking questions about where you come from, and who your parents are?"

It's my turn to shake my head.

"If anything ever happens, you call me first. Got it?"

I nod. The next hour is spent washing down the front porch with a weak water hose and dish liquid. Surprisingly, Uncle Silas is an especially efficient cleaning partner and when we're done, I thank him.

"Sure," he calls from over his shoulder as he makes his way to his car, "and let's keep this between the two of us. No need to get Summer all riled up, huh?"

I shake my head.

"Good girl. And it's probably a good idea to stay away from too many new friends, especially boys, but I'm sure I won't have to worry about that with you."

I shake my head again.

He climbs into his car, seals himself inside its tinted womb and drives off. Pins and needles creep into my toes before I realize I've been staring at the same spot for an eternity. Strangely, I feel safer outside than in. When I finally do go inside, I try to shake off the foreboding I feel, but it lingers just like the cigar smoke the old man leaves behind.

# CHAPTER FIFTEEN

Today, I'm as jumpy as a squirrel. On top of that, I'm mourning Mama and Brianna, carrying sadness around like a ball and chain. Although, dropping boxes of Cinnamon Buns off for the missing girls' families does make me feel a little bit better. I spent the better part of yesterday evening lurking around the backyard for Raphael and then baking to calm my nerves. Carlos's church had set up a donation center for money, gifts and that sort of thing. I finally buried that coin from Miss Miller's place too. I can't be too careful.

In the rush to get out the door early, I forgot the blessed tiny pills Summer gave me and now I'm paying for it. As soon as I get off the bus, I decide to see the school nurse before class.

As I walk, I start searching for Matt. I don't know why I do it, I just do. I haven't seen him in what feels like half a lifetime, but isn't this what was supposed to happen? I was so rude. He's probably on to someone else by now. It's fine. I'm losing my mind. Since when do I give a hoot about boys?

I think about asking around, but I beat that idea down like it was a thief after better judgment and crippling shyness takes over. Add it to my list of things I should do, but am scared to.

I practically stumble into the nurse's office and plop down into the first seat I see. After checking my pupil's she reluctantly gives me two extra strength Tylenol and a referral to a doctor in town.

On my way back to class, I run into Carlos coming out of the gym.

"Hey, what's up? What are you doing on the Freshman hall?" he asks.

"I had a headache. I got some Tylenol," I groan rubbing my temples.

"You must have been near death then. That witch doesn't give out so much as a glass of water to most people."

I shrug. "She was nice to me." I elect to change the subject.

"What are you doing in the gym?"

"Don't ask. No one wants to go into the boy's locker room so early in the morning. It smells like big foot's moldy jock strap in there."

I laugh hysterically. "Ewww!"

We get to the Forensics lab pretty quickly, and I follow Carlos to his regular seat in one of the large heavy desks in the back of the room. There's only enough room for four people at each table, and we're sharing our table with a rather large girl with a rhinestone nose ring named Salt (yes, I know) and a rail thin boy in a camouflage jacket named Finn.

The teacher, Ms. Mundy, is old, I mean really old, and I wonder if she was teaching when I was in school. Her wispy white hair is clipped into a short afro and she sports a lab coat. Once we get settled into a seat, she surprises me by bellowing out my name in the voice of a sport's announcer, "Colette Hognose?", she asks looking up from her grade book.

I sit up straight. "Yes, ma'am?"

"Hognose. Unusual name, still…" she squints a bit and looks at me. "You look familiar. Are your people from around here?"

I swallow and try very hard not to let on that I've stopped breathing. I decide then and there to never sit any closer to that woman as I am now. "No, ma'am," I answer sweetly.

"Well, then. Welcome to Forensics Part A." She steps off her stool and points the remote to the projector. A slide appears on the board, "Practical Forensics in Cold Cases", it reads. She slowly makes her way to the light switch when to my surprise Chamberlain walks in and with him, Lilah.

She's in that same white bow and pearl combo I saw her in the other day; decked out in a simple white shirt dress and to my surprise moccasins. Is she...? No, it couldn't be.

"I am so sorry Mrs. Mundy," she says in that accent I can't place. "We got held up talking to Mr. Lee about the Search for Brianna Charity Event."

"Do you have a pass?" the woman asks sternly.

Lilah steps closer to her and smiles. She's silent for just a second too long for me and a strange feeling comes over me.

"We wanted to make it here as soon as possible. A pass would've taken too long to write. We wouldn't want to disrupt class in the middle of a lesson."

Pfft. Flimsy lie. Her performance is subtle, but I can tell she's staging an act.

"Hmm. Alright, take a seat. Don't make this a habit Ms. Taylor," Miss Mundy says with slight hesitation. I can't believe she bought it.

Carlos must have registered the confusion on my face because he jumps in and whispers, "Lilah's suing the school district. When she got here last year, she claimed the old Soccer coach felt her up or something. They fired him, but until the suit is tied up, she's virtually untouchable. She doesn't get detention, she shows up late. She's the Teflon Don."

"What's Teflon?" I ask.

He shakes his head and pats me pityingly on the back. I see it coming and try my best not to flinch.

Carlos isn't a good projector, but when he touches me I get a surge of quiet playfulness with an undercurrent of sadness, like a slick film of oil in a sink full of sudsy water.

110

Chamberlain smiles serenely at no one as he holds Lilah's hand. She leads him to an empty desk in the opposite corner of the room. Like a robot he sets both his and then her backpack on the floor and gets notebooks out for them both. She kisses him on the cheek in thanks, and I watch him light up like a Christmas tree.

"Alright scholars, today we will discuss the various methods of forensics available to us after time has eroded our evidence. As you know, today is just your introductory meeting. You'll have to meet on your own after this so use your time wisely." She clears her throat. "Okay, today we'll discuss the examination of written documents, Blood Splatter analysis, and the advent of DNA testing. Afterwards, you'll break into your groups, which I've randomly assigned."

Groans break out across the room. Mrs. Mundy raises her voice, "Which. I've. Randomly. Assigned." She waits a beat. Silence. "You will then discuss your assigned closed case."

Once she dims the light we all get to scribbling down our notes. I steal glances over at Lilah and her lovesick puppy. What is it about her that has girls and guys enslaved?

The presentation drones on and a kid in a skull and cross bones t-shirt keeps trying to bait Mrs. Mundy into the finer details between semen and blood samples.

Soon, Mrs. Mundy turns the lights back on and with just a few minutes left before the bell rings, she begins calling out the groups and their chosen cold cases. "Salt and Finn, you'll be working with Rachel and Denise. The case: Charles Way. Sumter. Homicide, 2008."

Someone giggles in the back of the room, at what I don't know.

"Okay, Carlos and Colette, you'll be paired with…Lilah and Chamberlain." My eyes go wide and her voice fades to a muffled 'wah, wah, wah.'

Lilah smiles in my direction as if she knows just what I'm thinking. She's got a self-satisfied smirk on her face like the cat that's just got the cream.

Carlos gives me a weird look and hands me my bag. We're about to stand when the happy couple make their way to our side of the room. All eyes are on Lilah, her hair swaying from side to side as smooth as a bell as she dances over to our desk with Chamberlain in tow. Some people are visibly shocked and a riotous chatter dims to dull whispers.

"Hello again," she says sweetly and offers her hand. I brace myself and reach up slowly to shake it. The situation is tense, and I can't avoid being polite this time.

She slides her cool hand into my gloved one and ....nothing.

I feel nothing.

"Mrs. Mundy?" a staticky voice calls out from nowhere.

"Yes?"

"Can you please send Collette Hognose to the front office for early dismissal? Her grandmother is here."

Carlos leans over, "I didn't know you had a grandmother in town?"

"I don't."

### 

I'm still a little shaken by Lilah's handshake as I make my way out of class. As I walk down, something tells me Uncle Silas is behind it, but of all the possible scenarios running through my brain not one of them involves Miss Collins charming the front office so well that they don't question if she is really my kin or why she would need to pull me from school in the middle of the day.

"Did they ask you about my dad?" I ask in whispers as we make our way through the glass doors of the foyer.

"Why would they?" she replies smugly.

Because I'm a delinquent. Because he's been dead for over half of a century and well beyond making school visits.

"No reason. What are you doing here?" I ask hesitating at the door of her car.

She looks me in the eye and squares her shoulders. "I was wrong. It wasn't fair what I did to you the other day. I didn't act as a sister, and I apologize. I've been so long without a mentee, and I've forgotten what it was like to be a young sister."

She says it with sincerity, but without shame. This is honesty, and it flows real and solid from her frame. I nod in acceptance. I need to know this woman. There's power in her and maybe I need power, 'cause all I've got now is fear and questions.

I open the creaking door to her wood-paneled station wagon and get in. She nods with a slight smile and does the same.

She turns the key in the ignition and the beast roars to life, kicking up not a little bit of smoke as we charge down the school driveway. The interior smells of some sort of soup, not unpleasant, just—odd.

"I heard about the Thumper demonstration over your way."

I wonder how she even knows where I live, but then again I'm sure Miss Collins knows everything. That's it. She just knows. One of those old women who deals in secrets and sleeps with her ears alert and eyes open.

"There's a change in the air," she says ominously. "Lessons begin today. Lesson one: Self-Protection."

# CHAPTER SIXTEEN

"What is all this?" I ask as Miss Collins and I stare into the trunk of her station wagon parked outside of my house.

She reaches deep into her trunk to pull out three small potted plants and a small trowel. "Insurance," she replies.

"Insurance?" I can't help but think of Uncle Silas' little packet of money. It could be worse. I could have no one in my corner looking out for me though these two different people have very different ideas of what protection means.

"Yes, you can never be too careful and the balance in the air is off." She lifts her head and smells the air. "It's wrong. If I'm not crazy I'd venture that little Baxter girl is dead."

I swallow hard and my eyes go wild. Thankfully she doesn't see me. Her head is buried in a burlap sack that smells like—

"Garlic," she replies before I even ask and loops a string of it around her neck. "We'll hang these by the door. It wasn't pudding the Thumpers plastered this place with yesterday it was fear. And fear makes you susceptible to all kinds of nasty things."

"Did you bury that coin I gave you?" she asks.

I nod.

"Hmm. Guess it hasn't taken yet. Maybe it's a dud. No matter. We have other means. You see the Thumpers are laboring under the delusion that there is another angel war coming. We will not suffer under such silliness. The only war going on is the war between the light and the darkness in every man's heart. In this we are equipped," she says reassuringly.

I follow the little woman up my walkway and set the rosemary plants she's given me on the stoop before letting her in.

"Look at cha," she says while shaking her head from side to side. "Wide open. Not a lick of shielding."

I look around the house, trying to see what she sees.

A few more trips to the car and my kitchen table and counters are covered in herbs, plants, rosary beads, weird stones, a few dusty books and bibles she wants me to read and what must be the bones of a dead cat. Maybe a bit of fur too.

"This smells awful," I offer.

"I know," she agrees. "We'll open the windows after a bit." She grabs a handful of dry herbs tied with twine and lights it over the gas stove. "And, this will drive most of it away, as well as anything else that's lurking in these dusty old corners. I don't know how you stand it."

"What?"

"The footprints left behind, past hurts and arguments still lingering in the air. It's like spider webs you can't see. Makes my skin crawl." She hands me a vial of oil and a rag while the bundle in her other hand smolders.

"No need to stare. It's holy oil. Rub it on the windows and the doors after I clear with the sage smoke. Do you know the Psalms?"

I was an excellent Sunday school student. I reply excitedly, "Yes, ma'am. I can recite Psalm 23 and.."

She cuts me off with a wave of her flaming hand. "No sweetie, you need to know all of them, backwards and forwards, without thinking and without blinking. We'll do..." she thinks on this for a second or two and then continues, " 91. Yes, 91! Repeat after me..."

She speaks a line, and I follow behind her playing altar boy and repeat. She waves her bundle over every window, and stuffs it in every corner. I trail and do as I'm bid. Before long we've covered the entire house, save the attic, and we're both exhausted.

Now it's my turn to offer the old woman tea and cookies. I expect her to make some comment or joke about it, but she remains polite. I guess she knows better than to expect anything but blind obedience from me.

"Ooowee! That was a job," she huffs as she stuffs another thumbprint into her mouth. "These are delicious. What flavor is the marmalade?" she huffs.

"Orange Basil. My friend Summer inspired me to try something different."

"Well, you do have a talent."

My cheeks flush at the compliment. In the silence of our weariness, I take a deep breath and realize that Miss Collins was right, there is a difference in the air. Even with the cluttered counters and table, the air smells cleaner and feels lighter.

She yawns, stretching a bit and then sets her eyes on me. "Now let's get down to business. We're hardly done, but I need you to be honest with me," she demands.

"Yes, ma'am." I squeak.

"When did you get here? And by here, I mean this year. This time."

I gulp hard, teetering between spilling my guts and lying through my teeth. Why should I tell this woman anything? Maybe she knows too much already.

Fingers snap in front of my face and force a decision. "Don't sit there and try to think up a lie little girl."

I shift uncomfortably in my seat. I take a deep breath. "Two Saturdays ago? I think."

She gasps and reels back in her chair.

"Lies," she croaks.

The old woman's face goes ashen, and I close my eyes and let everything fall from my lips. I tell her who my grandmother was, what I remember on my last day of life and how I sprang up from the lake only a few weeks before.

"Stop," she whispers. "Stop!"

My eyelids snap open, and I look at her through a bleary haze.

"Don't tell me anymore. Just let me think a moment."

I open my mouth to respond, but she shakes her head and gets up from the table and paces for a bit before making her way outside and silently beckoning me to follow.

This time she pulls out a small wooden box with the Virgin Mary carved into its top. "I'll need a match, Sweetie. Then, meet me on the first step."

I think I prefer it when she's scolding me. I oblige her and when I get back she's snipping the tip off the end of a fat, hand rolled cigar. When I hand her the match she strikes it on the stone of the step and puffs loudly till the thing catches, releasing a thick, white tendril of perfumed smoke that I know is not tobacco.

She sighs loudly as she fiddles with a latch on another compartment of the box.

"I can tell when someone's lying. It's one of my gifts. I have other gifts too, you know." Her voice is weary and her tone has changed in a way that I haven't figured out yet. "I'm a manipulator."

My face must have changed without my knowing because she laughs. "No, no it's not as bad as all that. It's a gift, though when I was younger I thought it a curse. Some days I still do. I can influence people. Make them do what I want, even if they don't want to. Most of the time, I can control it like today in the school's front office. Other times it's such a part of me I can't tell when I'm doing it. It's one of the biggest reasons I never married. I couldn't tell if they proposed because they wanted to or because I wanted them to."

She pauses and puffs heartily, and I notice that the cloud of smoke above her isn't dissipating; it's collecting, as if it's afraid of the air around us. She looks at me as wistfully as a mother looks at a child. I will my knees to bend and sit next to her. In this moment, she looks so much like my Gran with her white shirt and skirt billowing out around her. Midnight blue clogs cover her small feet.

"It's also one of the reasons Mama said I shouldn't spell cast," she says softly, apologetically. "Casting isn't an exact science. The mood of the witch matters, the position of the moon matters, even the witch's tone of voice matters. I may have made a mistake."

"Mistake?"

I look at her quizzically as she fishes a folded newspaper article out of her pocket and hands it to me. The headline reads: The Doll Snatcher. Pictures of fourteen girls, some in school uniforms, line the length of the paper along with the dates they went missing. They smile out at me silently.

"There are fewer Willows now than there have ever been but that doesn't mean that we are powerless. And this," she taps the paper in my hands, "is what we are gifted to fight."

With a final jiggle, a drawer on the wooden box she's been fiddling with pops opens and three moths spring lazily from the compartment, floating into the cloud of smoke as soft as whispers.

I focus my gaze back on Miss Collins' relieved face. "I don't understand," I ask.

She watches the moths disappear into the thick cloud and nods as if she's agreeing with someone.

"Negligence! These girls goin' missing are gettin' no more attention than a dog lickin' his hind parts at any time of the day.

County police say they ran away. If we don't stop the evil that is snatching these girls, no one will."

We. This is the optimum word. We. What does she expect me to do?

With one last puff she clips the end of her cigar and sets it down to rest behind her. "I did a casting. I called. It was supposed to draw the Willows together, maybe even call an angel down. I think I may have made a mistake in the arrangement." She's staring into the cloud above us as it tumbles in slow motion on its own spit.

"I don't understand." I say again, because I'm truly confused, but I don't take my eyes off the cloud.

"I know. I wish I could make this all make sense to you, but I can't. At least not yet, but I'll start with this."

She points to the cloud above her and we both watch as the moths, who I thought had been consumed by the mass emerge on opposite ends of each other, and quite naturally, as if this is what I should have expected to happen, they float, each with an end of the cloud like a blanket, out from under the awning of the porch up to the highest point of the house.

"This what?" I squeak.

"This is a smoke shield. I traded one of my best love potions for it from a Colombian Santera I met a few years ago. Had a desperate daughter who was uglier than sin. I was happy to help."

The moths flutter out in opposite directions, softly, quickly, stretching the smoke like gauze so that it forms a dome around the yard and house.

"Trade?"

"Yes. A witch's spells are her own and eventually you find your niche. Mine is potions. Hers were protection spells."

The moths, done with their work, flutter back to the wooden box on the old woman's lap and she closes it softly. If you squint you might notice a thin haze that stretches over the fence and house, but you would most likely miss it.

"Miss Collins, I don't mean to speak out of turn, but I am really confused. You put this smoke shield up; you talk about these missing girls and Santeras. What does this have to do with me?"

"I am a witch. Your mother was a witch. You, God willing you live long enough, will be a witch. You are gifted, yes?"

I swallow. No one outside of my family knows I'm an empath, but then again, even I didn't know Mama was a witch. I used to pray all day and all night for God to make me normal, so I could just live like other kids, but that never happened and I don't ever think it will.

I take a deep breath and answer, "I'm an empath," I squeak.

She breathes a sigh of acceptance. "Ah, that's a strong gift."

"Hmm, not much gift at all. I can't manipulate people or make things move like Mama could." The sight of seeing Mama move that vial is burned into my brain. If I could do that, I'd never be afraid of anything. As it is, I can't go out into public without gloves on. Fat lot of good being a witch does me.

"It's not like that. Every gift has its rewards and responsibilities. I've never known an empath, but there have been great ones in my family line. It's a powerful gift, more powerful than I'm sure you can understand right now.

She picks up the remnant of her cigar and places it back in the top compartment of her box and fixes me with a compassionate glare.

"I wish I could tell you more about who you are right now, but I need to see an old Willow in Charleston, a telepathic sister, for advice. She's the oldest Willow I know, and her Fountain Book may hold answers mine doesn't. She may be able to tell me what mistake I made in calling you here and tell me if I should send you back."

Back? I never thought that was even a possibility. Back where? Back to my own time where Mama is dead. Back to the Void, where, where I am dead?

My tongue remains glued to the top of my mouth.

"I'll be back tomorrow or the next day to help you garden and get everything in order. The oil and smoke should hold you till then."

She gets up from the step and hurries into the house for her purse. Suddenly, every year of her age shows.

"Wait, you can't leave. You just… I mean we're just getting started. What do you mean by *back*?" I plead. "Maybe I should come with you."

She touches my arm and as I flinch concern, guilt and sadness seep into my muscles and flit across my skin in goose bumps.

" Willows have rules. You're a daughter of Odion, but you don't even know what that means. Willow girls train to hone their gifts and then work to be worthy of them. Your situation is completely unique. It's a dangerous time, and I can't leave you unprotected, but…Like I said. There are rules."

I walk her to her car and hug my arms against an imaginary wind. She pulls out a slim volume of psalms from her purse and hands it to me.

"Memorize it," she demands.

I nod.

"Don't look so worried. You're stronger than you think and more powerful than most. You prayed up?"

I give her a tiny nod.

As she lurches down the street in a puff of exhaust, I wonder if she'll make it to this sister for answers and what in God's name I'll do once she does.

# CHAPTER SEVENTEEN

"Whoa, Collette! What happened to this place?" Summer asks.

"One of the older ladies I met at Carlos' church said she'd help me with my garden."

I'm betting that it's enough of the truth that I don't trip over it later. The less Summer knows the better, and it's nice that I'm just another girl to Summer. It's uncomplicated.

"Uh huh. And your garden needs Belladonna?" she asks accusatorily, holding up a limp flowering plant wrapped in a wet paper towel.

I shrug and make room for her to unpack her soap making materials on the table. Summer knows enough not to ask too many questions, though I hate to make her aware of that. Who wants to share a secret with someone who's basically a vault of half-truths and plausible fictions?

She doesn't know that I left school early today and I'm not about to confess. We had a soap making date and despite my conversation with Miss Collins, I'm going to keep it. I'm still sixteen. I choose to live a sixteen-year-old's life. I didn't get to make that choice before. I was kept away. I was lonely. I'm not doing that anymore. Who knows how much time I have left to do it?

"What's up with that face?" she asks.

"What?"

"You just looked angry for a second. Never mind. Umm, so I have to apologize ahead of time for something."

"For what?"

The doorbell rings and her face pinches in a wince.

"That."

I can count on one hand the number of people who know where I live. Who could that be? I fix Summer with a deadly side-eye and try to settle the nervousness in my spine.

"Hey, beautiful," Matt croons as I open the door.

My lungs constrict, and I can only sip air. Lava churns in my belly and my cheeks flame. A smile wants to creep up onto my face, but I wrestle it down. I have my pride.

"What are you doing here?" I sputter.

"I was invited," he says smugly. "I would never show up to a lady's house without an invitation." Sarcasm drips from every word.

I look over at Summer who's mouthing 'I'm so sorry' over and over.

"Summer and I are collaborating on a special project. She needed our help," Matt cries in apology.

"Our?" I ask.

Matt leans to the side so I can see he's brought a friend. The same boy from the lake house is hovering around the front fence with a scowl on his face. Buck? Is that his name? I am not going to ask. It might give the impression that I care.

He reaches out for the fence as if he's about to open it and then shrinks back. He does it a few more times before he gives up. Weird.

"I'm out Fuller. Gonna see a girl on the other street," the boy yells when he catches us both looking at his little performance.

Matt nods and takes a step forward.

"Hold it right there! I don't *need* your help, you offered it. There is a difference." Summer responds from inside, jerking our attention to her.

"Fine" I say with as flat a tone as I can manage. "Come on in."

I can do this. I can control this situation. All I need is a moment alone. He crosses the threshold, and it's suddenly too hot to breathe.

*He's in my house! Keep it together, Collette.*

"So, about the project. Matt thought that it would be cool if I created a cream for guys as well as girls. The football team is always getting cuts and bruises and stuff, soooo, what about a scar cream for guys?"

I fix her with the soft smile usually saved for children who've just tried to serve you a mud pie. "Aren't guys supposed to have scars?"

She's smiling so brightly that I should have known not to give her my most honest answer, but it's already out there and I've just thrown a dirty diaper at her parade. Her shoulders fall and if I'm not mistaken I can see Matt holding back a chuckle. Wasn't this his idea?

"Shit! You're right. Why did I think this was a good idea?" She turns to Matt. "This is a crappy idea."

He shrugs. "Sounded good at the time."

"It did, didn't it?" She's genuinely confused, which is better than hurt so I take it and try to change the subject. It is *my* house after all, and its feeling too close for comfort in here.

"Hey, uh, Matt. Can you do me a favor while you're here? Since you owe Summer back for wasted creative energy."

If he had a tail, it would be wagging. "Sure!"

### 

"Ummhmm, and that patch over there."

Matt isn't unhappy, just shrouded in a gray cloud of confusion. He's probably wondering how his little plan to trick his way into my house has led to him pulling weeds out of an overgrown flower patch in the front yard. New grass looks like it's sprouting in a few dry places, so I figure my coin must be working to some degree.

"Wow, he's really goin' at it, "Summer observes between sips of iced tea.

"Serves him right. He had ulterior motives," I reply.

"And you don't? You're staring at his butt right now."

"Am not!"

I give her my best shocked face, but in truth I am a little mesmerized. In the dying light of the day, the sun is hitting Matt in a way that makes the hair on his legs look as fine as spun gold. It's going to take quite a bit for me to call him back inside. Even in the change of the light you can't notice the shield over the fence. I can't say that it doesn't make feel safer than those stupid security alarm signs that they have in the yard of the house across the street.

Summer says something I don't get. I turn to her. "What did you say?"

She laughs hysterically. "You know what I like about you?"

I shake my head, smiling.

"The way you look at people. At me. At him." She cocks her head in Matt's direction and I let my eyes fall back to where they're comfortable. "You look at people like all you can see is the good in them... like we're in Technicolor."

I look at her. I don't know what to say.

"Hey, Matt! Come get some tea!" Summer calls.

I frown at her. If he comes over now, he may never make it back out there.

"Thanks!" Matt says before bounding up the stairs and downing an entire glass of the stuff. "You really got me out there workin'!" he says with genuine joy. He smiles and my mouth fills with lava. Is this how all girls feel when they have a...crush? Is that what this is?

I clear my throat. "What can I say? I have a passion for gardening."

"More like punishment."

"Same thing," I reply.

"Oh! I have to use the little girl's room. Don't mind me, it might take a while," Summer says animatedly, and I wonder why she's being so crude until I realize she's left us on the porch alone.

"What are you doing here?!" I hiss with as much contrived irritation as I can muster.

"I, uh, wanted to help Summer," Matt stammers as he sets his clinking iced tea-less glass on the banister.

"Uh-uh. You wanted to weasel your way into my house. Did you know my Daddy wasn't home? Is that your game, Matt Fuller?"

Even if this is a crush, Matt is dangerous for me. Maybe Miss Collins found out about him, and he'll factor into the decision on whether I get to stay.

"Whoa! It's not like that at all."

"Then what is it like?" I say, folding my arms across my chest and feeling very much like I'm on a roll.

His face goes serious. "I had to see you."

"You always say that. *You had to see me.* Why?" I ask.

He's suddenly nervous and a yellow-greenish pallor rises in his cheeks. "She's dead," he whispers.

"Who?"

"Brianna Baxter." His face is sad and serious.

I should look shocked, but I know this already. "How do you know?" I ask in a small curious voice.

He's hesitant. "I can't tell you."

"You can't tell me?! Then why should I believe you," I hiss.

"I know it's hard for you to believe me, but you'll have to trust me on this."

"Trust you? I don't even know you!" I begin.

He places his hand over mine and my breath escapes as lightning shoots up my arm.

"They're gonna come after you too," he confesses.

I snatch my hand back and stare at him. He's being completely honest. I know it. Concern, like an aftertaste sits in the same spot where his hand just left.

"How do you know?" I whisper.

"I just know. I just. I can't tell you everything okay, I just wanted to warn you, and if you let me, help protect you."

I chew on my bottom lip. All of my bravado has been stamped into non-existence. I don't even have a good chance to absorb everything he's said because Summer chooses that moment to bound back onto the porch.

"So? Set a date yet?" Summer teases.

"For what?" I ask.

"You guys' first date," she sings as if it's the only thing we could have been discussing while she was gone.

"Oh, well…no. Matt was just saying how he had to get home and finish some homework. Weren't you Matt?" I ask.

His eyes are pleading, disappointed, but he plays along.

"Yup! I'll have to catch you girls laters," he smiles as he bounds off backwards towards his—

"What kind of car is that?" I ask Summer.

"It's a jeep."

"Oh."

We both wave as he pulls away, and I feel as cool as a pie set on the sill; feeling more and more like myself the farther he gets down the road.

"You're crazy you know that?" Summer chides, catching me off guard.

"What? Why?"

"No one and I mean no one has been able to turn Matt Fuller's head for months and from Day 1, he's been locked on you. He's stingy with his attention, ya know. What everybody wants just fell into your lap." Her eyes are hard if not still caring.

"Well, maybe I don't want it."

"Yeah, and maybe you're *a dang fool.* At least that's what my Granddaddy would say. You know why Tressa Lancaster was the envy of all of the girls before she went missing?" she pauses, "because *she* was dating Matt Fuller. All-State Matt Fuller. Dripping in his Daddy's cash Matt Fuller."

"Gorgeous Matt Fuller." I add.

I can't look at her. Maybe she's right.

"You know I'm right. Even Lilah was jealous. Unless getting a boyfriend isn't on your precious To-Do list. By the way , cross anything off lately?"

I give her the stink eye. Sometimes Summer can see right through me.

"You know…. I can see straight through that dress. I'm just glad you wore panties."

I nearly drop my glass in horror as she winks, and I chase her inside.

# CHAPTER EIGHTEEN

I resumed my search for Raphael again last night and expanded the territory to include the entire block. It was just me and my flashlight until I couldn't keep my eyes open anymore. He has a lot to answer for when I finally see him.

Grief leaked from the news about Brianna's death like yolk. The walls of the school are coated with its sticky foulness, and it doesn't help that the front office keeps a television tuned to the local news station all day. Even if it is on mute, the parade of pictures of missing girls does not help any of us focus on our studies. Now that Brianna's added to the mix, I don't think the county police can ignore the links to the other girls. Maybe Miss Collins is wrong. I want her to be wrong so she can forget about the help she needs and leave me be. The police can handle whatever mission she's on, and I can just live a normal life. My gift is tiny and more trouble than its worth if it means that I can't live a boring uneventful life that every other girl takes for granted.

By the time lunch rolls around, I've added another half-page of To-Do's, mostly having to do with Miss Collins, to my bucket list.

"Wow, those two should get a room. I know they're hot and all, but who wants to see that while they're eating," says a girl standing in the salad bar line ahead of me. The stress of everything is making me forgetful. I left my lunch at home and now I have to suffer through this God-awful lunch.

I don't even have to look to know who the girl is talking about. Lilah and Chamberlain are standing just outside the lunchroom, kissing passionately, ravenously, almost obscenely to the point where they must be out of breath. They look as if they're trying to consume each other.

Chamberlain and I haven't really spoken since that day I'd seen him walking the Reverend's dogs. He's so different from the guy that I met that day to the point that I'm beginning to think I dreamed it all together.

Lilah plants kisses down his chin and along his throat. His eyes roll back into his head, and I don't need to touch him to know that he's in ecstasy. I'm staring, but I can't help but be fascinated. When his head drops forward to kiss her I notice that his usually dark colored eyes have gone glassy, not just dark but black and large as an animal's. I blink to make sure it's not a trick of the light, but I'm sure of what I see before he closes his eyes again lost in another kiss.

Lilah bares her teeth and nips his chin in a snarl, and I'm suddenly afraid for him.

I turn away. When I turn my head again, they're gone.

I convince Carlos and Qutey to abandon their posts in the lunchroom for the tables in the quad near the fountain. It's more a broken water fountain than anything, but the location is a change, and I feel less boxed in outside. The grief is oily in the air and by lunch I'm aching to take a breath that's not soaked with emotion. Some girls still burst into tears for no apparent reason, and if my shields weren't up to full capacity I'd probably be doing the same.

"Feeling better?" Qutey asks.

I nod. "A bit. Thanks for the advice."

"What advice?" Carlos asks.

"Mind your business," Qutey retorts.

I decide to change the subject before they start their antics. "So what was with the yellow envelopes this morning?" I ask.

"What envelopes?" they both ask in unison.

I pull mine out from my bag and wave it at them. Qutey pulls it from my fingers as a deep frown blooms on her face.

"This isn't good," she says. "Can I open it?"

I nod.

"It's from the front office. It's an attendance citation," she tells me.

Carlos whistles and grimaces.

"And?" I ask.

"It's like a cross between a school summons and a traffic ticket. Your parents have to respond within a few days or you can't come back to school," Qutey answers. "I don't know how you'd get one though. They usually don't give these out until you've missed like two weeks of school," she mumbles while reading the letter.

My mind races at the potential for disaster this little piece of paper brings. I don't have parents to respond to a summons.

"Oh! I see what happened. There's a code at the bottom from the office. 299." Qutey points to the bottom of the letter to the hand written code. I look at her quizzically.

"She doesn't know what 299 means. I don't know what 299 means." Carlos jabs.

"It's the code for the social worker. If someone reports abuse or neglect or something like that, the summons gets a 299 code. I interned in that office two weeks ago before I got moved to the nurse. It means somebody reported you. It doesn't even matter if the report is true or not, the social worker has to follow up. The police get involved. Collette, this is bad," she says.

This is worse than bad. This is horrible. I don't need any more attention than I've already gotten. Didn't Uncle Silas tell me to keep a low profile? I close my eyes and groan inside as my appetite disappears. I'm still cringing inside when an idea presents itself.

"What do you know about Lilah?" I ask Carlos.

"Not much, other than she's a bitch," he replies.

"Language!" I snap.

Qutey taps her fork on the table, loud and hard as a gavel. "Here! Here!"

I have to say I'm a bit surprised. There aren't that many people out in the quad, but half of the girls who are there have copied her mourning outfit of black cigarette pants with matching sweater and headband. Of course the true Bells sport their customary oversized pearls to distinguish themselves from the peasants. "Everyone seems to love her. Why are you two the exceptions?"

"Cause we're not dumbasses. We had the same schedule and she thought she could weasel her way into my hard won place as Star Student. No, ma'am! No, sir!" she says with flourish.

The idea that's been running around in my head finally slows down enough for me to catch it.

"Qutey, you said that they rotate the interns around the different offices."

She nods in the same rhythm of the chews of her taco.

"Who replaced you in the social worker's office?" I ask.

She thinks for a second until recognition stills her jaw. "Lilah."

"I've got to go!" I spit as I hastily grab my bag and tray.

"What?!"

Carlos is calling after me, something about the project or a swim thing, but I don't hear him. I'm running. I only have five minutes before the bell rings and I've got to make it across the quad, through the cafeteria and out onto the other side. I run so fast that by the time I reach the parking lot I'm out of breath, but not so fast that I outrun my shyness and as my fatal flaw fills me up, faster than my lungs can recover, I've completely forgotten what I was gonna say.

My heart is still pounding from the run, legs still burning, hiding the familiar tingle in my spine.

"So, are you running from something or towards something?" he asks.

Matt.

"I umm. I…" Shoot! I don't know what to say. He's happy to see me. He's glowing with it. I smile brighter. I did have something to ask him, didn't I? "I wanted to ask you something."

"I know," he says with a smile.

"You know?"

"Yeah. You wanted to ask me out. I accept. I have to admit I was a little upset when Chamberlain Todd got to brag about your sweet buns, until I found out what he was really talking about."

"N-No, uh. That, I'm sure was not what I came out here…" I retort with my half eaten lunch still in my hands.

"No, I think it was. I'm a little taken aback myself. The guy usually is supposed to ask the girl, but as it is our second date so I think we can let it go." He's cocky. This is the golden boy everyone wants to be with. Sun is blazing behind him again creating a crown around his head and makes his skin light from the inside. He's beautiful.

"Really, I.."

"No, really, Collette." He's serious now, eyes soft with concern. "We do need to talk."

He's right. Not only do I need to find out more about Lilah, but I need to know how he knew about Brianna. Why does he know so much? Why does he think I'm in danger?

"How about now?" I ask in a voice so small I'm sure he hasn't heard me. I clear my throat and fake a bravery I rarely ever feel and say it again. "Now. We can talk in the dugout."

He gives me a sly smile and a fireball of lust shoots across my hips and turns the whites of his eyes pink. I don't know what he's thinking, but I can guess.

"J-just to talk."

"Nah, I know a better place." He takes my hand and I have to swallow hard not to cry out at the sensation.

### 

We drop my tray in a bin and walk briskly weaving through the crowd and downstairs through a hallway I've never been on until abruptly he opens a door and we're in a room covered completely in darkness.

"W-where are we?"

Matt doesn't answer. He just lets my hand go and the loss of him feels pulls out a chunk of me. In a second, lights go up, and I see that I'm looking directly into the face of a saxophone.

Matt jogs back up to me and leads me to a bench in the middle of the room.

"It's the jazz band room. They don't use it till spring so it's almost always empty."

Our voices echo slightly in the room, and while I want him to hold my hand again, I'm nervous. So nervous my palms sweat and silence snuggles in close as a too-fat friend on the bench. I break it.

"I love jazz."

What? We have serious things to discuss. Lilah. Someone or something coming after me. What was that? *I love jazz.*

"Really? I do too. Sarah Vaughn, Count Basie. That's my shit," he exclaims.

"Language!" Shoot. My hand slams over my mouth. Who corrects a boy in *the moment?*

He laughs. "Yeah, I need to work on that. But, yo, my Dad loves jazz. He put me on to it."

"Oh, is he a nice guy?"

He thinks for a moment. "Nice? Um, he's, uh…principled. He believes in honor and obligation. It's why I have that big, beautiful house all to myself."

"He doesn't live with you?" Why am I being called in to the attendance office then? Oh, yes, sabotage.

"In and out, more so now since Mom died."

My hand flies to my mouth again. "I'm so sorry."

His mouth turns down and his shoulders slump oh so slightly. "I'm supposed to say it's okay. That's what people expect, but it isn't okay. Not in the least. I still cry over it. My dad still cries over it, though he won't admit it."

"I know that's hard. My Mama passed on too." Her face flashes before me, smiling, freckles dancing. A moment passes.

"What?" he asks.

"What?"

"You were staring at me for a second," he states, not unkindly.

Heat rushes to my armpits. "I…Your freckles. My Mama had freckles. They're n-nice." It's the first compliment I've ever given a boy.

He laughs. "Thanks. I don't think anyone's ever noticed them. Definitely the first compliment I've gotten on those," he says, his voice bouncing off the walls. Pictures of past Band Majors look down on us in perfect rows, first in black and white and then later in color. Rows of dust covered white boys in uniform give way to Black, Hispanic and even one or two girls stare down at us angelically.

"So how do you like it?" he asks.

"Like what? The band room? I guess it's…"

"No," he interrupts with a laugh. "The school. Summer told me you were homeschooled."

"Oh! Well, it's nice to be around people, but it can be overwhelming. I spent a lot of time alone. Reading alone. Studying alone. Playing alone."

"It sounds...lonely."

I look at him and smile. "It was. I really hated it. I used to come up with these fantasies where my Dad would show up unexpectedly and take me away to live with him in Paris or Mexico, someplace exotic and completely foreign."

I should be asking him the hard questions. Getting to real answers, but I don't want to right now. It's just nice to sit and talk. Without anyone else around it feels as if we've landed on a different planet where everything is simple and girls and boys can have nice chats about nice, simple, normal things. I want to hold on to it just a little bit longer.

"Tell me about your Mom."

He tells me about her love of old movies and how she and his Dad first met. He confesses that his Dad really isn't his Dad, but some guy he's never seen. Mr. Fuller adopted him when he was a baby, the only father he's known.

"People think you shouldn't talk about the dead, but that's the best time. It's the best thing for people who miss the ones they love. They can't tell them that they love them anymore 'cause they're gone, but the next best thing is to tell someone else how lovely they were."

"What do you remember most about her?" I ask.

"Her laugh. If something was really funny she'd hiccup." He chuckles. "I miss that. You?"

"Her voice. She sang. Sang all the time. Sometimes in different languages. Hymns mostly. She had a beautiful voice. It was just...angelic." Something tickles my memory, and I know that this is important. I smile quickly and then frown. She had so many secrets.

"What about your Dad? Did he ever come rescue you like Superman?" he asks.

My jaw clenches, and I shake my head. "I didn't know him."

Thankfully, he doesn't give me a pitying look, just a smirk. "Too bad for him."

I've relaxed enough to let a smile creep onto my face.

"See, that's what I want to see," he says in appreciation, "that's like the sun to me."

I should smile brighter at the compliment, but all it does is make me feel uncomfortable. I may not be the peculiar girl anymore, but even here in my normal bubble I still feel like her.

"How did you know about Brianna?" I ask.

His warm demeanor washes away and seriousness straightens his back.

"I can't tell you."

I frown. "You've said that, but how do I know that you're not the killer?!" My voice bounces back at me, and I shrink as if it's going to whip around the corner and give us away.

"Don't say that!" he hisses and a seed of fear germinates in my belly. "I'm sorry."

He pauses and rubs his hands across his face and into his shoulders. He's conflicted and when he looks at me his expression is pained. He grips my hands in his, gently, and my whole body goes warm.

He wants me to trust him and I shouldn't. There is no way that he could lie to me and I not know it so I nod. He squeezes my hand and lets it go. I almost ask him to hold it again.

"I guess you can ask me now."

"Ask you what?" I ask.

"I know you want to ask me some big question. It's why you were out on the lot today. I knew it as soon as you walked on the asphalt."

Am I that obvious?

"No, well…How well do you know Lilah?"

"Lilah? Don't tell me you want to join her little cult?"

"Absolutely not!" I spit out exasperated.

He chuckles. "Uh, well. She loves to party, that's for sure. She hasn't been here that long. She got here just before…"

His voice trails off and something sad grips him. "Everyone just falls all over themselves when she comes around. Chamberlain being the number one stunna in that category. I figured that was because she had some good-good, but…"

I knit my eyebrows together. "What's good-good?"

"You know?"

I shake my head. At this, he really starts laughing.

"Ahh, I'm not saying. You really were homeschooled weren't you? Yeah, baby steps with you."

I'm missing the joke.

"Do you know where she lives, what classes she takes?" I rattle off a little too eagerly.

"Whoa! No, I don't, and to answer your other question. I don't like her. She's vain and conniving, and she dresses like a milkman," he jokes.

At this, I laugh; violet peals of it dance off the instruments. I'm still laughing when the band director opens the door and my heart skips not one beat, but two.

Busted.

# CHAPTER NINETEEN

Matt convinces the band director that everything was innocent, and we don't get into any trouble.

"I'll see you later?" he asks.

I nod and allow him a small smile.

"Cool. Baby steps. I'm cool with that."

Fourth period has been cancelled today in order for the school to engage in "small group counseling" as they put it. Today is supposed to be a day of remembrance, so classes are truncated so that we can all spend time in homeroom at the end of the day and talk out our feelings.

As it had been since the first day of school, I share a homeroom with Qutey. She rolls her eyes as soon as the grief counselor walks into the room, her face a model of irritation, but a nervously tapping foot, clad in a fuchsia-colored sequined sneaker gives away her true emotions.

The room is thick with anxiety, and I can't help breathing with my mouth open so that I don't pass out from the lack of air. The desks have all been pushed to the back of the room and the chairs arranged in a semi-circle. Miss Laura, the grief counselor is sitting at 12 o'clock, her long peasant skirt billowing out around her.

"Hello, everyone," she says in a pleasant, but appropriately cheerless tone. "My name is Laura Ingles, but you can just call me Laura, if you like."

Not gonna happen, but go on *Miss* Laura. I try *not* to imagine her on the prairie.

She tells us that she runs an after-school therapy group for teens at Greater Rehoboth Baptist nearby, but all faiths are welcome.

"Why don't we start by getting to know each other?"

"We already know each other," a boy in a grey Carolina Panthers hoodie and flip-flops offers, with not a little bit of snark.

"Well, introduce yourselves so I can get to know you," Miss Laura replies, ignoring his disrespect. "Tell me your name and one word that describes how you feel right now."

She nods her head so that the boy in paint splattered camouflage sitting next to her knew to start. Most kids say they're sad or scared. A few bold ones here and there, like the boy in the sweatshirt, say that they're bored. I mean to follow the trend and say that I'm sad too, but something stops me, and I can't think of the correct response. I want to say I'm sad so that I fall in line, but I can't. I've stopped the flow of things and my mouth is hanging open while everyone stares. After a too long pause, Qutey pulls on a lock of my hair.

"Ow."

"Sorry, you had some lint," she lies, a fake smile spread on her face. This was my cue to come back down to earth.

"I..I'm Colette," I croak. "I, um…"

"It's okay to be confused," Miss Laura finishes for me.

"Yes! Confused." I shout as if it's the winning answer.

Qutey gives me a side look as if I've grown another head.

"Alright, let's return to the moment and think about why we're all here. Brianna, a bright, young girl, who may have been just like you is gone and whether we knew her very well or not at all, we can't help but be affected by her death. Death isn't something we have to think about very often, but it is something we can't escape."

Maybe, maybe not. My current situation is proof of that.

She goes on for a bit and then walks over to the wall to dim the lights and leads us into a meditation exercise.

"We have to be silent to learn how to heal," she says in honeyed and husky voice, one she obviously had been saving for this activity. Her steps are silent as she walks throughout the room. "You're in a room. A room not unlike this one, except you're all alone. You're completely safe here and warm. All of your muscles are relaxed and breathing is easy."

I breathe in and out evenly and let everything but Miss Laura's voice fall away.

She tells us to walk through the door in the room to a place and a time that you felt safe.

My hand is on the door, and I know that on the other side I'll be in my Gran's house in Eastover. It will be Easter and Mama, my Uncle and Gran will be dying eggs for the church Easter Egg hunt. I can almost smell the vinegar as I turn the knob, but when I do I realize I'm not in the room anymore. I'm not at Gran's either. I'm in a train station with Mama. I'm seven or eight years old, and I can see my reflection in the windows. A plaid skirt skims my shins and I've got a limp white bow in my hair.

Mama is arguing with the ticket operator about our seats. She's angry, angrier than I've ever seen her, and a little scared too. Her hands are shaking and tiny red sparks of rage flake off of them when she moves.

Where are we going?

I remember now. We visited a cousin in Kansas City for a few weeks. It was one of the only times I was allowed to enroll in school.

Mama looks at me and her frustration dissipates enough to allow her to smile at me. Her Willow pendant sits perfectly at her throat, like some ancient jewel. Sometimes I think mine looks silly, as if I've been rummaging in my grandmother's costume jewelry.

She looks so young. A second later the operator hands her the tickets, and she's rushing over to me. When she grabs my hand I'm filled with love that swallows me like a warm bath and makes everything horrible melt away. We're running to catch our train and my legs are moving too fast.

We're almost there.

We're going to make it. She's happy.

"Wait!" someone yells behind us, but we keep on moving.

"Wait!" the voice yells again.

Finally we turn and my bow has fallen off. Mama smiles at the Nun whose running to catch us. I reach out to take the bow from her but when I look down it's not white, but red. Blood drips down my arm and over my shoes as I run. In shock I trip and almost hit the floor when I jerk awake and fall out of my chair.

The lights are still dim and everyone else is still in their happy place. How long have I been out?

Miss Laura looks at me strangely while everyone is still lost in their own worlds.

"I need a minute," I manage.

"Oh, fine dear. Take as long as you need. I'll be out in a minute," she whispers.

"No, no. Thank you. I'll be fine," I say running out of the door. My heart is pounding as I round the corner and through the double doors on the way to the 10th grade hall bathroom. I try and try to shake the last image of blood running down my arm. I run faster.

That wasn't an ordinary vision. It was wrong. Almost as wrong as a flushed and disheveled Lilah ferociously kissing Buck, which I just happen to catch as I clumsily burst through the senior hallway doors.

### ###

I stand motionless for a split second. Just enough time for Lilah to lean back and slap Buck across the face so hard that it makes *my* palm sting.

Buck looks at her with shock and betrayal before letting it melt into white hot rage. But his anger isn't focused on her, it's directed at me.

"I…I'm sorry. I was going to the bathroom. I…"

Lilah cuts me off. "Buck, I can't believe you. Leave. Go. Away!" she shouts, as much as you can shout in her tiny sing-song voice.

If looks could kill, I'd be dead right now. He stares at me for a full minute before she shouts again. "Buck! Go!"

He tears his gaze away from mine and brushes past me sending a weird jolt of energy, like he's just hit my funny bone, except my funny bone is my entire body. It only lasts a second before he mule kicks the double doors behind us and disappears.

"Oh-Em-Gee, Colette. If you hadn't come through those doors I don't know what would have happened."

Well, *I'm* absolutely sure, *you* know.

"He…he just went crazy." And then, the talented actress begins to cry.

Now this entire performance may have worked on a lesser mortal. And I must admit she is really performing, but I know better. What I saw should not have been seen by anyone and even though I can't *feel* her I know she is full of it. I decide to play along. Besides, I need information.

"It's okay. Do you want me to get someone? A teacher? Officer John?" I offer in an equally stunning performance of concerned bystander.

"No!" she spurts, too aggressively, too quickly and too loudly. "I…I…I'm too embarrassed."

I would be too. Girls these days really have no regard for their reputations. Some things have changed, but some things remain the same, and people still talk as much as they always have.

"Alright, do you want me to walk you to the bathroom and help get you cleaned up?" The shock of seeing her and Buck made me, *momentarily*, forget my nightmare. I mean daymare.

She nods and grabs my hand like a small child leading the way. I jerk at the contact, but it isn't necessary. When she touches me I still don't *feel* a thing.

"What lovely lace kid gloves," she says kindly, but without the real kindness to back it up.

Once inside, Lilah sets to the task of fixing her smeared lipstick and runny mascara. By the time I relieve myself and step out of the stall she's resplendent again, as if nothing had ever happened.

I turn on the faucet to wash my hands and ask her, "Are you alright?"

She smiles brightly at me through her reflection in the mirror. "Why wouldn't I be?"

I blink. For a second and it's just a second, I could swear that perfect smile was a fanged grimace, but then my imagination could be running wild. If I think she's evil, then my eyes see it too. It doesn't help that she's aura-less. Maybe my gift is on the fritz.

When I'm done drying my hands, I steel myself for confrontation. I've done my Christian duty by walking her here. The time for concern is up. I may be homeschooled, and I may be shy, but Mama didn't raise no punk.

"Why did you report me to the social worker?"

She looks at me incredulously, eyelashes batting. "I didn't tell anyone anything, Colleen."

She knows darn well what my name is.

"I hardly even know you, why would I do a thing like that?"

Well, that's my question. I'm about to dig further when the bell rings and two of her carbon copies burst through the doors, laughing wildly. The girls squeal when they see her and if she's as excited to see them as they are to see her, she doesn't show it.

In the presence of the Bells she seems even more poised and regal. Without a word, she grabs her white book bag from the floor and walks out into the hallway. The girls follow, obviously abandoning whatever business they'd had in the bathroom in the first place.

I could go after her, but she's waded into the ocean of emotion just outside the door. My chance is gone. I'm left there. Alone. Frustrated. Again.

# CHAPTER TWENTY

The Richland County Public Library is a massive structure made of thick green glass and solid silence on the corner of Assembly Street and Hampton in downtown Columbia. I'm still kicking myself for wasting my chance to confront Lilah when Carlos and I commandeer a small table near a microfilm machine in one of the research rooms.

"So I got most of this done, but I want to dig a little deeper. I saw in the textbook…"

Carlos is droning on about the project and possible leads, but it's hard to pay attention when I know that the murder is no murder at all. He's already printed out an article for me to summarize while he works on laying out the presentation on his laptop.

*February 17th, 1950*

*Bloody Holiday Comes to an End*

*COLUMBIA, SC - Churches breathed a sigh of relief as last Sunday came and went without the disappearance or burning death of any women in the surrounding county.*

*"We're just glad it seems to be over," says Mother Bernice Clayweather of Greater Ascension Baptist Church.*

*After a brief and fruitless investigation, the disappearance of sixteen-year-old Collette Thigpen will remain a mystery as the Thanksgiving day burning death of her mother Evelyn Thigpen, 36, has been ruled an accident by the Richland County Police Department. While in isolation the event seemed to be a tragic accident, many other people in the community thought otherwise as eleven more colored women in the county and surrounding areas have either succumb to mysterious fires or disappeared themselves, one every week to end last Sunday.*

*Authorities refuse to connect the events as there is no evidence that the women knew each other.*

*The women counted among the dead and missing are as follows:*

"Hey, Carlos. Do you recognize any of these names?"

He peers over my shoulder and reads down the list of women and points to the second name on the list.

"Cartwright. Qutey's a Cartwright. She'll probably know who that is. And…" he trails off for a second," Clement. Fuller. Wait, these names are familiar." He stops to think a minute. "Oooh! This has gotta be worth extra points. Culbreth. That's the link. That's the 'A' sweet spot. Unh!"

He punches the air and does a little shoulder dance.

"Collette? Do you know what this means?"

I shake my head.

He pulls his laptop over so I can see the screen and types something into the search bar. A list of names pops up, along with pictures. It's the missing girls.

"Look. Clement. Fuller. Culbreth. They're all there."

He's right. With the exception of Baxter for Brianna and Tressa Lancaster, there is a matching missing woman in my time to match a missing girl today.

"Okay. Okay. Okay. Whoo! Alright, we've like cracked a cold case. What do we do next? Uh, uh, uh, we gotta call the police."

He fishes his cell phone out of his backpack and kicks the chair in frustration once he realizes he doesn't have a signal.

"Okay. I'm gonna run outside and try to get a signal. You cool to stay here?"

I nod and before my head pops back up he's out the door.

A connection. We found a connection. This is a good thing right, but how can they be connected? Mama killed herself, she wasn't murdered, but that seemed to be the first death in the string. I'm missing something. I put a sticky-note on our research page to remind Carlos to add a nationwide search for missing women or missing children during my time.

It's there tickling the back of my mind, but I'm not getting it.

But isn't that the story of my life these days. Me, just not getting it.

### 

By coincidence, Carlos saw Summer outside on the way to pick up some dry cleaning for her Mom. Hey, I'm always up for a trip to Vikki's.

Summer picks through a rack of jeans and pulls out a pair of bell bottoms and holds them up to her waist.

I'm waiting for the bomb to drop. If she hasn't heard about my mad dash across the quad earlier, I'm going to have to confess before she finds out from someone else. Ugh!

"What do you think?" she asks.

"I think you should try another pair." I pull out a long narrow pair of dark colored jeans and hold them up to her waist. The hem hangs past her ankles and on past her toes.

"They're too long," she counters.

"You cuff them up really high."

"They'll make me look too skinny," she says.

"You *are* skinny. Only skinny girls look good in them." Compliments. That's the way. What do I have to be nervous about? She's my friend, she's not my mother.

She thinks for a minute and puts them back on the rack. "Not my style"

I know, I think to myself, that's why I recommended them. I take a deep breath and jump in the cold pool of truth.

"Okay. I'm ready."

"Good. So what were you and Matt doing fourth period? Did you guys make out?" I guess my interrogator is coming out swinging.

"What? No. We were just talking," I croak.

"Talking? Sheila Thompson said Mr. Bowler had to have the benches wiped down because of you," she practically yells.

"Ssssh! Are you crazy? That is a bald faced lie and you know it," I whisper.

"Do I?" Her voice is stern, but she's smiling.

Ms. Vikki comes out of the back room in a floor length cotton sheath, and bangles of all colors reaching halfway up her forearms. They clink as she walks across the store floor. "Girls! How are you?"

"Fine," we sing out in unison.

"Good. We've got some fabulous new pieces in. Collette, isn't it?"

"Yes, ma'am," I reply.

"I know you love scarves so you should check out some of the selections in the corner. One of the old Debs passed recently, and her daughter brought in a lovely pair of Hermes pieces. A little pricey, but worth it," she says with a wink.

"I will. We're just looking. I'm trying to get Summer to try something new."

Summer shakes her head with a smile.

"Well, you girls let me know if you need anything."

"Okay," Summer assures her while Ms. Vikki walks behind the checkout counter. We make our way to the corner while she pulls out an old rag and some solution and begins polishing some old pocket watches and bangles that she'd had lain out on the counter. I hadn't noticed them before.

"She must be really trusting to leave those out in the open while she works in the back," I whisper to Summer.

"Surveillance cameras. And don't change the subject. I can do that all by myself. I, uh... joined the Chemistry Bowl Team. I mean my Mom made me join," she reveals.

"That's swell! You should meet people who are all into potions like you are."

"Potions," she says flatly, and I know she's rolling her eyes. "It meets twice a week. Tuesday and Thursday until six, and..." she trails off.

"And what?" I ask while I slip off my flats and try on a few strappy heels left behind in the dressing room.

"My Mom doesn't want me hanging out with you so much."

I feel as if someone has punched me in the gut.

"What? Why?" I manage to breathe out.

"It's Uncle Silas. He's got the FBI calling the house again asking questions about him and she knows that I met you through him... and, she might think that you're a bad influence because we've been out past curfew so many nights," she confesses.

"What are you talking about? You're always gone before 6," I sputter.

"I know. I might have told her it was you I was hanging out with and not my boyfriend."

She starts absentmindedly organizing the shoes by color.

"What boyfriend?!" She's purposely not looking at me. "Oh, so who's keeping secrets now?" I say abandoning the shoes and making my way to clearance accessories counter Vikki keeps hidden in the back.

"Don't think of it that way. He's just…We're just…Please don't be mad at me," she begs.

I flop down in the seat next to the counter and feel sorry for myself for a second before responding.

"I'm not mad," I murmur.

"Oh good! You're my best friend."

"I'm your only friend," I declare.

"I don't want you to be lonely. I know what that's like. Even if you do have some secret thing with Matt," she says, trying her best to console me.

"Really, we're just…friends," I urge.

"Whatever. I'll feel better when you have something else to do besides read and hang out with old people."

At that moment, I want to hug her. I give her a grateful smile and say, "I'll be fine."

As soon as I say it, I know I'm not. I tell Summer to wait while I pretend to try on more cardigans in the dressing room. I don't allow myself to get angry or cry, but I do sit, drop my shields and just be for just a moment. I try to shake it all off and plaster a little smile on my face.

When I pull the curtain back, Summer is standing there with the biggest smile on her face and big red and white "Help Wanted" sign.

"I've got an idea!"

# CHAPTER TWENTY-ONE

"Under no circumstances."

"What?"

Miss Collins is pounding something foul smelling and dry in the mortar and pestle while I copy tea recipes from a musty book she's brought by. She hasn't mentioned anything about her trip to Charleston yet, and I haven't asked.

"You don't have time to work. You waste enough time at school all day. Again. D is for?"

She must be kidding.

"D is for Djinn, a shape-shifting invisible demon made of fire. They dwell in fireplaces and the desert. They can be disarmed by saying grace and throwing salt." I wait a beat.

"I'm sixteen. Sixteen-year-olds go to school. We get after school jobs. We date!" To-Do #55, go on a date.

Her laugh is hollow. "You are not a normal sixteen year old. You're a Willow. Y is for?"

"Y is for Yuki-Onna, a Japanese female demon with pale skin that sucks the life out of her victims. She's also knows as the Lady of the Snow. There is no known deterrent." I sigh.

"Why can't I be normal? Who says that I am who you even think I am? You said yourself you made a mistake. Maybe this is all a coincidence. You could be wrong."

"Little girl, you are smellin' yourself. Once you learn more than how to talk back you might understand. Until then, *I* will be your mentor and *I* will decide when and where you spend your time, Apprentice."

Her eyes bore into me disapprovingly from across the counter, and I finger the willow pendant at my throat. It's funny how I don't even notice it until she comes around.

"Are you gonna send me back?"

She stops pounding. I meet her gaze with one of my own that's just as intense if not more. Why can't I be normal? If this is all gonna end or if I have to be something I'm not sure I am or if my mother wanted me to be then she needs to say it out right.

As if she's read my mind, her gaze softens. She walks over to the stove and turns the kettle on.

"If my mother killed herself then maybe she didn't want me to be a Willow?" I manage to choke out. I don't care what Miss Miller said about the Klan. The Klan's always been around, my mother had to have been afraid of something world crushing to kill herself and to send me away for however long.

"Ssssh! Let me speak, girl. Let me tell you a story."

She slides a dusty cloth-covered book over to her side of the table and turns to a page.

"This is Odion." She points to a pencil drawing of a beautiful woman with close-cropped hair. I study the woman's face as Miss Collins makes her way back to the pestle to resume her rhythmic pounding.

"She was a Yoruba girl. The favorite of her grandfather, the village shaman."

I wonder if she ever cowered in her room for an entire week afraid to touch even her mother.

"She had visions, she could influence, manipulate, and she could even see the colors of the soul and discern the truth in a man's words without him having to speak at all. Some legends even say that she could even bend time. As always happens, this girl met a boy, a young warrior from a neighboring village and chose him over her chieftain's son." She pauses and looks at me, I assume to make sure I'm paying close attention and then makes her way to open a window, letting a breeze full of the scent of honeysuckle and azalea that bloomed overnight in to perfume her tale.

"It was on her wedding night that the slavers came, undoubtedly sent by her own chief. She'd been married only hours before she saw her husband's blood spilled on the hut floor. She prayed for death that never came and by the time she arrived in Charleston, grief had stolen her voice completely, and she was pregnant with the boat captain's twins."

She pauses and stops the scrape-bump, scrape-bump rhythm of the pestle.

"Odion did not have to endure the auction block. She became the captain's personal maid and when her time came, he sent for the finest of the slave midwives, a French creole slave named Collette. She told her what kind of life lay in wait for her and her children and the all but extinguished life in her belly sparked and she remembered who she was. She could not accept that her life was not her own. She could not accept that her children were not her own and though power had been stolen from her, she could gain it back, but it would require sacrifice. A great sacrifice."

"Still weak from birth she gazed down upon her children and spoke for the first time in nearly a year. Part prayer, part incantation the words rose into the air in a trail of sacrificial smoke and the birthing bed became her altar. As dawn approached to end her service, she did the only thing that would break the thing inside her and loose her awful power. She killed her son."

The tea kettle whistles right at that moment, and I nearly wet myself. I want to speak and can't. I want to cry, but something holds me still.

"If she did not love her son this would not be a sacrifice. The spell could not have worked and oh did it work. Her natural gifts became magnified. The captain suddenly became overcome with love for his new daughter and broken over the grief of his now dead son so he released Odion from her bonds and gifted her a generous amount of his fortune before dying mysteriously soon after. Apparently, this same affliction fell upon all of the crewman aboard his ship. Fearing this mysterious illness, no one wanted the remaining slaves left to be auctioned from the voyage. Fortunately, she was newly rich. And if you think this is a fairy tale and her young son was the only sacrifice you haven't been paying attention to your studies. There is no magic. Magic *is* science. All energy, life, spirit, and force is about balance. When Odion sacrificed her son, she had to give more than blood and life; she had to give of herself as well. We are descendants of her, gifted like her, and cursed like her. We are the fruits of that sacrifice."

"Cursed?" I whimper as if that's not the only and right payment for murdering your newborn son.

"When she sacrificed her mother's love she also sacrificed her lover's heart. All Willow born are gifted and cursed. Any love we share is doomed, dangerous to us, dangerous to those we love. The best we can hope for is the love of our sisters."

She gets up to pull two mugs from the cabinet.

"I'll fix the tea," I croak.

I've learned my lesson with her. My tongue is heavy in my mouth, and I feel dirty knowing my blood is contaminated. I hand a steaming mug to Miss Collins afraid of what she has left to tell.

"What about my Mama?" I ask.

She looks confused. "What about her?"

"I don't ever remember Mama having any friends. If she was a member, like you think she was, why don't I remember any of them visiting on a birthday, Christmas? Sometimes, the prayer circle would come once in a blue moon. She was lonely."

"This is a lonely life!" She points to my teacup.

"A young sister will learn how to make Forgetting tea before her first blood. Maybe she didn't want you to know certain things. If your mother was called to something she wanted you protected from she made sure you knew only what you needed to know."

"If she didn't want me to know then why are we doing this? Aren't you going against her wishes?"

She shakes her head. "You can't outrun your destiny. I tried to do it and people suffered. We live a life of service, Collette. We serve."

Her eyes press upon me, and I can feel her will burning away my resistance.

"You will serve or others will suffer. You will suffer. This is not a threat. It is as certain as math, an unshakeable truth. Don't immerse yourself too much into the cares of this world. You're in it, not of it. Shake off your distractions. Drink your tea."

I do as I'm told and think about everything she's said. I want to be normal and the universe keeps reminding me that I'm not. How many hints will it take before God takes more drastic measures? Maybe I don't get a second chance.

"So if I'm here to help the order. What am I supposed to do?"

"What you're supposed to do is as you're told. You'll know what you need to know as soon as you need to know it and not a minute sooner."

She gets up from the table and resumes her pounding, and I'm left staring at Odion. The soft rhythmic crunch fills the house. Odion was a killer. I think of the evil in men's hearts. What about the evil in hers? I frown thinking of everything she gave up, what my mother must have had to give up. Can I do that? Will I have to?

"Stop it," Miss Collins says halting her pounding.

"What?"

"Just stop. One day a week," she concedes. "Work will be good for you. A learning opportunity."

I smile, much brighter than I should be for something so small and notice the book she's had to set aside, the demon encyclopedia.

"Miss Collins? I read the encyclopedia, but it's incomplete."

She raises an eyebrow.

"It doesn't have an entry for imps."

I've searched for Raphael for days and there's no sign of him. My urge to see him is never so strong as just after a meeting with Miss Collins.

She rolls her eyes. "Fool girl. There are a lot of things in this world you don't know about and then there is make believe. There's no such thing as imps.

"Now, on to Lesson, what is it now, 22? Did you know you can pull memory from cloth?" she asks.

Dear Lord, how much don't I know?

# CHAPTER TWENTY-TWO

Sunday church services are an all-day affair for Miss Collins so after attending the early morning service with her, I meet Summer at the Sports Pavilion for the dedication of the new pool. Carlos has been talking about the off-season opening nonstop, but I guess I've been too wrapped in my own world to really pay attention.

Summer's Mom's weekday ban against me is still in effect, but the weekends are fair game. Balloons are attached to the handles of the double doors, and you can smell the chlorine from the parking lot. We walk in and make our way to the bleachers at the diving board end of the pool. Qutey waves at us from across the room.

"Hey!" she yells from the stands.

"Hey," I smile in reply.

"Why they decided to do a dedication on a Sunday I can't figure out," she remarks as she slides over. "You don't look so good."

I shrug. I was up half the night with Miss Collins, feeling fabric and trying to recognize my seventh sense. I'm exhausted.

"Especially for someone who was showin' the world all dat azz in the band room." She erupts into peals of laughter and Summer joins her.

"Oh my God! Is that what you heard?" Summer asks in chuckles.

I lose two inches from my height. Mortified.

I try to tune them out as Mr. Sandal, one of the rarely seen Assistant Principals, welcomes everyone. I secretly thank God that the rumors he would do an inaugural kick-off swim were unfounded. Seeing this man in swim trunks would not be pretty.

Before long the air gun pops and Carlos, the man of the hour and friend that brought us all together, shoots under the surface like a dolphin before bobbing up mid-lane to begin his breaststroke. Chatter echoes and bounces off the walls and fills my ears so that my own thoughts can't fit inside. It's sweet relief until Qutey's voice slices through the noise as clumsy as a rusty ax.

"My gawd. I didn't notice until you said something."

Summer gasps, "And look, look, look. Is it possible to smirk under water?"

"Goooo number 6!" Qutey yells.

"Number 6! Number 6!" Summer chants. Eventually all of the girls in our row take up the chant and when Number 6 is announced as the winner they all cheer. He bounds up with inhuman speed and grace and waves to the crowd, water glistening over six pack abs. The only problem is that Carlos is *not* number 6, but I know who is.

Raphael.

### 

Raphael winks at me as he emerges from poolside, and I silently make my way under the bleachers.

It only takes a few moments before he meets me there with a hug. He's chosen his usual form and looks to be about nineteen, a little over six feet tall with, ironically, a swimmer's build: wide shoulders, slim waist and all hard, lean muscle. He's hairless from head to toe, save two bushy, but manicured eyebrows and dark as volcanic rock.

I should be excited to see him, ecstatic even, but some-thing tells me this is just another sign of trouble to come.

"Are you being good?" I ask. Raphael scoops me up and gives me another sopping wet hug, all the while sniffing my hair, an odd gesture for anyone other than Raphael.

"Of course!" he chuckles and begins to speak telepathical-ly.

*You smell like my own, my dear. It is…intoxicating.*

"Try to use your words Raphael. Not everyone can speak without talking and kids to think it's weird when we stare."

*Very well.*

He puts me down as gently as he can, and beams at Qutey, who, consequently has been struck dumb by his brilliance and stares blankly at us through the bleachers.

"Um, let's go get some coffee," I suggest, before he blows my cover along with his own. "We can sit in a corner away from all of your throngs of admirers. If you walk around any longer in that Speedo, I'm almost sure someone will try to attack me to get to you."

"That would be a mistake on their part," he replies a little grimly.

At the coffee house, I order myself a cappuccino and Raphael a white chocolate macchiato. The waitress, a college student with cropped black hair and boxy glasses practically trips over her work boots to serve us. If she pokes out her chest any more, I'm sure that gravity will have no recourse but to take her down. Raphael doesn't seem to notice.

"So, Colette, are you enjoying your return? It was hard won," he asks before sipping his macchiato.

Raphael's wearing a pair of pressed khakis, boat shoes without socks and a gleaming white t-shirt that stretches over his build and creates an eye-catching contrast with his dark skin. I'm glad the waitress has shown us to a corner so that we can minimize that eye-catching. She's staring so hard from her pastry counter, I think she might bore a hole in my head.

"Mmmm. This is delightful - almost sinful." He winks and flashes me a glorious grin. As he sips, the dark pools of ebony at the center of his eyes floods into the whites until I am looking into nothing but blackness in his sockets.

"Where have you been?" I ask, feeling very much like he's had more than enough time to get settled.

"What do you mean? I've never left your side."

"I've been looking for you every night!"

"How many times do I have to tell you? Just because you cannot see me it does not mean I am not there."

Frustration seizes me and won't let go.

"I've been losing my mind, and I've been all alone while it was happening! You could have warned me about all of this. You could have told me that there was a whole world I knew nothing about."

"I always told you that you were special."

"Every child is told they're special."

"Well, in your case it just happens to be true," he says matter-of-factly and takes another sip of his coffee.

I blow out an air of frustration.

"I saw...I saw Mama kill herself. Was...was what I saw true? I thought I saw you...well, look at me. Did you?"

He gives me a look of pity that I immediately hate. I need help, not pity. I need answers, not sad looks.

"I saw you. I exist in all planes of existence, in all timelines. What you saw was true, but it's what you didn't see that matters. Your mother was the greatest witch of her time, and she sacrificed herself to save you and her sisters. Unfortunately, it didn't work as she had planned."

"Her sisters died anyway," I whisper remembering the list of missing women that Carlos and I found in the newspaper. I think of the missing girls today.

"It's back isn't it? Whatever, whoever Mama was running from."

He nods tersely.

"Well, how am I supposed to help? What is it? Who is it?"

His lips purse tightly, draining of all color.

"I am not permitted to say," he growls.

"Excuse me?" I say in disbelief.

"There are rules Collette," he says tightly.

"Rules? Whose rules? This is my life. Girls are dying. Someone maybe trying to kill me." I think of the danger Matt's so worried about.

"I am aware."

"You're aware. Is that it? What if I decide I don't want to play this supernatural game with you people who don't want to let me know anything? It's like everyone knows the rules to the game, but me, but I'm the one who has to live or die by them. Well, I don't want to play anymore."

*There are things you must find out on your own. Things I am not allowed to tell you.*

My eyes are cold. "Did Mama want me to join the order?"

"I think you know the answer to that question."

Why can't I get a simple answer? I look into his eyes, they have returned to normal, or his guise of normal.

*Precious One, she could not outrun her destiny and neither can you.*

"So I have no choice," I whine.

"You always have a choice. Your mother taught you that."

"I choose to be normal, I want to have children. I want to work!"

"Children? Is that what this is about? I could give you children."

"Uh, nuh-uh. I have no desire to lose my mind or give birth to a full grown half-bull half-man. Isn't that what happens to women who fall in love with mythical creatures?"

"Mythical! Who have you been talking to?" he asks suspiciously. "The situation with the bull was… unfortunate and only happened once," he says with a dismissive wave of his hand. He pauses, thoughtful for a moment.

"So you've actually done that!?" I exclaim. It takes a second, but I actually laugh to myself. "No seduction of the lovely virgins these days?" I tease.

*As if there were any left.*

"I beg your pardon. Hello!" I gave myself a showgirlesque once-over with my hand. I saw it on a game show late one night. "You can believe in fairy tales. We do exist," I say, my voice thick with vinegar.

I'm sure that anyone overhearing this conversation is wondering if we've both escaped from a mental institution, but what can I say? I take stock of the room. It doesn't seem like anyone is noticing us, besides the stalker waitress.

"You're doing what you always do."

"And that is?" he coaxes.

"Distracting me. Miss Collins says I need to avoid them."

"Ah, Young Odion. She made her choices."

"She's not so young anymore. She's a lonely old woman," I offer.

"She's also a hero. She's saved countless lives. I can say this from a perspective of impact on generations to come. Her kindness will reverberate long after she is dust. Any cow can bear offspring."

I think about that and without warning images of Matt's face, his amber eyes, even the golden hair of his legs appear in my mind.

*Handsome.*

"You know I don't like it when you read my mind."

He holds up his hands in apology.

"Is it true about the curse?" I ask.

"The English language is so limited and your understanding of power even more so. A curse is little more than an idea. Would you not find this idea to be suspiciously ineffectual given your very existence and the continuence of the willow born line each passing year?"

"So it isn't true then," I sigh.

"I didn't say that."

Uggh! He shrugs and takes another long sip of his macchiato. He really is enjoying it because his irises cloud over and expand again. The liquid pools of oil spill out and cover the whites. These are the moments when Raphael's otherness becomes abundantly clear to anyone who had a mind to pay attention.

"Have you kissed him?"

"What?!" My voice raises several octaves.

"Have you kissed him? You don't want me to read your mind and you've claimed to hold your virginity intact so you can't have taken him as your lover."

"No, I haven't kissed him. Not yet." I whisper the confession and Raphael beams. I think I have an unlikely ally on Team Life, although as head of Team Obligation Miss Collins is more aggressive.

*I am glad to see you adjusting well, but I need to warn you.*

He fixes me with a look that says, but doesn't say that I should listen and not talk.

"You have upset the balance," he says flatly.

"Your return, while not the first, was…unexpected. There is a delicate measure of energies in this physical realm. The natural and supernatural can either coexist or collide based on a holy algorithm that your human brain could never comprehend."

In an instant he downs his entire cup of steaming hot macchiato in a gulp that would have hospitalized anyone else.

"So why are you telling me all this?"

"Prophecy and tradition is a lost art in these modern times. As much as it pains me, as much as it pained your mother you should stay…close with the Collins woman. With your particular 'gifts', you're at risk and you may need her assistance if things go badly."

"Badly?"

He waves his hand as if shooing a fly. "What does this have to do with Mama?" I plead.

"You should pray more. You should study more," he says lightly as if that is an answer.

"I don't understand," I whimper, hopelessly confused. "I don't know what I'm supposed to do? How much danger am I in?"

"I would say that you *are* the danger." He laughs as if he's made a joke. "The hour draws near and the day wanes. Show me what you have done with your new home."

This feels like a ploy to escape my interrogation. I am about to say as much when he tenses and his eyes go black in the span of a second. He's no longer looking at me. His eyes are pinned to the gaggle of white bowed girls bouncing through the doorway, a nest of depressed bunnies, with Lilah at the helm.

With a flick of his wrist the room grows cold.

*Gather your things.*

"But, I have to pay," I object.

*She has already forgotten us.*

I look over to our previously stalking waitress. She's perched on the counter, reading some vampire novel. Now I know why we never got a refill.

He gently pushes me towards the door, and I realize that *no one* is noticing us. When we walked in, I could barely contain my wonder at the shameless lascivious stares and too loud whispers. Now there is nothing. We are invisible.

We are almost to the door when Lilah turns and meets Raphael's eyes.

A look of sheer horror leaps into her face. Her beautiful olive skin goes ashen in seconds and if I didn't know better that pretty bow at the top of her head shoots up for a moment. A chill blows through me and even though there is no breeze goose pimples erupt across my forearms. My ears pop as the air pressure changes and the world seems to slow as if we're all under water. I hear a scream, horrible as a war bird diving to attack, but the sound doesn't fill my ears. It's in my head, drilling into my brain.

I don't have time to process what is happening because Raphael is dragging me out of the front door, but what I do see is Lilah's angry and distorted open mouth, and just before the door slams to cut off her stare I hear the bird-voice screech a word. Is it spy? Lie? But as soon as we're outside and I can hear again I'm absolute sure that it was...

"Die!"

# CHAPTER TWENTY-THREE

"What in God's name?" I say, blinking furiously while opening and closing my jaw to make sure my ears have popped back to normal.

*Don't blaspheme.*

*Sorry*, I reply silently, duly chastised. *But I could hear her! I think it was her. How can I hear her?*

Raphael walks briskly as he crosses the street, but not as if he is afraid, that would be too unsettling. Raphael isn't scared of anything, but more with purpose. I have to double my pace to keep up.

"Hey," I say after a few minutes of walking in silence. "Hey!"

Raphael stops so abruptly that I crash into his back and stumble over his heels. He reaches down to grab my elbow and help me up.

The imposed silence presses in on me and builds up a bubble of anxiety in my chest as he leads us back to the school and towards a late model Triumph Bonneville motorcycle. We have to shoo away a crowd of boys and a few men who've attached themselves to the thing.

"We're going to ride this?"

He nods quickly, still serious.

"I don't have a helmet," I say and as soon as the word spills out of my mouth he fits his own helmet onto my head.

With eyes as black and flat as dried tar he speaks, "There are things you will never understand. Things that will save you and things that can destroy you."

I nod solemnly, bracing myself for what is sure to be devastating news.

*You are as great and terrible as anything on this earth, Collette. You always have a choice. Remember that.*

"Okay," I manage, completely confused.

We ride silently, and I'm so wrapped up in my own head that I almost miss my own house.

Raphael slows down to a stop, and we both have to marvel at the sight.

"I see Odion has been busy."

Bougainvillea has bloomed so riotously that it has crept up to the second floor and blotted out all of the windows in pale blue bursts of soft petals. Roses the size of grapefruits with thorns as big as a man's thumb have wrapped themselves around the iron fence, and in the moments we find ourselves staring no less than three magnolia blooms burst so loudly and pungently that the perfume makes both of our eyes water.

"Uncle Silas is gonna kill me," I whisper as much to myself as to Raphael.

Serious up until this point, a titter escapes from Raphael's lips and then another until he's in a fit of giggles as he makes his way to the porch.

He takes a seat on the second step, and I move in close to him on the cold cement just in time to get a front row seat to the Thumper van ride through the neighborhood like the devil's ice cream sales team.

"Repent! The end is upon us! Repent!" blares the bull horn atop the hood. Aluminum wings fashioned out of scraps are attached to the back doors and gleam in the sunlight.

"Crazies," I mutter as they pass by the house.

"Do not discount the warnings of those who the people despise," Raphael replies, not bothering to turn to me.

What does that mean? Does he think what they say is true? I'm about to ask when quite suddenly he wraps me in his arms for a massive hug. I'm flooded with calm and love and a peace that I can't remember ever having. I swim in it. I soak it up so that it reaches my bones and I lock it away in my heart for a time when I'll need it again.

"I must go. My appeal…Well, I must go. I should return soon. Please know it is not my wish to leave you."

He stands, dignified and regal. His eyes return to a semblance of their human façade.

"Wait! You just got here. Aren't you going to…"

I want to say "stay", but I know that is impossible before the word even passes my lips.

His eyes dart around quickly as if he's afraid and he whispers, "Follow your mother's instructions."

"Instructions? I did. You know…"

He cuts me off. "To the letter!"

He bends down and kisses my forehead with lips as cold as ice. A shiver ripples through me. He smiles at me and kisses me once, very lightly on the lips before turning and disappearing into thin air, his body popping like a soap bubble.

Just that quick. I'm alone again.

# CHAPTER TWENTY-FOUR

*Get thee to a church.*

Vikki Vintage is slow on Mondays, so slow that Vikki is letting me handle the place on my own on my first day while she runs an errand. After my visit from Raphael and Miss Collins' horrible bedtime stories, I need some peace. Mama's letter is light in my hand, and it's a wonder it hasn't burst into flames with all the intensity I've been giving it.

After organizing the racks and do a little homework, I slip Mama's letter into a Willow children's book I'm supposed to memorize, some fairy tale, and pull Vikki's bible out from under the desk. I read the chapters before and after the one Mama tore out to see if there's something missing. I'm almost blind with a headache at the mystery of it all when the bell dings over the door and Qutey walks in.

"Hey!" I shout, genuinely excited to see her.

"Hey back at you. I thought I'd come and see what you were workin' with in here, once I got past your bodyguard."

I roll my eyes. Matt's idea of baby steps seems to entail dispatching a phalanx of JV Football players to walk me to and from all of my classes. The boy outside is the late shift. "He's sweet, just a little serious."

She tosses back her fuchsia extensions and sets her book bag on a chair next to the checkout counter.

"Mmmmhmm. Well, I wanted to find out what the hell happened to you in homeroom Friday. I meant to ask you at the pool, but I forgot somehow. You're always kinda spacey, but when you ran out and never came back I worried."

"Aww, you do care." I mock.

"Whatever," she says and smiles, fingering a rack of scarves I'd just set out.

"Yeah, I, uh, I guess you would call it a daymare? A nightmare, but I wasn't asleep. A nun gave me a bloody hairbow."

"Sick!" she snorts walking slowly through the racks.

"I know. It really shook me. Did you make it to your *happy* place?"

"I made it to sleep, is what I did," she quips.

The lie turns her tongue green, but I don't press her.

"How about this?" I pull out a black peasant shirt with tiny embroidered flowers on the collar.

"What am I? A hippie?" she laughs. I shrug and put it back. I pick up a slim cotton pencil skirt, also in black, and hold it up.

"It could work for your college interviews," I offer.

She gives me a frown and shakes her head. "Too sexy. Besides, I don't have enough booty to make it look good."

The way she says booty makes me laugh, though I'm not sure why. We go through a number of items before I realize that she's not really here to shop, so I give up on the saleswoman act.

"You know Matt Fuller has been asking questions about you."

My stomach hitches. "What kind of questions?"

"You don't even sound surprised. He heard about you running out. He asked if you were alright. Again, something I meant to mention at the meet on Saturday. I asked him why he doesn't just call, but he said it was complicated."

She's got a look on her face as if she's just swallowed bile.

"What's wrong," I ask hesitantly.

"Nothing, he's just gotten a little weird since he got sick."

Sick? Is this the head injury thing Summer mentioned? I'm about to ask her some more questions when the bell rings over the door and Lilah and Chamberlain walk in, hand-in-hand.

"Oh, Hi! I didn't know you worked here," Lilah croons with that sugar-glazed smile practically spraying that creepy feeling onto my skin as her presence fills the small store. It's the first time I've laid eyes on her since the coffee shop. My eyes linger greedily on her face, that perfect smile and that stupid bow. Is she supernatural?

Chamberlain looks on blankly.

"Sweetie, say hi! It's Colette from class." She pulls on his arm gently as if he's touched in the head.

He nods slowly, politely, glassy-eyed. Each step is labored as if he were the Tin Man in need of oil.

"That's better. Oh, ooooh look at this!" she chirps to no one or all of us, I'm not sure.

I guess she doesn't think Qutey is worth a hello, because she ignores her. Qutey conversely decides the whole exchange isn't worth her time so she asks for the wi-fi password and retreats to a desk in a back corner. Before she passes out of sight she mouths "He's hot!" and throws me a bright smile.

Lilah dumps a brown bag in the consignment bin and pulls a flapper dress off the wall from the high-end section and squeals. "I have to try this on."

She leaves Chamberlain in the middle of the store and runs off to a dressing room. He's a lost puppy.

"You can go back there if you want," I tell him, even though Vikki would be livid if she knew. Couples are never allowed in the dressing rooms alone. There had been *incidents*, as she tells it.

He looks at me confused for a second and questions softly, "No?" and then louder and more firmly in his normal baritone,

"No. I'm fine." It's the soft rumbling voice I remember from the first time we met and, oddly, it has been missing ever since.

"How long have you been working here?" he asks.

"It's my first day! I always wanted an after school job."

He nods his head. He looks uncomfortable, as if he's not completely sure what's going on.

"How long have you and Lilah been going out? She seems nice." Okay, I already know the answer to the first question and the last bit is an outright lie, but I need something to go on.

A confused furrow cracks his brow. "Uh…it feels like a really long time. Maybe six months, maybe more. As soon as she moved to town."

"That's fast," I admit.

"Yeah."

I catch Qutey out of the corner of my eye making lewd gestures, urging me to tackle the guy or swallow him whole. I'm not sure. I don't think I'm good at this game.

"You and Carlos should come out with us sometime," he offers.

"Carlos?" I scoff.

"Yeah, you two are togeth…I thought," he stutters.

"No! What would make you think that?" I scoff.

"I don't know. You're lab partners. I saw you at Wingtastic the other day."

"Yes, of course, with other people. He's just my lab partner. *Believe* me. Besides, I don't think… Never mind." I want to say that I have my suspicions about Carlos, but that isn't for me to say. In any case, I think this may be my only chance to get some inside information into this girl who isn't just a girl. Maybe.

"Oh. Sorry," he says with as little consolation as possible and even a touch of laughter.

"Whatever. You guys were having a good time. Besides Lilah…"

"Lilah what?" I ask.

He looks nervous all of a sudden and his grin fades.

"Nothing. I'm sorry I didn't say hello. It was rude of me." He says mechanically.

What just happened? I thought he was coming out of his shell. For a second, I was too.

"S-so, how well do you know Matt?" I ask to get us back on track.

"Matt? He's my man fifty grand. We don't hang as much now that he's off the team, but we're still cool. Why? I'm surprised he hasn't shown up on your front step yet. Matt can't resist a pretty face."

Heat rises to my cheeks. He has shown up on my front step. I purse my lips and look away.

"C'mon? Don't play that game. You know you're pretty. All pretty girls know they're pretty. You dress different because of it. You talk different because of it. You even walk different because of it."

"Oh, like Lilah." I slam my hand over my mouth. Did I really just say that? "I'm so sorry."

To my surprise he laughs out loud and hard.

Just then the curtain swings back from the dressing rooms and Lilah floats out.

"I have to have it. It fits like a glove!" she sings. "I had one just like…I mean my Grandmother had one just like it. Well, um…I hope I didn't take too long."

"No, we were just talking" I say politely, masterfully erasing the bees nest in my stomach. Can women smell deceit? I have known people with weirder senses. I am people with weirder senses.

"Talking?" she seems surprised and gives Chamberlain a quizzical look. He looks back blandly. "Hmm, strange, you know my Pookums isn't much of a talker."

I shrug. "We had a pretty good talk. I'm still meeting people you know."

"Really?!" her tone changes this time and something hard rises from inside her and settles into her eyes. I've said something wrong, though I can't imagine what. I'm just about to place the gown in the bag when she places a cool hand over mine to stop me.

"On second thought… Do you work on commission?" she asks.

"Yes." I am glad for it, because big sales, like this one, can double what I will normally make just on minimum wage.

"Well, I don't think I'll be needing these. It won't be too much trouble to cancel the transaction, will it?" she says with a honey-dipped flourish.

"Not at all," I say tightly. I try to avoid hers and Chamberlain's eyes as I get out the binder with the refund instructions.

"Great. On second thought, I just don't have anywhere to wear that dress. I don't know what I was thinking."

I finish settling her up and give her her money back.

"Thanks. Just curious, do you have a skin condition?" she beams.

"Excuse me?" I object.

"The gloves. You always have your hands and arms covered. Is it a skin condition or some Madonna thing?" she taunts.

"I don't have a skin condition," I say tightly. "Is there anything else I can get for you?" I ask through almost gritted teeth.

"No. I think we're done," she sighs.

She slides her slender fingers into Chamberlain's grasp and leads him out the door. He doesn't look back.

# CHAPTER TWENTY-FIVE

"It's the most wonderful time of the year!" Summer sings as I slam the door to her car.

"What time is that?" I ask.

"South Carolina State Fair time! You're not from around here, so you don't know and it is my job to teach you." She rattles on about how it's the event of the season while we make our way to the fairgrounds. I guess Chemistry Club isn't meeting today, or she's ditching them, either way I'm glad to hang out with my friend and ditch my JV escorts. It's weird that I haven't seen Matt in the last few days. If it weren't for the bodyguards, I'd think he'd forgotten about me.

I gave Miss Collins the bag of dresses Lilah dropped off. She was so intrigued by the energy coming off Lilah's clothes that she gave me the afternoon off so she could concentrate on reading them.

"We're here!" Summer sings.

Even after years of practice, and you're full and you've had a good night's rest and you've done all you can to make sure you're physically and mentally sound, if you're an empath, crowds are always problematic.

Missing posters are plastered on every free wall space at the gate, and the air is heavy with grease. Sugar soaked steam is rising from the concrete and dotted with the faint trail of straw and manure, all of which would be tolerable if it weren't hotter than hell's kitchen on Thanksgiving Day.

"Are you okay?" Summer asks as we make our way to the rocket ship just past the front gate to buy tickets. I nod, even though I'm very far from it, but when I look at her she looks about as anxious as I feel.

"What's wrong?" I ask.

She looks at me as if she's scared, and I know something is very wrong. "What's happened?" I ask in a panicked voice. She looks as if she's about to cry.

"Don't be mad."

"What did you do?"

She bites her lip, and waves to someone behind me. I blow the air out of my lungs and know who it is before I even turn around. Weaving through the crowd with the brightest smile on his face and joy seeping through every pore is Matt holding a candy apple as precious as a single rose. He's so happy to see me. So happy, that he can't take his eyes off of me. So happy, that he doesn't see the yellow traffic barricade right in his path and lands flat on his face.

"Are you okay?" I yell as we run over.

"Aw, man. That was smooth. Are you pissed?"

I want to be. I really do, but here, holding his hand, a hand hotter than the sun, all I feel is happy to see him too. I shake my head.

"Okay, so, Collette. It's my fault, but it's totally good for you."

"You're lying." The smile in my voice is hiding the betrayal underneath. Summer has got to stop doing this.

"What?" Matt asks.

"I can tell," I say as I strain to help Matt up onto his feet. "This isn't about me, there is another reason."

"No, this was my idea," Matt cuts in. "I knew you'd never just say yes to a date, so I convinced Summer to set us up."

"Summer?" I look at her accusingly.

She throws up her hands. "No, no. She's right. You just think this was your idea. I'm meeting somebody. Mama would never let me go out on a date. She hates boys waaay more than she distrusts you."

She leans in to whisper in my ear. "Pleeease! I wouldn't have done it if I didn't know you like him too."

I'm about to protest, but that would mean I'd have to let Matt's hand go, and I don't want to.

"Fine. So where is he?" I ask.

"Thank yoooou! I'm supposed to meet him by the Tilt-a-Whirl." Relief swirls around her in a mini-tornado.

"Alright let's go meet this mystery guy." Matt and I turn to follow her.

She stops. "Uh, you can't meet him." She says it as if she's sorry.

"Why not? Don't tell me you guys are still a secret? And besides, you're in public," I chide.

Matt yells to someone up ahead. "Collette, I want to introduce you to somebody. Summer we'll catch up with you later," He shouts over his shoulder as he nearly drags me down a walkway full of girl scouts.

"Wait a minute! I can't just leave her," I plead.

"Collette, she's already gone."

I look behind me, peering through the swirling crowd. I can't find Summer anywhere. What kind of guy doesn't want to meet his girlfriend's friends?

"She'll be fine," he says slowing down a bit. "You okay?" he shouts over the din of organ music.

The smell of boiled peanuts, manure and vinegar tickle my nose. Peals of laughter and an ever present buzz-buzz-buzz waft through the air like a thousand kitchen ovens crying out that Mama's roast is done, but more bothersome than that, is the cloud of exhalative joy that's hovering above the whole fairground licking at my skin, soft as silk pajamas in a steady breeze. Even with my shields up I feel light headed.

I nod just as a loud 'pop' explodes on the street nearby - a car backfiring. I jump and nearly scream when Matt touches my arm. "I'm sorry. Uh, crowds make me nervous."

I'm on a date. This is a date. To-Do #53. I look up at him and try to root out the truth from the lies. Is he saint or sinner? Distraction or destiny? He catches me staring, and I try to pretend that I was looking past him at a carnival game.

"Take a chance! Take a chance! Every third bull's-eye is a winnerrrrr!" a booth man bellows across the walkway. A gold tooth gleams as he smiles at the both of us.

"I see a winner right here, I do. Good afternoon!" he croons in my direction. "Lucky boy," he offers to Matt and winks.

Matt moves a possessive hand to my hip and positions himself behind me. My whole body hums at the contact.

"I know," he replies, agreeing without the least bit of politeness. He nods toward the huge stuffed University of South Carolina mascot and largest animal on the prize wall. "How much for the Cocky? It's a once in a lifetime day."

The guy smiles sinisterly, "No cost at all. Free to the winner. Every third bulls-eye wins you a first tier prize." He points to a row of hand-sized dolls and animals. "The Cocky, that's a tenth tier prize."

We both wait for him to continue. "And?" Matt asks.

"Oh, ho, ho. The man is bold. Confident. That's good. He must be to win you, eh?" He winks again. "Twenty bulls-eyes." He pauses. "In a row," he says and laughs.

If I could whistle, which I can't, I would have. There is no way we are going home with that doll.

"Okay," Matt says nonchalantly and shrugs. "How much for a game?"

I try to hide my mild shock as a guise of determination falls over Matt's face as he slides me gently to the side and takes the oversized football in his hand. Having gotten used to the closeness, suddenly being apart feels cold and anxiety comes rushing in with a vengeance. It's becoming clear that the longer we're together, the worse it feels when we're apart.

The guy explains the rules and moves from directly in front of us to the side so that Matt could choose from the three brightly-colored and freakishly small car tires suspended from the ceiling of the booth. His aim will have to be perfect to slice through any one of the tires just once, let alone 3 times.

"Ready when yew are son," he says with a mocking smile.

Matt rolls his shoulders and squares his hips. After a second or two his arm pulls back and he snaps, sending the ball slicing through the air and bouncing violently off the side of the first tire.

"Steerike one!" the man bellows from his stool. He's checking his cell phone and doesn't even look up as he yells.

Confusion visits for half a second before even fiercer determination takes hold. He pulls back and launches a second time. This time the ball circles the holes but ultimately teeters out before going in. I let out a puff of disappointed air I didn't know I had been holding in.

"Steerike two!"

Before the man can even get off his stool, Matt hands over another two dollars. "Just rusty, that's all, "he says to neither one of us in particular. This time he fires off both balls in rapid succession with the same results. Feeling the specter of a ruined afternoon creeping up on us, I pull on his belt loop.

"Hey! I don't need that Cocky," I whisper. "It's too big to carry around anyway."

Frustration is boiling in him and blue-black veins bulge in his neck.

The man slides the money in his apron and yells out to the crowd, "One man up. Is he a winner? Are you a winner? Step in line."

He's already reeling in his next kill, confident these shots will go on like the last. I grip my pendant hard and smile at Matt.

He tosses the ball up once, twice, three times. When it drops he pulls back and sends the ball through the air and to the other side of the tire smooth as thread through a needle.

"Yes!" I yell and clap my hands before self-consciousness returns, and I shrink at the sound of my own voice.

In the next minute, he fires off six perfect throws, one after another without the slightest pause. By this time, the operator doesn't need to catcall, because a crowd forms and soon it is standing room only in our little corner of the fairgrounds.

Zeroing in on his target Matt pulls back one last time and stops. His gaze falls on me and he walks over without blinking, without stopping, without seeing anyone or anything else but me. Time slows and anticipation lifts me off of the ground. My cheeks tingle as he leans in, his mouth a hairs' breath away. His soft lips graze my ear as he whispers, "See. Once in a lifetime." His eyes gleam as he pulls back leaving me breathless.

He backs up with that same unblinking stare and launches a heat seeking missile and the crowd erupts.

### 

"Hey!" he says, using Cocky's head to peek around the corner.

"Hey to you, Superstar."

He walks around to stand in front of me. "That was quite a show."

He shrugs nonchalantly and drops to one knee. "For you, my Lady" he says as he offers up the toddler-sized toy like an engagement ring.

"Ewww, get up. The ground is covered in God knows what," I giggle. "Thank you, sir," I say and nod regally.

"Carnies and Cocky. A memorable first date, eh?" he asks and waggles his eyebrows.

"And here I thought candlelit dinners were the rule of the day," I joke. He fakes a shot to the chest, but smiles at my jab.

"You really like that don't you?" I ask taking his elbow and helping him onto his feet bracing myself for the familiar zing that zips through my funny bone to my arm.

"What?" he asks guiding my fingers to his belt loop and leading me back into the flow of the crowd.

"The attention."

He purses his lips for a second, in thought and takes a deep breath "Ah, it has its moments, but I can't say that I can't live without it. Now ask me six months ago and I would have told you something different.

"People expect too much. They always want you to be on and then when you're not, they feel like they have a right to call you on it. Like they've bought a piece of you."

I spy a cluster of policemen talking with a group of boys up ahead and get an ominous feeling. They've got them handcuffed on the curb. The boys are scared. The policemen? Bored and frustrated. I'm about to mention it when my purse buzzes.

It's a text from Miss Collins: *Call me as soon as you get home.*

I frown and shove the phone deep into my bag. I don't need any reminders about what I *should* be doing right now. I'm doing what I want, and it feels good.

"Anything wrong?" he asks.

"No. Let's go back the way we came." I turn around in the opposite direction of the policemen.

"There sure are a lot of policemen here," I comment. It's sad that I'm more afraid of the policemen than demons.

"Yeah. It's the missing girls. There was talk that they wouldn't even open this year because of it, that, and the curfew cutting into profits."

According to the new policy, anyone under 18 has to be home by 9PM every night. I look back over my shoulder at the boys and the policemen. The boys sit on the dirty sidewalk, embarrassment plain on their faces. The boys, all black. The policemen, all white. It strikes me who the curfew might really be for.

"Why did they open then?" I ask turning back, a knot building in my stomach.

"Why do they do anything? Money. Hey, I got a fun idea."

With victory upon him close as second skin, all his nervousness slips away, and we walk in brisk steps up to a booth.

"Karaoke madness?" I ask. "What's kar-a-oke?"

"It's a singing booth," he says quickly as he feeds tickets into the side slot and pulls back the curtain. It's close quarters inside and a large light beams down on both of us as our pictures pop on the screen in front of us.

"So what do you want to try?" he asks.

"What do you mean try?"

"Sing. We're gonna sing."

I shake my head violently and laugh. "Oh no, we're not."

He nods his head just as hard. "You said your Mom liked to sing, so I know you have to have at least some talent at it."

"I never said that," I argue.

He shrugs. "You didn't have to." He's scrolling through a list of songs on another screen below our pictures. "How about this one?"

I shake my head. "I don't know that song." He tries several more, and I shake my head at all of them. I've missed nearly a half-century of music. There isn't much I'll be able to get. I think he's about to give up when he snaps his fingers.

"Aha! Got it!"

I'm about to ask what when the music cues up and fills the little booth as the words pop on the screen.

"Really?" I ask.

He nods and in seconds his face distorts into a toothy grin and the most awful Louis Armstrong impression pours out of his mouth. "It's jazz baby!"

I laugh. I mean really laugh. "Can anyone see us?"

He shakes his head, still affecting a ridiculously wide grin.

"Okay." I say.

"Alrighty boo bop boo bay!" she scats just before it's my cue to sing Ella Fitzgerald's introduction to "Let's Call the Whole Thing Off."

At first, I'm nervous, really nervous, but by the time the second chorus rolls around and he's had a chance to really impress me with his horrible impression I let go. I let go and sing as loud and smooth as I want. I feel light. Lighter than I can ever remember feeling and when the song is over, my toes tingle with the excitement.

"Wow! I didn't know you were that good. How do you feel?" he asks.

"I feel….I feel great. I know I couldn't do it in front of an audience, but this was…"

"Fun, right?"

I nod and giggle again.

"Wanna go again?" he asks.

"No. It was a surprise the first time. I want to end on a high note."

As soon as I say that, he pulls the curtain back and a crowd claps as we emerge.

My cheeks go hot. "I thought you said no one could see us," I hiss in his ear.

"They couldn't, but that doesn't mean they couldn't hear us. Guess you're the show stopper now."

# CHAPTER TWENTY-SIX

Matt pulls off a piece of the elephant ear and feeds it to me. The sugar melts in my mouth and in his eyes, I feel the safest I've ever been. A shock of energy from where his finger touches me leaves my lips buzzing.

The next hour slips past slow as honey and just as sweet as we ride the Ferris wheel, just in time to see the sun slip behind the horizon and the moon rise like a nightingale. Matt's letting me try to win him a tiny plush hound dog when Summer appears out of the crowd and rushes over.

"Hey!" she squeals, and I can't help but squeal back. Again she wants to hug and I feel the pull too, but we just stop short and bounce high as Ping-Pong balls in front of each other.

"Sup, Summer?" Matt says coolly smiling. She gives him a big smile and a quick wave.

My smile falls a bit when I realize that it must be time to go. "Time's up?" I ask.

"What? No!"

Matt pulls my fishing rod, not unkindly, from my hand and leaves us to our girly ramblings.

"I need Matt to take you home," she says.

"Why? Where are you going?"

A wicked smile crosses her lips.

"Oh no! Absolutely not. Your mother already hates me," I argue.

"She doesn't hate you she just doesn't trust you," she offers.

I roll my eyes. "So, I'm just supposed to abandon you to some guy while a known killer-kidnapper is on the loose? Where is he anyway?"

I look behind her to see if I pick him out among the throngs of kids, small families and packs of middle-schoolers.

"He's in line to get us some polish sausages," she says quickly, glee shooting out of her in a fine mist.

"Does he at least go to our school?" I say, side stepping a little boy who's escaped from his mother's side. Some burly man in a dirty Sonny's t-shirt and construction boots clouds my vision.

"I can't tell you that, but I can tell you not worry. I see it all over your face." She waves her hand in front of my eyes as if she's casting a spell. "*I've* known him for a very long time. He's not a serial killer."

I drop my hands with a snap across my sides in defeat. I look in her eyes imploringly, willing her to see the silliness of all this secrecy, the danger of it all.

Matt tugs on my elbow, and I giggle at the sensation. Summer gives me a sly look.

"I'm gonna get us some fried pickles." I breathe in his smell of sandalwood and ocean water, the fragrance from Summer's latest line of shampoo for guys.

Before I can answer gunshots pop like firecrackers around my feet, and Summer and I both scream, seconds before we realize that the sound actually is firecrackers. Matt, the consummate hero, takes off in pursuit of the 8-year-old assailant.

I find a bench and wave Summer over. "This is bad. I've got a bad feeling. I don't like it."

"It's fine. Really. Just be happy for me."

Head still shaking she touches me, softly on the knee. Joy radiates through my blood.

"Look," she beams as she slowly separates the tangle of bangles and leather bands on her arm to reveal a thin chain of silver wrapped twice around her wrist. I can tell that it is supposed to be worn as a necklace and has a small oval pendant attached.

"What's that?" I ask.

"He gave it to me," she breathes. " Its Saint Christopher."

"You're not Catholic," I said flatly.

"So," she says harshly and pushes the bangles down in a flash, hiding the necklace in plain sight. I've upset her.

"Christopher is the patron saint of lost things." I remember from my religion class I took the single semester I attended St. Martin de Porres in Kansas City. Just for the briefest of moments, I get a flash of the bus depot.

My mouth forms to say something, but I let the night wind snatch the words away into the din of prize bells and synthesized bass. I can't bring myself to snatch her back to the earth when she's flying so high.

"I see him!"

I crane my neck behind her to see if I can pick him out from the crowd.

She steps in front of me and for the first time, I notice how pretty she looks tonight. Her red curls are pulled back with a woven gold band I hadn't known she borrowed, and there was a flush to her cheeks that made her look virginal and pure, as if she were on her way to her first communion.

"What?"

"Nothing. Have fun. Tell me everything later."

She smiles and runs into the crowd. I stare after her for a minute before I glance around and search the crowd for Matt too. He's been gone for half an hour and I'm beginning to miss the now-familiar buzz of energy I feel whenever he's around.

I weave precariously through the crowd in the direction I saw him run in. Something is pulling at my gut. Gnawing. I don't walk for too long before I feel that familiar buzz bloom from the biting hollow in my stomach. I follow it like a homing beacon.

The noise dies down to a loud, thumping muffle and the light spills through spaces between carts, casting a sickly yellow and green color to the asphalt, wet with dead slushies and....other fluids.

A niggling feeling of dread squeezes my heart as I reach a chain link fence. My rational self tells me to go back and wait, but the charge running through me propels me forward. It's not too long before I hear voices and the pent up nervousness dissipates. A few more steps, and I recognize Matt's voice, but I've never heard it like this.

"This has nothing to do with me!" he hisses.

I hear the whimpering of a wounded animal and then the voice growls and laughs wickedly. I slow down and peer around the last corner of a storage unit near an exit so small and well-hidden it can't be on the fairgrounds map. I suck my teeth and then clamp my hand over my mouth so I can hear.

The laugh fizzles and high-pitched voice retorts, "Maybe. Maybe not! Look at me!"

"I see you," he says calmly.

"You see me? You see me! Do you see this!"

I notice a security mirror attached to the corner of a nearby storage unit and get a perfect view of the pair. The girl is rail thin and as tall as country sunflowers so that her gaze meets Matt's head on. She would look formidable if it weren't for the desperation that settles on her like a trench coat. She tucks a greasy strand of brassy blonde weave behind an ear smudged with dirt. Her lip cracks and blood shines through as she grins maniacally and grabs Matt's hand and presses it to her swollen pregnant belly.

# CHAPTER TWENTY-SEVEN

Matt jerks his hand back, but she's got an iron grip. My stomach lurches, and I cover my mouth and heave silently. Nothing comes out.

Her bloodshot eyes are pleading and wild.

"This," she says softly, tears springing from her eyes, "is your fault." She lets go as her voice cracks.

Matt stumbles back at the release and rubs his wrist rhythmically. He opens his mouth to say something and then stops and then starts again. "Tressa, I'll help you however I can, but this...this is not my fault."

Thick bile rises in my throat and a mix of shock and anger and something old and as simple as the instinct to hunt, to kill courses through my blood and seeps out of my skin, and I can no longer stand. I land in a pile of dirty water with a plop, but no one notices because in that same instant, the girl, Tressa begins wailing.

She wails as if someone has died, as if she is dying. It lasts too long, and she is too loud.

"Tressa, calm down," Matt pleads wearily, quietly, as if she's done this before, as if she were no more than a little girl who didn't get the candy apple she wanted before leaving the Fair. Molten steel fills his eyes and hardens as he pins the girl with a fierce stare. Still rubbing his right wrist, he speaks clearly, firmly, "Tressa. Stop. Crying."

It is not a request. It is a command. The girl's wailing dies to a trickle. She wipes her nose with the sleeve of her threadbare shirt. Her eyes ask a question, though I can't imagine what it could be.

He leans in to whisper something to her, and I can't decipher the words though I'm willing whatever supernatural power I have to give me superhuman hearing. Whatever it is, it breaks something inside the girl and her knees buckle. If Matt hadn't been there to catch her, she would have collapsed entirely. He bends to help her sit when a voice rings out.

"Hey there!" the voice calls from the darkness. "Don't even try it! I see you," the voice continues, but this time I can see that it is attached to a bouncing beam of light that eventually reveals a security officer. He's fat, balding and clearly in no mood to be disobeyed. Matt reverses his trajectory and helps Tressa stand.

The officer clucks his tongue. I am about to thank God that he hadn't seen me, that I could sit here in my dirty skirt and process this colossal failure of a first date.

"You too young lady!"

The flashlight rises to the security mirror, and I'm busted.

### 

The rain tap dances on the roof, and I try to imagine something, anything to distract me from the police lights casting blue and red ghosts through the windshield. He has miraculously convinced them that we just got lost looking for the bathrooms. Tressa will have to make her own explanations.

My thighs feel sticky, and I'm glad for the rain.

Matt runs back to the car and slams the door just as the sky opens up for a torrential downpour. The front gate belches people out into the street, making my hoped for speedy getaway impossible.

190

I don't look at him. I am not going to cry. I am stone. That current that runs between is as frenzied as ever, but I fight it. I push at that nerve until my whole body trembles with the effort and a headache tickles at the back of my neck.

I can hear his mouth open to say something, and the beat of the rain pounds those first words into nothing. Soon, the lot clears and we're able to pull out into the street. I count the slosh of the windshield wipers and chew the skin on the inside of my cheek.

"I owe you an apology."

No you don't. This is my fault for thinking I could go on about my life as if things were normal, as if I were normal. I say nothing.

"I...," his voice is small and manic, "I had no idea this would happen. She's been gone so long. We all thought she was dead. I thought she was..." His voice trails off.

A few times I think I hear him open his mouth to speak again, but he is silent. Finally, we pull up to the house, and I practically leap out of the car before it comes to a full stop.

"Wait!" he shouts.

I ignore him and run up to the porch, cursing myself for not leaving the light on. He follows me.

I pick up speed as he nears, being careful not to slip on the wet stone. I don't have to see him to know that he is just a few inches behind. I bound up to the top step and whirl around.

"Don't you step foot on my porch, Matt Fuller!" I bellow. The command stops him in mid-air as I stare him down with lakes of fire in my eyes, a rod straight finger pointed at his heart.

"Let me explain," he begs.

"No."

"Let me apologize."

"No!"

"Let me come up out of the rain?"

"Hell no!"

My blood boils at his boldness, heat coursing through me so much that I can feel the water on my arms turning to steam as my anger pulses to the beat of the storm, and the headache blooms to full capacity. I need to get inside. I need to take one of Summer's little pills and forget. Forget this night. Forget him.

Rain has plastered his shirt to his chest and the suede on his shoes is irreparably damaged. He looks at me confused.

"Really?" he pleads.

"Yes really. You don't get whatever you want here, Matt Fuller. You need to leave."

My voice is surprisingly calm. The confusion is still crawling all over Matt's face. Though, I can't imagine why. I am being quite clear.

"She's my ex-girlfriend."

I huff. "I gathered."

"We thought she'd been kidnapped or killed. I thought...I thought she was being held..." His eyes were pleading now. "I didn't take it well, but...I knew."

My mouth is a flat line, daring him to step on the porch so I can donkey kick him in the chest and run into the house, take my pill and disappear.

"We were together for almost a year. Her Dad works with mine. I thought she was cheating. I was gonna. We..."

The words dribble into the puddles streaming into the azalea bushes.

"I loved her."

My head pounds. My pressure is rising. Thunder rolls in the distance, and the rain continues to pound. I explode.

"I'm sure you did. What was wrong with her? Did she have a broken leg that needed mending? An abusive ex-boyfriend she needed saving from? Is that your thing? Girls with big problems. Well, I can't compete with a pregnant runaway. As needy girls go, she takes the cake."

His confusion breaks to offense. "Is that what you think?"

"Do you care what I think!?" I rail. "Obviously you don't since you run into your pregnant ex-girlfriend while you're out with me and then profess your love for said girlfriend on my FRONT PORCH!"

"I don't love her anymore."

His rebuttal is weak.

"I don't care!"

"It's complicated," he whimpers. Water streams down his face, his neck, his chest. He is so beautiful.

"Get off of my property!" I seethe through clenched teeth. My hands are balled into fists, and my keys dig into my palms so that I'm sure they will break skin. I literally see spots I'm so angry.

His eyes bore into mine. Searching. Pleading. But I am a stone wall.

Before I can blink, he's cleared the steps in one leap. I'm about to scream when soft, wet lips cover mine and silence me.

I have no bones. I am a puddle of water dripping from my hair, trickling down my tingling spine past blazing panties to collect at the bottom of my feet.

Fingers squeeze into my sides, and I exist only in the small space where lips meet lips, tongue meets teeth and the only sound is a heartbeat thumping.

I want this. I don't want this. I am better than this. There is *nothing* better than this moment. I. Am. Alive.

Slowly, excruciatingly, exquisitely I return from the ether into my body, lifted slightly off the ground by arms, stiff and insistent. I dig my nails into the flesh there, and realize I can feel the nail scratch skin. With each ticking second we press closer, are closer, one breath, one heartbeat.

I float back to earth slow as the first snowflake of winter. My heart is still running a marathon when Matt sets me down. A porch light across the street cuts on, and we both realize our time is up.

"You have to go," I say quietly. He nods.

"Can I come back tomorrow? To just talk."

I study his face and memorize each line. I close my eyes and feel the hum in my bones from having him near. I touch my lip that was kissed for the first time. I answer.

"No."

# CHAPTER TWENTY-EIGHT

The radio news reporter's voice floats through the kitchen on coffee scented air. "Detectives in the case have issued a statement. Quote: While we are happy to return Tressa Lancaster to the loving arms of her family, her appearance confirms long held suspicions that the so-called "Metro serial killer" is a manufactured fiction created by hopeful, but misguided parents and self-professed community leaders who would prey upon them. End quote.

"Insider sources in the police department say the curfew enacted just days ago could be lifted as soon as this afternoon."

Miss Collins sucks her teeth loudly as she dumps sugar violently into her mug. "Imbeciles," she hisses. "I don't know why I'm even surprised."

She stomps back over to the kitchen table mumbling to herself. "C'mon now. We need to do this before you go to school."

I slide slow as an arthritic cow over to the table. Miss Collins was none too happy about me not returning her text last night so this crack of dawn session is my punishment. I yawn loudly.

"You remember what I said about distractions?"

"Yes ma'am," I croak. She has no idea how much I've taken our discussion to heart. She rolls her eyes at me as if I didn't agree with her.

She dumps the brown paper bag I'd given her onto the table and spreads the dresses out. "Where did you get these?"

"A girl at school. I thought we might practice pulling memories from them."

I keep thinking about that weird situation at the coffee shop with Raphael.

"Girl? These are not the dresses of a girl, there are too many memories on them. In fact, there are too many memories on them for an old woman. There are lifetimes in this silk."

I look at her confused.

Irritated she throws her hands in the air. "Did you read the book I gave you on demonology?"

I swallow hard. "No, well, not completely."

"Umhmm. You not gone be happy until you're caught falling without a net. This girl of yours is no girl at all," she chastises pointing a bony finger in my face.

I think about the screech inside my brain that day.

"What is she?"

She shakes her head. "I can't tell yet. I need to consult a friend. In the meantime stay away from her."

"But we have classes together. Well, a project together. I don't see her that often. She's been excused indefinitely from gym."

"Do like I say and avoid her." She walks over to the table and places her duffle bag of Willow goodies on the table.

"I want to show you something."

She pulls out an old book wrapped in linen and a stick of incense. The book rattles the wooden table with its weight when she plunks it down in front of me.

I finger the worn leather and onion skin-thin paper. I can see its identical twin resting on a podium in the hallway, Mama hunched over it, a wrinkle of confusion deep in her brow. How did I miss all this growing up? Was I blind? I lose myself in guilt for long, sad moments before I notice Miss Collins staring at me.

"You've missed so much," she muses and takes a deep breath. "Look here," she flips to section partitioned off by a cloth bookmark, "Uh, yes. Read this. It's about Empaths, like you."

I lean towards her and squint at the tiny script and read.

> *The gift of Empathy is the strongest of all the Willow gifts. The root of all power is energy and only an Empath can discern between emotional energy and natural energy. They can see it, absorb it, reflect it and manipulate it. It is emotional energy that connects this physical realm to the spiritual realm. Because of this they are the messengers.*

"There. Stop," Miss Collins breathes in my ear. "That's the mistake I made. I can't call the angels. I'm not an Empath. There is no way that my spell could have worked. This is why we study, so we don't make mortal mistakes."

"This explains why I'm here?" I ask. It seems so simple, but still clouded in absurdity. I don't know how to manipulate emotions. But...there is that bit about absorbing. I've done that. I did it with my grandmother, I did it with Summer.

She rolls her shoulders and walks back into the kitchen. "Did you memorize those tea recipes?"

I nod, grateful that I've at least done that.

"Mix yourself a cup of Discernment tea, heavy on the lavender. You should have everything you need in the cabinet."

I get to my work while she turns the radio up and curses under her breath. "I'm gonna put up some extra wards on the house while you're at school. Remember now that the tea will make it easier to recognize anyone who's gifted around you. If this girl is who I think she might be you'll be able to see her better to avoid her. Call me as soon as you get a glimpse and tell me what her aura looks like."

I pour the hot water over the leaves and the steam makes my nose wrinkle. "Are there any side effects?"

"Always, sweetheart, but as reactions go this one isn't so bad. You'll be able to see her better, but she'll also be able to see you. Don't worry though. With any luck, the clothes came from an auntie or a grandma, or someone pretending to be an auntie or a grandma."

I sip my tea and let Miss Collins fade into the background. I'm supposed to be paying attention, but either I've lost the energy or the ability. I'm not sure. I throw on a maxi dress and some flats, cover myself in a chunky knit hood and follow Miss Collins out the front door. With my 299 situation, it seems best to have her pick me up and drop me off to school. At least I can pretend to have some family.

"Father in heaven!" She stops short. "Well, he must be guilty as hell if this is his response."

At first I don't know what she's rambling about, but then I peer around her and see. There are a dozen roses in every color I know and didn't know roses came in on my porch. I bend down to pull the card nestled in one of the bunches and then think better of it. I walk off the porch. Miss Collins follows me.

"Aren't you going to read the card?"

I shake my head. "I know who they're from." She fixes me with a questioning stare. "It's just a distraction, I'm handling it."

### 

You would think that I would have learned my lesson. You would think that I'd be a less willing participant in Carlos' 'pick-me-up' shenanigans, but you don't know Carlos, and he is very convincing when he wants to be and right now, I want him to be because I'm tired of peeking around corners like a cat burglar and that niggling sense of doom is growing wild as kudzu in my belly. The walls at school are too closed in, and people don't even have the decency to whisper when they gossip about me.

"Scalini's Scare House?"

Carlos nods. "You're too tense. You have a problem, and I'm the problem solver."

I look up at the rickety structure, almost four stories high. The building is creepy, yes, but more so for its near crumbling façade, rusted bolts and general abandoned appearance. After lunch, Carlos smuggles us off school grounds. According to him, the last place they'll look for me is the scene of the crime.

"Don't judge a book by its cover. This, my friend, is THE scariest place on earth."

As if on cue, a screaming boy, as pale as dryer sheets bolts from the exit door on the front of the structure, his eyes peeled back as if he's seen death itself. His fear slams into me in a thick fog. Even with my shields up, I stumble back and sneeze.

"Bless you. See? That kid knows what I'm talkin' about," Carlos says gleefully.

"Welp, that's my cue. See you guys when you come out," Qutey announces and makes her way toward a fried mushroom stand she's been eying since we walked through the gate.

Carlos calls after her. "You're missing out!"

In the most monotone voice imaginable, the ticket taker speaks up, "Scalini's Scare House is not a ride; it's an experience. Management is not responsible for resulting nightmares, bed-wetting or even death should you enter these horrifying halls. Step right up," he drones.

Carlos leaps up the steps two at a time. "Two please!"

I can't place it, but something about the place makes me feel uneasy, not to discount the ten-foot wide blood covered clown mask affixed to the sign atop the building.

I follow Carlos up to the black drape that separates us from the unseen inside. I hesitate.

"And how is this supposed to make me feel better?" I inquire.

"It will trust me. It's scientific. You go in, you get scared, and the rush of endorphins floods your system, boosting your serotonin levels, thus making you happy."

"So I have to get scared to get happy."

"Yup," he affirms happily.

Something inside is ringing high as a bell, urging me to stay outside, but Carlos has already paid for the ticket and he's been so sweet. I don't have the heart to say no. I square my shoulders and nod. Besides, how long could all this take anyway?

He reaches for my hand, but I ignore it and plunge head first into the darkness. I'm only able to make two steps before I have to stop and allow my eyes to adjust the total blackness that now surrounds me. I call out to Carlos.

"Carlos!"

"Right here."

I jump at his reply, so close he might be standing directly in front of me.

"I can't see anything," I whisper, unsure of how I should conduct myself. How does a girl act in a haunted house?

"That's the point," Carlos whispers back, matching my tone. "You're supposed to use your other senses, feel, hear, smell."

A faint smell of old fish tickles my nose, and I snort. Another nudge by Carlos at my back and I make tiny but determined steps forward. With permission to "use my senses" I let my shields thin to a whisper's breadth to help me relax. With the ability to "feel" those around me, I don't feel so vulnerable. Carlos' giddiness appears in a ball of static to my back, and I know exactly how far behind me or beside me he is. His excitement fills me up as tight as a shaken soda can, and I find myself grinning in anticipation of I know not what.

A second later the sound of a chainsaw rips through the darkness, punctuated by a splatter of something wet and warm. Carlos screams and bolts ahead of me.

"Wait!" I cry, and wipe futilely at my face to clear my unseeing eyes. I try not to get the blood or whatever it is in my mouth, but a few drops make it in anyway.

Cherry syrup.

It's already drying to a sticky mess when I begin walking again, annoyed that the stuff will probably not come out of my dress.

Even still, exhilaration and fear course through me, less and less so as Carlos gets farther away, but still there. I walk cautiously, still unused to the darkness surrounding me. A cackling laugh pierces the blackness, and I jump. My heart pounds and I, disbelievingly, laugh.

After a few more paces, the anticipation of what will come next builds and little nervous insects begin to crawl inside my belly. I let my shield thin to cheesecloth and keep moving. Soon I stumble over something and reach out to touch the wall and my hands come away with slime. It smells rancid. Why would someone think gross equates with scary? After a few more paces, I come to a stairwell, and I have to feel my way up. Instead of darkness, there is a faint red light cloaked in fireless smoke. Skeletons hang from the hallway, and I can feel at least three people hiding somewhere in the near darkness, three extremely bored people, so bored that I don't even feign surprise when they jump out to scare me. I quicken my pace to make it to the stairwell on the opposite end of the hallway. I'm almost there when something stops me cold. There's someone else here.

I didn't notice this other person before and weirder still his/her energy feels different, more primal, animal-like even. I squint to try to see if there's someone waiting on the stairs, maybe even behind me or crouched near a sliding door like the other carnival workers, but it's no use. There's so little light here. My skin feels clammy, and the cold from the A/C swirls around me and snatches away my short-lived confidence. It's getting closer.

A pulsing, nagging anger builds in my chest, rising hotly and quickly. Whoever this is they are enraged. I hear a growl and spin around; searching in the darkness for the source before realizing it was my own voice.

"Get a hold of yourself," I whisper fiercely. I suck in a deep breath and hug myself willing my shields to drop into place heavy as an iron curtain. Soon, I'm myself again, but with my shields up, I'm cut off. I can't see or feel where the anger is coming from. I pray it's just a disgruntled employee and head quickly for the staircase. I shuffle down the steps and can see someone shadowed in the faint light of the outside at the end of the hallway.

"Carlos?"

The figure doesn't respond. I try again, "Carlos?"

Nothing. Instead it rushes towards me with lightning speed. My breath catches and instinctively I turn heel and run in the other direction back up the stairs. I almost make it when a rough hand snatches me by the hair and hurls me back down. My back cracks against the floor, and I see stars. A second later a boot kicks me in my side and I scream. As the pain takes center stage in my brain, my shields crash down, and I'm flooded with a mix of fear and liquid hot anger. A rough hand clamps down on my mouth and I bite ferociously, growling with murderous rage. I draw blood and he draws back. He's squatting over me, and I take the advantage and laser in on his privates, not least because I can't see his eyes. Thankfully, he's wearing shorts and it's easy to find what feels like hard boiled eggs. I dig in my nails, twist and pull as if I'm snatching plums from a tree.

He cries out this time and scrambles to the side. I kick my legs out from under him and flip over to my knees to crawl, but a hand snatches my heel. Volcanic rage erupts from my pores and bile fills my mouth. My eyes roll around in my head and I flail wildly, shaking my attacker loose and momentarily gaining myself again.

"Help! Someone please!"

My voice sounds garbled and desperate in my ears, and it may be the fall, but I think I can hear Carlos in the distance, laughing. I throw my arms out to try to grab something to keep me from this man, but the walls are slick and my eyes cloud with tears so I see next to nothing. The hand that was on my heel finds my calf and soon nails are digging into my thighs and my back is pressed against a hardened chest.

I scream, roar, and growl again. Louder still and nothing. A demonic rage overtakes me, and I hate this man and realize he hates me. He wants to kill me. I shrink in my own conscious-ness, and I am small within myself, a tiny soul at the bottom of a well of someone else's emotions, and I realize that no one will come. They are used to screams here. This man can kill me and no one will know until someone stumbles over my body.

Thick fingers grip my neck in a vice and a stinking mouth opens and a wet tongue glides over my cheek.

"You taste good," a gravelly voice says, and I fight the rage giving me energy the pain had sapped. The real me is deep inside of me. I'm looking out at this raging beast I've become from the bottom of a deep pit that I don't know how to get out of. Pressed so close, I am him, so intertwined I can feel his intentions and see out of his own eyes. It's from the bottom of that well that I get an epiphany. With my free hand I jab my thumb in my/his eyes. A split second later his hand loosens and I yell.

"Fire!"

That does it. Immediately the house lights go up and I'm blinded. Through slitted eyes, I see the man, hooded in a sweatshirt nearly trample Carlos as he shoots through the exit.

# CHAPTER TWENTY-NINE

"Are you okay?" Matt asks. An EMT is still dressing the small cuts on my forehead and thighs with gloved fingers. It stings.

I glare at him as I wince. I must have hit my head pretty hard because he seems to be glowing. Sydney, my fourth period escort is hovering a few feet away. I'm assuming he followed us here and then called Matt because it wasn't more than 45 minutes before he appeared, face drawn with concern and simmering anger.

"Alright Miss Hognose, we're almost done," the youngish paramedic says while giving Matt a glare that rivals my own in its ferocity.

"I came as fast as I could," he says.

"I see that," I reply coldly.

He leans in close to me firing off synapses in my spine that I wish would just die, regardless of the resulting possible paralysis.

"Please don't be mad. It's complicated."

"I don't think it is," I say in a normal, read quite loud, tone.

"But it is," he protests. "It's the baby isn't it?"

"Among other things I'm sure." Not the least being the army of journalists on my lawn.

"She's five months along," he says coolly, regaining some of his original swagger.

I shrug as if to say AND?

"She's been missing since last winter. That baby cannot in any stretch of the imagination be mine."

I stare at him without expression.

"I still care about YOU!" he protests and tentatively, slowly, oh so gently slides his hand over mine. I will myself not to smile as the paramedic knocks his hand away and points angrily at the riotously beeping heart monitor that I've forgotten I was attached to.

"Mr. Fuller," breaks in Officer…?

"Officer Moody," Matt replies, his voice cracking in his nervousness.

"It is quite odd to see you here. Especially, considering you were being questioned all morning."

He bristles at the comment. "I don't think so. Colette's my girlfriend. I came to check on her."

I open my mouth to protest and then close it. Now is not the time.

"Hmm. It seems being your girlfriend is a dangerous occupation. Miss Hognose is attacked and Tressa Thornton is kidnapped," she snaps. Her nostrils are flaring and her hands are digging into the flesh where she's crossed them. "And it's a might convenient she's claiming amnesia for the time she was gone. Says the last thing she remember is being at a party you and a a…Lilah Clemens threw."

"I'm not sure I know what you're trying to say," he retorts.

The officer steps closer to Matt so that they are almost nose-to-nose. She speaks quietly, venomously, "Oh, I think you know exactly what I'm implying. Especially, since every missing girl can be connected to you in some way, shape, or form." She takes a step back and continues. "And here you are before even the girl's grandmother has been able to get here. I think I'm going to need you to come down to the station again."

It's at this point Matt takes a step towards her, he smiles and there is an air of determination that wafts off in a fog. He whispers something and leads her out of earshot. That glow around him seems to be getting brighter. I rub my eyes against the effects of the pain medication. They talk animatedly for a minute or two before he makes his way back.

Matt walks back over to me. He reaches out his hand to try to grasp mine but I slide it out of reach.

"Don't touch me," I say quietly.

He looks hurt. "Why?"

There is a look there. A straining behind his eyes. He has something to say. It's ballooning in his chest, but he blows it out and says nothing.

"What did you say to her?"

"Nothing," he lies as the tell-tale signs of it bubble up on his upper lip.

I pull the heart monitor off my chest with a whimper, thank the paramedic and find Carlos baking in the dying sun near the entrance of the ride.

"Can we go now? I'd like you to take me home." I tell him. Matt is still on my heels. Carlos looks at him for approval, but I assume his face is blank. I feel his eyes on the back of my neck.

"You sure you don't want Matt to take you. I thought that's what he came down for," Carlos asks.

"You were wrong."

# CHAPTER THIRTY

"So you think the boy has some kinda power over you?" Miss Collins asks.

"Yes. No. I'm not sure," I waffle.

"What color was his aura?"

"Gold," I reply. I wanted to dismiss it the first time I saw it, but I can't discount the tingly feeling I get from him. I don't want it anymore.

Miss Collins was livid when I got home. We've spent the next few hours walking the perimeter of the house and sprinkling holy water by the bucketfuls.

"Hmmm, that doesn't say much. Gold isn't malicious. And you're sure he's not the one who attacked you."

"Yes," I affirm.

She taps a teaspoon on the table. "It was late in the day so the tea may not have been able to tell you much, but it's better to be safe than sorry."

She scrawls out a short spell on a post-it note and hands it to me.

"This is simple," I murmur.

She laughs. "You just think it's simple. You've never done spells before and this one is deceptive. It's a stripping spell. It will strip someone of their gifts. Handy if someone is trying to overpower you.

"For it to work, you'll need a talisman. Your willow pendant will do, some holy water and a sacrifice."

I look at her with grave eyes. Ever since she told me the story of Odion, I hate the word. Sacrifice. It sounds bloody to my ears.

"Don't look at me like that. If the boy's influence is small, the sacrifice can be as small as a stick of incense. The holy water is the conduit. Toss it on him and you're done. I don't think he's influencing you though. I think he's a charmer and you like him too much and you don't like that."

I frown.

"Now, if the person you're trying to strip is very powerful, you'll need a lot more water and a much bigger sacrifice. A full moon doesn't hurt either."

Something strikes me, a solution to everything. "Can the spell be used on another Willow? I mean can a Willow use it on herself?"

She looks at me fiercely and then her eyes soften. If anyone knows how hard it is to be gifted, she does. She's admitted it.

"I don't know if anyone has tried. I wouldn't think so." She pauses a second and mumbles, "A Blessed Willow maybe."

"The children's book?" I ask. I remember the handful of children's books for Willows that she'd given me. One was called *The Blessed Willow*, the one I keep Mama's letter in.

"It's just an old wives tale. Some old legend says that each generation will bare a Blessed Willow. She'd have all the powers of Odion, which means pretty much all powerful. Thing is, I haven't come across a single Fountain Book that mentions one in real life."

I stroke the pendant at my throat. "Where do I get holy water?"

She shrugs. "Tons of places. Any Catholic church will have some. If you're so inclined, the pure of body and heart can make some. That takes a blessing from an ordained minister though. There's paperwork, and you have to be tested. Takes a while. Ah, you know? I'll go get some from the house."

"You're leaving?"

She smiles at me. "Just for a bit. There is still a good bit of daylight out and with the vegetation growing up so nicely those rose bushes are as good as guard dogs."

I nod. "You're right."

I help her gather her things and wave as she coaxes her way through the vines that have completely covered the walkway. I've been a hostage in the house for two days, Uncle Silas' orders, and Miss Collins has been my only contact with the outside world. I've come full circle. I'm back to being locked away again.

I spend the next half-hour cleaning my prison, and then the next two hours experimenting with ginger and honey for a new sticky bun recipe. I begin to worry about Miss Collins when there is a knock at the door.

"You can't come up on the porch! My lawyer said so!" I yell, thinking it's just another tabloid reporter or worse, a Thumper. The knock comes again.

"Delivery," a voice calls out from the other side of the door.

I roll my eyes. What is it this time? "Leave it on the porch!"

"Sorry, ma'am. You'll have to sign."

I'm irritated when I swing open the door to a visibly agitated delivery boy who nearly shoves a heavy white box into my arms. After setting the thing by the door, I sign and smile in apology.

Clearly, it's from Matt and though my first reaction is to ignore it, curiosity wins out.

In short order, I haul the package to the table and with a quick motion pull the ribbon apart. Set atop the tissue paper is a note.

It reads: *A beautiful girl needs BIG protection*
"It's a gun."
I turn the note over in my hand. No signature.
I pick the gun up out of the box. It feels solid and reassuring in my grasp. I cock the empty barrel and point it out of the kitchen window into the backyard. Now this is what I call a gift.

# PART THREE
## Trials and Tribulations

*Purgatory*

The cherub stood, red-cheeked and nervous. "This hearing is called to order in the matter of deposed angel, Raphael, currently serving a suspension of one hundred years for dereliction of duties," he called out to the assembly in a crackling soprano.

In the great room, Raphael stood motionless before his judges, the Archangels. He had come in his battle uniform: a metal breastplate, tunic, gladiator sandals of gleaming gold leather and his halo; not to impress, but to drive home the point. A sundial sat before him as a golf-ball sized sun and moon moved in sporadic circles around it, monitoring a time that didn't exist on this plane.

Michael sat at the center of the seven who would pass judgment on the angel. Three sat on his left while one seat remained noticeably absent on his right. His voice rang out to the heavens, "We see that you have sought an appeal to your previous sentence. What say you in your defense?"

Raphael looked each angel in the eye before he spoke. "These are grave times, and I have served my sentence humbly, but the time for humility has ended as war approaches. The era of secrecy has fallen away and angel-kind once again appear before believers and unbelievers alike to meet out justice and do God's will. I ask for a full pardon so that I may be reinstated as a full guardian angel. The Blessed one is, even at this moment, in mortal danger."

A deep baritone laugh crackled across the wall-less room like thunder. "A pardon? You ask what has never been received, nor shall be."

Raphael's face was serious. "That which has never been done does not mean it never will be." He paused. "I implore you to revisit the facts of the case. Succubi are nesting in plain sight, abducting young ones by the dozens. One is cause for alarm, but an entire nest is a sign of a demon uprising."

The judges shifted uncomfortably in their seats.

Raphael continued, "We all know who the succubi answer to and their reemergence in Carolina was no accident. They sought out the Blessed one in order to eliminate her. The mother made a choice. I agreed with her."

"You don't make choices! You don't agree!" Gabriel bellowed. "You follow orders!"

"I followed protocol. I received no answer. A choice had to be made. I made it! The girl lived and the mother died. It was her own sacrifice. My hands remain clean. I continued to protect the girl, and I, to this day, continue to protect the girl, even in my weakened state, but help is needed. She faces the same threat again, and she is ill prepared. She is in need of a guardian, and I am no longer such."

A flicker of shame coated his words but his back remained rigid, his eyes focused on the judges.

"Enough!" Michael called out and held up a rigid hand. "The Great I Am remains silent, though his law remains. It is clear that war is upon us..."

Gabriel interrupts, "Clearly he is insubordinate and..."

"And I am the lead on this matter! War. Is. Upon. Us. The case is clear. All of you have reviewed the facts. Look in your souls and pass judgment." Michael said quickly and then paused before setting eyes on Raphael again. "Have you any more to say?"

"No. My conscience is clear. I know the soul of word behind the law and it is that soul that I have followed," Raphael said clearly for all to hear. He did not look at Gabriel.

Michael raised an eyebrow and the tiniest flicker of a smile tickled the corner of his mouth before he spoke again, "What say you heavenly body? How do you vote?"

"Pardon."

"Pardon"

"Pardon," the first three angels sang out, and then Michael himself joined the chorus to end at Gabriel, who remained silent.

"Gabriel you know the pardon must be unanimous. What say you?" Michael asked.

The angel looked down at Raphael with a fearsome grimace and then he passed judgment.

# CHAPTER THIRTY-ONE

I set the gun, quite possibly the best gift I've ever been given, by the door and stare at the note. Matt is persistent if he's anything and as distractions go, he is getting harder and harder to ignore. I hear a murmur outside, and I wonder for a second if the delivery man has forgotten something.

I steel myself and draw up my shields before I open the door to an agitated Carlos. He's caught in one of the rope-thick vines, his leg flailing as the thing winds tighter and tighter. I charge down the stairs with a pair of scissors so that I can saw him free before it drags him out of sight.

"Jesus, man!" he huffs. "What kind of fertilizer are you using?"

I shrug my shoulders and smile. "What are you doing here!? Somebody must be dead if you're willing to wade through that," I joke, really glad to see him.

"That's just it." He stops for a minute to shake his head. "There was a fire. It's Mother Johnson. She died."

### 

I expect to have to swim through a sea of family members and security when we get to the hospital, but after hours of waiting, and a vending machine dinner there isn't anyone near Miss Collins' door in the Intensive Care Unit. She'd been there when the fire happened; getting the holy water I wanted.

When I step into the room, an overwhelming smell of oil and herbs envelopes me like a mist, accompanied by the crunch of something gritty covering the floor.

"You made it," Miss Collins hisses through her oxygen mask with obvious relief.

"Yes, ma'am," I reply guiltily. She went back to the house on my account. Isn't this even a little bit my fault?

"What is this?" I ask, shaking off the bottoms of my feet as I make my way to her bedside.

"Rock salt and a little brick dust. Protection." she wheezes.

I reach out my gloved hand to hold hers wondering how she had time to do all this.

"I'm sorry about Mother Johnson. I say softly."

She whimpers a little and tears run down her face.

"They killed her," she groans. I pull a handkerchief from my bag and wipe her face. Before I can pull away she grabs my wrist, inadvertently pouring searing pain into my arms followed by cold yellow fear. "Collette, you have to listen to me. I thought there would be more time, but I may be dead before the week is out."

I look into her eyes, deadly serious and determined. "Don't say that."

She shakes her head emphatically. "No, no. It's true. I can feel a presence here. It is foul and hungry. I know it's what killed my sister."

I shake my head. "You said yourself she wasn't well. Sometimes stress can…these things just…"

She cuts me off. "No! Listen girl, and do not interrupt again. Get me that quilt on the counter over there."

The quilt, old and soft with age is black with smoke and charred in some places. I unfold it, thinking she must be cold, but inside sits The Fountain Book, as pristine as it had ever been. This is the only thing that survived the fire. The only thing she saved.

I place the book on her lap and sit on the edge of the bed. She glides her wrinkled fingers over the cover and seems to draw energy from it. She sits up and removes her mask.

"Remember, I told you The Fountain Book has three sections," she says clearly. "The first is the Holy Bible. King James was a fool and so were his scribes," she spits with haughty indignation. "The Willow translation is more accurate."

She closes the book and slides it towards me. I look at her with questioning eyes.

"I'm giving this book to you," she says soberly.

"You can't. I'm…I'm not your daughter," I say weakly.

She strokes the cover lovingly. "Yes, but you are a daughter of the order, even if you are just now becoming aware of it."

"But you're not dead yet."

She chuckles. "I know that. Keep it until I'm well enough if that makes you feel better. It isn't safe here, for that matter neither am I. You," she gasps, "can be the solution."

She falls into a fit of coughs and replaces her mask to take a few deep breaths.

"I know who burned down my house," she says, struggling for air.

"Who? Did you tell the police?"

She shakes her head, rubbing the thin fabric of her gown across her chest with a frail hand. "No point. She used Daemon Fyre to cause the explosion. It's the only thing that could have burned that hot, that fast. As I was running out of the side door with the book, I saw her run away."

"What did she look like?"

She shakes her head slowly. "Young, like you. In a white dress and…and," she struggles again. I pour her a small cup of ice water from her tray and put the straw to her lips. She takes a long sip and rests back on the pillows for a minute.

"A limp…white…bow in her hair."

The temperature in the room drops and time slows for just a split second.

I squeeze Miss Collin's leathery hand and hold it. "I think I know who it was."

Miss Collins nods her head and removes her mask again. "Then I am right to give this to you. You will need to banish her."

"What? I don't know anything. I…" I stammer.

"That's why I'm not telling you to kill her. A banishment is simple and completely within your depth," she says with confidence.

She flips open the book to a place in the second section and points a bony finger at a passage.

"Here. This is your spell," she coughs.

She pulls my fingers to her lips and blows onto them with her eyes closed. I've never seen the gesture, but I know as sure as I know my own fear that there is power in it.

"You are smart. I know this because you made it in here through three levels of security. You are kind. I know this too because you never would have made it past my wards if you were not. You can do this."

I don't believe her. I want to. I really want to, but I don't. The smell of rosemary oil and incense is making me dizzy. My eyes water, and it looks like I'm crying.

"Oh, don't cry child. We are blessed warriors. You are a blessed warrior. Even our mistakes are correct," she says haughtily.

I laugh at her arrogance in that.

Miss Collins eyelids begin to dip, and I know I'm running out of time. "I have a question. There are some kids at my school who don't act like the others do around her. It's like they're immune to whatever control she has over people."

She thinks for a minute and then laughs. "If they've got a bit of color it could be sister's blood. It means they're not

Willow, but they're in the Willow bloodline, maybe nieces or nephews or daughters who weren't chosen. I guess that's a gift of sorts."

That explains Qutey and Carlos, but something tells me Matt is completely different.

It isn't long before I hear the soft snoring that lets me know it's time to leave. Even on my tiptoes, I still crunch loudly out the door. Like before, there is still no one in sight. Not even at the nurse's station.

I'm almost to the nurse's station when out of the corner of my eye I see a girl turn the corner. A girl in a candy striper's outfit. A girl with a limp, white bow.

"Hey!" I call out and run to catch her, the Fountain Book bouncing heavily in my bag. I round the corner just in time to see her dash into the stairwell. I follow. As I peer over the railing I can see her ponytail bounce down the stairs one floor below me. I practically, fly down the stairs but I'm just not fast enough. By the time I make it to the ground floor, she's nowhere in sight and I'm winded beyond belief.

I drag myself to the lobby where I run into Carlos at the vending machine.

"Did you…" I heave, "see her?"

"Who?" he asks. "What's wrong with you?"

"I ran down the stairs. I saw… I thought I saw."

"You know there is an elevator, right?" he jokes with a quizzical look on his face.

I lean against the wall and slump to the floor. "Never mind."

# CHAPTER THIRTY-TWO

"Wow! I mean, just wow," Summer gushes.

"Well, I do clean up nicely," I say and laugh. Eventually, Uncle Silas said I could go back to school. I readjust my stockings so that they don't smudge the eyeliner I used to make the seam on the back of my legs. Working at Vikki's had its benefits. It wasn't hard to piece together an authentic 40's style outfit for my presentation with Carlos. I almost teared up when I did my hair this morning. I look just like my mother. And it didn't help that there wasn't any update on Miss Collins.

She isn't doing as well as she should. She only had some minor scrapes and burns but she isn't getting any better. I'm beginning to believe that she was right, and there is something in the air feeding from her, sucking the life out minute by minute. I scoured the halls at school and at the hospital for Lilah, but she always seems to be two steps ahead, but today she'll have to be there. It's project day.

"If you guys don't get an 'A' I'm staging a protest," Summer pledges.

"I hope so. Carlos has been stressing about this for weeks, and I haven't been the best partner." I'm planning on making it up to him today though.

"You better."

###

"Team Number 2- Carlos, Collette, Chamberlain and Lilah," Mr. Lee calls from his perch in the corner of the darkened room. Carlos really has put in a staggering amount of effort. He's transcribed our conversations with Ms. Miller and Mother Johnson, made a slide show of the crime scene and an animated reenactment of the murder using some software I've never heard of. I would feel guilty were it not for the fact that his delivery is as dry as toast. When it's just Qutey and me he's like a strobe light, but in front of the class he's a dying candle on a windy night.

But what he lacks I make up for in showmanship, from my *authentic* outfit to my truer-than-they-know stories about what it was like to live in the neighborhood at that time. I even hum a pretty good rendition of "Caravan," that receives a few giggles and claps from the band geeks in the room. When I'm myself I can't seem to speak right, stand right or act right, but when I'm someone else, performing, it's like a mask. I put on a fantastic show, despite my nerves, because I know I'm doing it for a friend and not myself.

"Miss Hognose. Mr. Diaz. I must say that I am impressed. That was a fantastic presentation," Mr. Lee says flatly. Carlos beams.

"Unfortunately, it is incomplete. If I remember correctly, the groups were of four," Mr. Lee chides.

"Yes, but…" Carlos tries to interrupt. Mr. Lee raises his hand.

"We'll discuss your grade and the group requirements after class."

We sulk to our seats and I can't look at Carlos without letting my relief show. While I want to, *have to*, confront Lilah. I don't think I'm anywhere near ready. I keep telling myself, just a few more minutes.

When the bell rings, I see a Bell dart by the open class-room door, and I jump up to follow her.

"Where the hell are you going!?" Carlos asks, shock on his face.

"I see…Brittany or Tiffany or Buffy …uh, one of the Bells. Lilah's friends! I'm going to ask them where she is. You don't need me here."

He starts to object, but I don't stand there long enough to hear it. Instead, I run out of the room into the crowd, losing Matt's assigned escort, a tight-end named Victor, in the melee. I think I've lost my target until I see the tell-tale white bow pop up like a buoy in the sea of quick-weaves and kool-aid dye jobs. I'm almost there when she turns a corner onto the Art Academy, and I crash head first into Matt. We both tumble.

"I know you like me, but you don't have to be so aggressive," he jokes, helping me up off the floor. He looks behind me with a grimace. "Victor's a dead man," he grumbles.

Once I'm on my feet I scan the hallway for my target, but she's gone and it's just as well because the current running through my spine probably wouldn't have let me leave Matt's side anyway. His eyes bore into mine and even though my body is on fire I don't return his smile.

"Thanks for helping me up. I'm gonna be late. Sorry for bumping into you," I say politely, formally, without a hint of affection to give away the quivering in my knees.

"Whoa, wait! Aren't you going to at least let me walk you to the nurse?" he says pointing to my ripped stocking and bleeding knee.

Shoot! I can't refuse him without seeming like a complete jerk, so I nod. He bends to …

"Are you going to try to carry me?" I hiss in disbelief.

"Of course," he says as if it's the most logical form of transportation available, and I laugh hysterically. I barely let anyone, and I mean *anyone* touch me and if he thinks I'm going to let him carry me, well…

"Absolutely not! You can *walk* me to the nurse. That is it!"

He smiles that mile wide grin and waves an outstretched hand. "It would be my honor," he says.

I'm determined to remain stoic, not to encourage him, even though I can feel him smiling next to me.

"You're avoiding me," he says cheerfully.

"We don't have any classes together," I say matter-of-factly.

"True, but I got your number from Summer weeks ago. You never called me back. I left *my* number with all of the flowers."

Why does he keep trying? It would just be so much easier if he just gave up.

"Thank you. You've been…" I search for a word that's grateful, but not too encouraging, " very kind."

"Kind," he mimics and chuckles.

The nurse's station is in the oldest part of the building, down a dusty brick hallway and a small set of stairs. I limp down each step and stumble. Matt catches me, and my heart stops. Suddenly, the temperature in the hallway is stifling and the only thing I know for sure is how good his minty toothpaste smells as his lips hover in front of mine.

"Gotcha," he says righting me on my feet.

"Thank you," I whisper dryly, still trying to get my bodily functions back in order. I see the station door straight ahead so I quicken my pace and slip by him to push open the door, but he grabs the handle.

"Hey, "he whispers. "I…know I've come on a little strong. It's just that when I'm around you, my palms get sweaty and I feel like I can talk to you. We have…I feel…Don't you feel a connection?"

His eyes are pleading and sad. He can't know how much I want to fall into his arms, how I can't control my body around him. Whatever he feels, for me it's ten times worse. I drop my guard.

"I do feel a connection," I whisper to the ground, avoiding his eyes. "But it doesn't matter. I just, can't."

I push past him and into the nurse's station, shutting the door behind me and him in the hallway. I only get a second to feel sorry for myself when I lock eyes with Lilah, smiling beautifully, maliciously at the reception desk.

"My, my, aren't we a mess."

# CHAPTER THIRTY-THREE

Lilah's voice reverberates against the brick walls in a stale echo.

"Where were you? Our presentation was last period," I say doing my best to impersonate someone fierce and self-assured. The outfit helps.

"Didn't you hear? We got an extension."

"That's impossible. I literally, just left Carlos and Mr. Lee to find you."

She squints and all the lightness leaves her eyes. "Now, you would be the authority on impossible things, now wouldn't you? How old are you now anyway?"

She knows.

"Good morning!" the nurse sings, emerging from her office just as the air becomes thick with truth.

"Oh, looks like you took a bad spill. Lilah's in our dual enrollment Health program so she is going to patch you up while I supervise. Is that okay?"

"Oh, I don't..." I start to protest, but the nurse isn't listening and pats a hand lightly on a stretcher.

"Take a seat on the bed over here in station one," she mumbles in my direction and then goes to whisper some instructions to Lilah.

I shuffle to the station, never letting my eyes off Lilah. She coos and demures to the nurse, disarming her completely, immediately letting me know who is really in charge here. Soon, she's gliding like a ballerina in my direction. Where her movements once seemed lithe and preternaturally graceful, they now seem as choreographed and sinister as a snake's before it strikes.

"So are you going to answer my question?" she asks through gritted teeth so only I can hear her.

"I don't know what you're talking about," I lie.

She soaks a cotton ball in alcohol and presses it firmly on my knee. I hiss loudly in pain.

"Gentle!" the nurse calls from her place at the reception desk.

I scowl at Lilah, but resist the urge to slap her.

"You know what I am talking about. How do you know Raphael?" she asks.

"Who? You mean the guy you saw me with at the coffee shop? As far as anyone knows he is my cousin." My voice is cracking. Keep it together, Collette.

At this, she laughs and something desperate creeps into her eyes. She will never get me to admit to anything, but we both know that she knows. The question is how *much* does she know.

"What were you doing at the hospital?" I ask my tone low and menacing.

She smiles deviously and shrugs. "I'm a volunteer candy striper. I'm at the hospital almost every week. I don't remember seeing you there. Next time you should stop me."

I imagine strangling her with that stupid white hair ribbon.

"Are you interested in volunteering?" the nurse asks over my shoulder, startling us both.

I nod my head. "Yes ma'am. I have a passion for the elderly. They just have so much knowledge to pass on," I say staring directly into Lilah's eyes. "I've learned so much from them."

"That's nice to hear," the nurse replies approvingly.

The color drains from Lilah's face, and is then replaced by what I assume is good old-fashioned rage.

"Well, I like it when my face is the last thing they see before they pass on. It's like I have a hand in helping them into a good death," she practically spits as she wraps my knee.

She nearly rips her own arm off with the force that she uses tearing a bit of tape from the dispenser to finish my bandage.

"Whatever Raphael told you about me wasn't true. He lies twice as much as he tells the truth."

"How do you know he told me anything?" number one, and number two, she's wrong. Raphael never lies, but does omit the truth. I don't know exactly why she's here or what she is, but maybe I'm not so outgunned as I thought.

I decide to go for it.

"You killed Mother Johnson," I hiss fiercely, so low that only she can hear. For a second, I don't think she hears me because she walks away, but when she places her thin hand on the nurse's shoulder and freezes her in mid-step, eyes unseeing and mouth wide open, my stomach drops.

"I assure you little girl" she roars in a voice from out of this world, "that you have no idea who you are dealing with!"

It feels as if her soul is filling up the room like smoke. I can't tell if it is my imagination or if the canisters of cotton balls and tongue dispensers are really rattling in time to the breaths she takes.

Fear bubbles up in my gut, but I have to say something - do something. I take a deep breath and stand with as much fake grace as I can manage with a bum knee and a mouth full of sour fear-tinged bile. I give her my best blank stare.

"I don't need to know who you are. I know who *I* am," I say coolly.

A flicker of something dangerous flashes in her eyes and the air in the room shifts like a breeze. Something is about to happen, but I don't know what.

In a blink she releases the nurse and makes her way to me, but before she can get there the door opens and sucks the air out in a vacuum, nearly knocking me off my feet again.

"Chamberlain!" Lilah squeals nervously in her usual musical lilt.

A whoosh of air ruffles his shirt as he steps into the room and he's either surprised to see us or surprised to find himself in the nurse's station. I've never seen someone look so confused.

Lilah rushes to his side gliding her hand against the still frozen nurse's wrist so that by the time she's able to throw herself into his arm's the woman is back to normal asking him why he thinks he can visit his girlfriend anytime he pleases.

"Aren't you supposed to be in class?" she asks sternly.

"I, uh...I was on my way to study hall. I'm not sure how I got here," he says as he pries Lilah's arms from his neck.

"Oh, you're so funny. I told you to come by and pick up the list for the party," Lilah says playfully, looking very much the barnacle to Chamberlain's ship hull.

"Oh, yeah, right," he replies convincing no one that he remembers a thing.

Lilah crosses the room to pull a list from her purse, giving me the stink eye the entire way.

"Sup, Collette? Sorry I missed the presentation this morning. I was... Shit! I don't remember what I was doing."

"Language!" the nurse barks from her reception desk. "Are you about done here son?"

"Yes ma'am," Lilah replies, handing Chamberlain the list.

"You comin' to the party Saturday?" he asks me.

"Party?"

Lilah, who had been the fawning girlfriend two seconds ago, flips a switch and rips Chamberlain a new one.

"Whose party is this?!" she hisses.

"Mine," he replies matter of factly.

"But who's planning it?" she barks.

"You are, babe, but…"

"But nothing, I think…" she goes on but he cuts her off.

"…that because it's my birthday I can invite whoever I want. Collette come on out tomorrow, my dad's lake house. Bring Summer," he proposes.

Lilah's face flashes from red to purple, but she keeps it together.

"Okay. I'll call her. It should be fun," I accept.

He nods.

I flash Lilah my most winning smile in spite of the gnawing fear threatening to tear open my gut. Tomorrow it is.

I've run out of time.

# CHAPTER THIRTY-FOUR

I'm done.

This is it. I tried, but there is no way that I'm going to be able to deal with or defeat whatever Lilah is on my own. I don't have the skills, I don't have the tools and most importantly, I don't have any help, and what's worse is now she knows that I know. She'll be coming after me with all that she's got and with Miss Collins in a coma, I've got a fistful of nothing.

I sit on a bench outside and cry for what seems like endless hours until I have an idea. Insurance. I've got insurance. I can run away. Uncle Silas assured me that everything I needed would be in the little envelope he gave me.

I take a deep breath and wipe my nose. At least there's this. I can still call Summer when I settle... wherever I settle. It can't be too hard. People do it all the time.

I know exactly where I'm going when I dart inside my house and rip open the envelope Uncle Silas gave me. I'm already halfway up the stairs to pack when I start reading and have to stop at the top step as my legs turn to stone.

There is no money.

Inside, there is a note, a single rusted coin and two faded tickets.

*Dear One,*

*I took the liberty of providing you with some REAL insurance. If you're in the kind of trouble that would lead you to run away and I am not there, money will not be of help. I have given you two tickets to go see the only person who can. I've also provided you with tribute.*

*Take care,*
*Raphael*

This time there is no room in my heart to cry. All the space there is crowded out by disbelief and hopelessness. I can't feel my fingers, though they grip the tickets that read: *Charleston City Greek Excursions.* I can't feel my feet.

Why?

Why do I have to be the one to out Lilah? Why do I have to be Willow and carry on a legacy my mother never wanted? Why can't Raphael ever be where I need him to be?

Questions run through my head, and I feel sorry for myself for exactly two minutes before I realize that this is a waste of time.

"Mama wouldn't tolerate this," I say to myself.

She hated a cry-baby. If you've got to do something, then do it, no matter how it hurts if it has to be done. She'd said it a hundred times if she said it once, and I *am* her daughter. Everything else may be up for question, but that I know.

With a fleeting moment of determination I go downstairs and dial Summer.

"Hey, can you drive me to Charleston?"

### 

In less than four hours, we are packed and on the way to the coast.

"So who are we seeing again?" Summer asks. I tell her it has something to do with the anniversary of my mother's death. I know it's a horrible lie, but I also know it is one she'd never be able to turn down.

To her credit, she doesn't pry too much and agrees to go on less information than I usually give for a trip to Vikki's, but I figure she owes me for lying to her Mom.

"When we get back, I'll take you to visit Matt if you want."

I give her a quizzical look.

"Why would I want to do that?"

"Wow, that's cold Collette. The guys' practically in love with you and you can't visit him in the hospital. He had a seizure for Chrissakes."

My mouth forms a silent 'O'. It must have happened after lunch, long after I'd left school for the day. I try to process the feelings I'm having, but they don't come out in any discernible format.

"Sure. I mean, yes, please. When we get back."

The air is salty and electric as if it were self-aware, full of knowledge of the coming days. Why couldn't I be gifted with second sight? Now that would be useful.

Raphael's tickets are for a boat tour at sunset. To get to the yacht we have to take a smaller boat to reach it. As we got closer, we notice a boy sitting in a chair next to a small placard with a setting sun inside a Grecian blue circle. This is our ride.

As we get even closer we notice the boy is not a boy at all, but just a very short man. He says his name is Michael and asks us for our gift.

"It's in my purse," I reply, wondering if it's weird that the first thing he's worried about is a gift.

"Well, as long as it isn't jewelry. Most people bring the goddess jewelry, as if she doesn't have all the trinkets and baubles she could ever want," he says in a guttural accent I can only faintly remember. Someone I know has the same accent, but I can't place it.

"I'm sorry, did you say goddess?" Summer asks disbelievingly.

"Yes. Of course, her worship has gone out of fashion, but that is the way of deities I tell her. No one and no thing is worshipped forever, not even the sea," he replies.

We ride in silence. Soon, we're at the yacht and climbing up the rope ladder to the deck. A bald man, who looks eerily like Mr. Clean, retrieves our tribute from Michael and leads the way to the far end of deck where sitting on a throne of rope sits Thetis.

I know this because there is a placard set in gold script in front of her: Throne of Thetis, in Greek.

For a supposed deity, she is surprisingly unimpressive. She doesn't shine like the morning sun, like you'd expect. She is average height with brunette curls that are cut short, much like my own. She's wearing a bronze halter dress with a simple gold necklace that loops into a small O at her neck. Plain is what my mother would have called her, except for two things. The palms of her hands and the soles of her feet seem to be covered in gold paint or glitter. And there is also the business of her mouth. While every other bit of her may have been purchased on sale, her mouth is custom made, both lips perfectly shaped into a pillowy rose-colored bow. It alone would cause men to stare, had she ever left her yacht, which I now knew she never did. Thetis is a sea nymph.

*N is for nymph, a female divine spirit of nature, neither good nor evil.*

Summer's calm giddiness gives way to nervous insecurity, and her heart begins to speed up and cast waves of pale yellow fog from her skin in its rhythm, as if she were a human speaker. I need to put her at ease. I swallow hard and plaster my most pleasant smile to my face.

Thetis is barefoot and though my shields are up it's clear that she is painfully and immovably bored. Mr. Clean walks ahead of us and kneels before her with great flourish.

"They have brought you tribute my Queen," he says in the same guttural tone of Michael.

"I see," she replies in the most musical voice I have ever heard. It is a kind of mixture between a jazz flute and children laughing at the pool.

He looks at me expectantly, and it takes a second before I realize that I'm supposed to give him my gift. I rummage in my purse and hand over the coin Raphael left with the tickets. I've wrapped it in a scarf with gold and blue trim, hoping that maybe together the modest gift will be enough.

Reverently, he takes the bundle from my hands and offers it to Thetis. She draws in a deep breath and blows it out of her nose slowly while she examines it in his hands. "I like this scarf," she says, and I grin inside.

"Oh, I'm so glad. I thought it might..."

"Shut up," she croons in soprano.

She pulls the corners of the scarf and unveils the coin inside. There. A flicker. For just a fraction of a second, excitement lights her eyes and dies like sleet on a sidewalk.

"This," she caresses the coin lovingly. "This is not tribute. This is payment." She sets her gaze on me and my face begins to melt under its heat.

"Insolence!" Michael barks and rises angrily.

"Stop!" Thetis commands with one hand raised in his direction. "You are too young to know whatever you need of me is so precious you cannot pay for it, whatever worldly goods you have acquired, but..." she pauses and lets the scarf fall to her lap, holding the coin up like a torch, "this has sentimental value. I have not seen the coin of my homeland for centuries. It is worth, to me, a great deal."

I nod stupidly, the smile still firmly in place. Thank you, Raphael. At least you didn't fail me in this.

At that Mr. Clean bows and quickly disappears. The sun follows, leaving deck torches and the young moon to light the scene.

"Did she say centuries?" Summer whispers. She's been so quiet all this time I almost forgot she was there.

"Come closer," Thetis croons. Reluctantly, I make my way to the throne. At first Summer follows, but I make it clear it should be me and me alone by pinching her on the arm.

Why didn't I notice her eyes in all the time I've been on deck? The whites are opal that flash lavender and turquoise like a fresh water pearl, the irises a deep and glowing jade.

"You have something to ask me my child," she says looking directly at me. Her gaze bores into me as if they are peeling back layers of my existence.

She can see the indecision in my eyes. "Think about what is most important to you and then ask."

It is simple really. I know what, or *who* I should say is most important at that moment.

I take a deep breath. If I am only going to get one shot at this, then I am going to make it good. "How can I kill a succubus?" I spit, the words shooting out of my mouth like spilled candy.

L is for Lilah, *a daughter of Lilith, mother of all succubi. These beautiful and immortal demons suck the life from their victims in order to maintain their own and can hypnotize at will.*

Uncle Silas said the girls didn't die like they should. And then there is Lilah, herself, she called me a little girl, like an old woman.

Thetis raises a perfectly arched eyebrow and settles into her thrown as I wonder how she doesn't chafe with the ropes digging into her back.

"A succubus you say." She stops and ponders.

It's then I realize she isn't breathing. I shift one foot to the other nervously. Summer mirrors my movements behind me, and I'm sure it must look as if both of us need to pee.

"A succubus is a solitary shape-shifting creature that usually maintains a nomadic existence, feeding off insecure virgins by seducing them with sweet words and then drinking their life force as a person sleeps or, more often, as they lie together. A common misconception is that they only lie with men."

"I don't know what you mean?" I ask. She flashes me a look of rage and I instantly recognize my error. I have interrupted her and she is not the kind who is used to pausing for others. I cast down my eyes and hunch my soldiers. With someone else an 'I'm sorry' would be enough, but this is not a some*one,* she is a some*thing.* Only the outward vestiges of shame would do and if crouching won't cut it, I am fully prepared to kneel.

She rolls those frighteningly beautiful eyes and releases the fist she's balled her hand into and continues tightly, "If a succubus creates a nest either by attracting other succubi or by enlisting them, she may create an unnatural balance and may need to feed more often than she would if she was alone, taking from whatever donors are available, male or female. She will also become more powerful, more difficult to kill."

She is quiet for a moment, unmoving like a living statue. I am grateful for the information, but she hasn't said anything about how to kill a succubus. I dare not ask her to repeat herself.

"And, of course, there is the Devil's Flesh. This is a rare succubus may be trying to bring about the time of the anti-Christ. In which case, she will be looking for a psychic to lie with. He's not completely without protection though. He'll have to lie with her willingly."

"Can it be killed?" I ask a little too quickly.

"Yes, of course," she replies as if I'd asked her the dumbest question on earth. "The succubus is of flesh as you are and she can be harmed as easily as you can be. But…"

There's a but?

"...the succubus is a shape-shifter and can take any form she pleases to evade harm unless death is her choice, and even then only the Seraphim or a high ranking daimon can end their existence in this realm. The possibility of a creature of their power and immortality going quickly or quietly into that good night is not very high though, most succubi are narcissists, *as you can imagine.*"

My mind is racing with possibilities. So much so, that I hardly notice Mr. Clean coming towards me out of the corner of my eye until he's driven the foot-long blade through my side. Thetis' face doesn't even register that anything out of the ordinary has occurred, and I probably would have dismissed the entire event as a wild daydream had Summer not screamed like a banshee and rushed to my side.

Suddenly, the onlookers realize that the party must be over and begin to retreat to the lower deck without so much as a glance my way. By the time they begin to move, I've tumbled to the deck and Summer's hands and shirt are covered in my blood. Oddly, what I feel most, other than the searing hot pain in my side, is the stunningly acute curiosity of Thetis. Her gaze is fixated on me, her eyes roving over me from head to toe hungrily like she is drinking information.

Someone drags Summer away while she spews the most god-awful curses I have ever heard. I try to cry out, but nothing comes out. I only have a few moments of consciousness left, and I don't know if they'll be my last on earth. I say a silent prayer for Summer and gaze at the beautiful night sky. I breathe in the cool salty breeze and try to let that be my last feeling. It is much more peaceful than you would think, much more peaceful than my last brush with death. I smile a tiny smile and feel Thetis' hand on my cheek before the darkness pulls me under.

# CHAPTER THIRTY-FIVE

I'm not dead. Again.

Pain, thick and hot as lava sits on my torso heavy and unrelenting.

"So, you are mortal," the tinkling voice says. I still haven't opened my eyes so I can't attach a face to a voice just yet. "You are not psychic, otherwise you would have known what Alric was planning to do."

I have to fight my way to understand what she's saying, to put together where I am. After a few moments, I remember what happened and find a face in my memory to attach to the voice, Thetis.

"Can…May I have a glass of water," I cough through cracked lips. Before I can unglue my eyelids to look around, someone is sticking a straw into my mouth. I drink and then promptly vomit.

"You need to heal and this will heal you. You will drink," she says firmly. She begins whispering to someone else in the room. I still haven't opened my eyes. I'm too weak and afraid.

With my shields down, I can sense this other person is brimming with compassion, Thetis' opposite.

"You have no need to be afraid," Thetis says as if she's read my mind. "You will rest and heal and then you will tell me who you are," she says finally. I have an urge to thank her before I remember that she is the one who's done this to me.

I hear the door close and without Thetis the room is an emotional vacuum. Suddenly, self-pity rolls in like a bad storm, and I begin to whimper. I want to cry, but when I feel the warm washcloth wipe the dried salt from my face, I realize that I must have cried myself out in my sleep. A cool hand rests on my cheek and again I sense the compassion. When I open my eyes to what looks to be an older, but more beautiful version of Thetis, she smiles at me.

"I am Ione," she says, her voice a mere trickle to the rushing waterfall of melody in Thetis' voice. "Thetis is my sister. You need to drink this." She puts the straw to my mouth again, and I will myself to keep it down. She giggles at my pinched face and occasional gagging between sips.

"Good," she laughs," good." She sets the bottle on a table behind me and glances around the polished wood room. I'm lying on a chaise lounge; a mirror is mounted on the ceiling along with a rendition of the night sky and opposite me sits an identical chaise where my best friend lies with her eyes closed.

I spring up and pay for it in pain.

"Don't sit up. You'll tear your bandages and you won't be completely healed for another few hours," she says while pushing me down.

I peer around her at Summer. "Is she? Is she dead?" I ask in the smallest voice I can manage, afraid of the answer.

"No, of course not," she laughs. "She is but asleep. She will wake before the day is out and she will not remember a thing unless you feel the need to enlighten her." She smiles again. She is so reassuring. I need to feel safe in the midst of this mess. How could I have gotten myself into this? Maybe Miss Collins is right. Maybe this *is* destiny.

No. I can't believe that, because if I do then that means I don't have a choice and the end is already written. It means I'm a moving piece in a game I don't want to play. It means I'm cursed.

Matt's face flutters before me involuntarily. I shouldn't even be thinking about him, but heat rises to my cheeks and worry scratches at my mind. I should be worrying about myself.

"You love deeply," she says knowingly, like she's reading my mind. Is mind reading a nymph quality? I can't remember from my reading. Ione has eyes exactly like her sister's, except they seem to be richer, deeper somehow, like she has hidden warmth her sister lacks.

"Ah, Thetis is not as bad as you think. Immortality does not suit everyone. I am sure you can relate." How much does she know?

"I can only glean what is at the top of your mind at any moment. If you would like to talk, we can do that. You seem to be uneasy," she says as she lifts my shirt dress to check my bandages. I wince, but try not to cry out. I've been dressed in the flowing style of Ione and her sister. Remembering how much blood there had been I am sure my clothes are ruined.

"Ah, those rags have been tossed into the furnace. This is much better. You like this?" She asks while pressing my abdomen. I think I might black out from the pain. "Yes, you like this, but you don't know it yet. Here, drink this."

She lifts a small gold cup, the shape of a teacup without the handle, to my lips. I sip the hot liquid, which smells and tastes like warm licorice, and let it run down my throat and make a direct deposit into my veins. This time, sleep comes quick and easy.

I wake up to the predawn, just a flicker of sun peering over the horizon and into my cabin from a single porthole I didn't notice before. I tentatively take a deep breath and am beyond grateful it doesn't hurt. In fact, nothing hurts; I feel as good as I have ever felt. I can tell by the gentle rocking that we are no longer out at sea but docked. I get up and swing my feet over and onto the polished wooden floor. Summer is still sleeping. How am I going to explain everything when she wakes up, especially if she isn't going to remember anything? What will I say to her mother? Is there anything I can say to explain what happened to my clothes and why I'm in a...*toga?*

"Actually, it is a stola."

I jump and my breath catches in my throat as I notice Ione standing in a corner of the room.

"You look well and rested."

I feel well and rested and thanks to the stola, waves and waves of the thinnest pale blue cotton, cinched at the waist with a thin gold belt, I'm sure I look like a part of the ship, like I belong here.

"You do..," Ione catches herself and gives me a knowing smile as she reaches into a corner and hands me a pair of sandals.

I guess she's partly right, I'm not normal, I've died and come back. I can feel what other people feel. I have a supernatural guardian who sets up trust funds for his charges. I know I'm not normal, but I am human and whoever and whatever may be on this ship, human they are not.

"My sister is sleeping. It is time for you to go, but I have something for you." She stands and slides a thin gold band, as slim as string, from her index finger.

"This is for you," she says and hands it to me.

"It's pretty," I say and slip the band on my finger. It fits perfectly.

"Yes, like you. It is very old. Not as old as I am, but still. We will not meet again."

I feel like I've been given a great gift though it is just a piece of jewelry.

"Thank you."

She nods.

While I'm grateful, I'm still uneasy. I've come here and I've gotten information, but still nothing that will help me in facing Lilah. That's if I make it home. I look at Summer and frown.

"What am I going to tell her?"

"Nothing. Michael will walk you to your, what is it called..." she thinks for a second, " ah, your automobile. Michael says it looks like an insect." Though, that doesn't answer my question I keep quiet until Michael appears at the door and scoops Summer into his arms. I nod in realization and smile to him in thanks.

Ione steps out onto the boardwalk with us but stops after only a few steps.

"This is where our chapter ends. We will not meet again. I have another gift for you. I believe it is what you came here seeking."

A young girl who I sense is not young at all rushes to her side with a small box. When she opens it, I see that inside it holds a dagger in its sheath. It is rugged and hulking, with a handle made of bone.

The girl closes the box and hands it to Ione, who in turn hands it to me then kisses me on my cheek. She smells like this moment: relief and seawater, the dawn and the mist of dreams.

*We will not meet again. Remember, who you are.*

My cheeks flush with the purity of it, and then she whispers in my ear, a blessing I know, in a language I don't understand and turns to walk back onto the boat and inside.

I stand in silence for what feels like weeks and then turn toward Michael who stands patiently waiting to be led to the car.

# CHAPTER THIRTY-SIX

There is no magic. There is no magic?

Miss Collins said this to me, but I still don't believe it. Especially since Summer drove almost the entire way home in a kind of wakeful sleep. She even bought the story that she hit her head on the door frame and slept all night. I sleepwalked through the rest of the day while she flitted around the house, overjoyed at the prospect of the party.

We're late, really late, not that I'm complaining. I haven't been able to keep anything down since breakfast.

"I'm so sorry," Summer apologizes.

"It's fine. I told you."

Summer practically exploded with joy when she found out we were invited to Lilah's party. It's Chamberlain's birthday, but everyone refers to it as *Lilah's* party (heavy on the breathy 'L') and only the most 'in' of the in crowd are invited.

"We're fine though. We're just an hour late."

She's trying to convince herself. Little patches of nervousness are growing like moss on every patch of her skin that isn't covered in fabric, of which there is a lot. Apparently, mystery boyfriend will be in attendance.

"Are you going to point him out if he's there?" I ask.

She smirks at me and I scowl in return.

"If you're going to be all weird about it then I'll just keep him to myself," she professes.

"I just worry about you. Anybody who cares about you should be happy to show you off to his friends. I don't like it that you're a secret."

"And you would be the authority on secrets," she mumbles.

I sigh. I don't want to fight. I'm trying my best to muster up the rage I had the last time I visited Miss Collins, to channel it into something useful to face off with Lilah again, but I can't. I sigh heavily. I'm worried. Tired — but mostly I'm afraid. The knife rests heavily in my purse.

"You don't look too happy to be going tonight. You're all…tight. Tighter than usual. No offense," Summer declares.

In a minute we're parking on a gravel road at the end of an impossibly long row of cars. Even blocks away we can hear the deep thump thump of the bass coming from the party. For a second, I wonder how the neighbors can stand the noise and then I remember who I'm dealing with.

The party's first victims are already bent over the porch railing, puking violently when we make it to the house. A girl without pants, but a very nice shirt and plastic devil horns runs by us laughing hysterically before she trips and bloodies her lip on the sidewalk. When we try to help her up, she growls like a trapped dog and keeps on running.

This is our first sign to turn around. Further up the driveway, we see two Bells barking orders in a strip Twister game on the front lawn with what looks like the school's defensive line. The boys are sporting pipe cleaner halos and giggling hysterically, but not at all in a fun way.

Sign two.

Eerily the house is dark, save porch lights that spill out into the night and cast shadows on the giggling fools that pop out of the front door every now and then.

We step up on the porch, and I nearly jump out of my own skin when a hand grabs my ankle.

"It's me!" Qutey says from a blanket of darkness on the steps.

"Jeeezuslovesme you scared me!" I sputter.

She laughs. "I know! I'm sorry!"

She has to shout to be heard over the music.

"What are you doing here?!" I ask.

"She's a Cartwright!" Summer replies in answer.

"I'm invited by default. My cousin and his 'crew' are automatically invited to these things."

"You're his crew?" I ask.

She laughs. "Hardly. I wanted to see how this Angels and Demons theme was gonna play out."

"Why are you outside?" Summer shouts.

"It is all shades of crazy in there. Every third song is death metal and there's a rumor she had a priest turn the entire pool into holy water. I'm just waiting for my ride before the whole place gets struck down."

We look at each other stupidly for a moment before Summer breaks the awkwardness. "Well, we're going inside."

I turn to follow, but Qutey catches my arm and mild panic hits my funny bone.

"Don't drink anything you don't make yourself."

"Why?" I ask.

"It's just good policy. Lilah's parties are legendary for a reason," she says lightly.

I nod in thanks and catch up with Summer, plunging myself headlong into darkness and danger.

We wade through red plastic cups and nearly fall over an angel-winged Bell carrying a tray of tiny paper cups filled with jello.

"Death?" she asks.

"What?!" Summer replies.

"Death! It's what it's called. Want one!" she shouts.

We both shake our heads and she moves on.

Outside it's early Fall, still hot during the day, but getting colder at night. Inside, it is July. The smell of sweat and insecurity is so thick it is like breathing soup. People are pressed from wall to wall and everyone is holding at least one red cup in their hands. We baby step like toddlers to some place in the corner that I didn't know we'd agreed to make our way to. With the press of people, it doesn't take long for the space between us to widen and soon she's too far ahead of me to touch, and I know that she's seen the guy.

"I need your bag!" I yell and she cups her ear to hear, but it's no use. She weaves through the crowd like a snake through grass. I try to catch up, but I keep bumping into people. Vacant stares and giggles greet me, and I want nothing more than to get out of there, but I need to find Lilah.

Even without the bottle of holy water in her bag, I've come too far to turn back. I think I've found her or at least a good candidate when a hand grabs me and pulls me into a room and slams the door.

"Lilah?! Stop!" I yell and in the darkness I don't know what I'm striking out at but I hit hard and hear a yell before the light is flipped on.

"Damn it, Collette!" Matt cries, holding his nose.

"Oh! Oh! Oh! I'm so sorry. I thought you were…I didn't know…What are you doing here? I thought you were in the hospital."

Matt stumbles over to the bed and rubs his nose. I kneel down in front of him to inspect it.

"It's not bleeding," I assure him, my face in a wince. Pain is pulsing from his enclosed hands like he's holding a twinkling star.

"I was, but I had to get out of there. I had to find you."

"That again," I sigh and let my bottom hit the floor. "I'm sorry, but I can't do this with you anymore. Whatever *this* is?"

He shakes his head violently. "You don't understand. You can't do what you're planning. It's not going to turn out how you think it is. I came here to stop you."

I fight the urge to roll my eyes. He has no idea what I've come here to do. How can he?

"Really Matt. I don't have time for this," I say as kindly as I can. "And you shouldn't be out. You're sick. Did you drive? Qutey is outside, maybe she can give you a ride home if…"

He cuts me off with a wave of his hand and stands directly in front of me gripping my shoulders as he speaks. "You're not listening. I know who you are. I've known since you woke up in the lake outside my house. You can't go meet with Lilah because she's going to kill you!"

That live wire between us pulses with an energy that crowds out everything in my mind, but his mouth, his words. I snatch myself out of his grip.

"What are you talking about? What do you mean you know who I am?"

He covers his face with his palm and mumbles, "I can't believe I'm telling you this." Embarrassment and fear pour out of him in great gusts. "Shit! I might as well…I'm psychic."

He waits for a beat. I look at him blankly.

"Okay. You didn't laugh. That's good", he pauses. "Ever since I started having seizures, I started getting these visions, mostly of a girl. A girl falling from the sky. I thought I was crazy. The doctors told me that it was unusual for epilepsy to come on this late and maybe football was the cause. Too many hard hits. I was already paddling on the lake when I found you. Think about it, I never could have heard you from the shore, you were too far out."

My hand goes up to my mouth, silence follows.

"I don't know why this happened to me and when football ended for me, I didn't know what I'd do, but if I can save you then maybe it was worth it."

He steps closer to me and the cloud of embarrassment disappears.

"Collette, you have to believe me. Lilah is going to kill you. I saw it as clearly as I saw you struggle to stay afloat, weeks before you actually did."

I shake my head. It's not true. I can't let it be true. She killed Mother Johnson. She tried to kill Mother Johnson.

"Look!"

He pulls a piece of paper from his pocket and hands it to me. It's a copy of a newspaper article.

"So?" I ask. "What is this?"

"Look at it!" he urges and taps the paper hard in my hands. "You dropped it yesterday on the way to the nurse's office. Look at the picture."

I look at the copy. It's one of the slips of evidence that Carlos didn't submit for our project. I'd asked him to do some research on Kansas City, but I forgot to follow up with him. This copy was from the *Kansas City Observer* February, 1940. There was a picture of a young girl in a sooty Habit, being comforted by a firefighter. The headline reads "Lone Survivor in Nunnery Fire".

"So?" I ask him fiercely.

"Look at the picture."

I look at it again and it's grainy, but now I see what he's talking about. I straighten the article out and look closer.

No, it can't be, but…it is. "It's Lilah."

"She's not human. Those were her sisters. Your mother killed them and then Lilah killed the Willows and now she is going to kill you."

"You saw all that?" I ask in disbelief. "You saw my mother?"

He spins and clenches his fists, anxious and afraid. "We need to get out of here. I can explain all of this later."

"No! Now."

Everything has been coming to me too late. I want to know what he knows, what he is. This is life or death now, and I can't take chances with anyone; no one is who they say they are or appear to be.

"Everything is 'no' with you! Sometimes you have to let go, Collette. This is one of those times! I only get glimpses of the past. The future is much clearer, but it doesn't work like you think it does."

"If you can see the future then you can help. You can help me stop her. Tell me what you see, and we can do the opposite." I argue, deciding to trust him for the moment.

"Like I said, it doesn't work like you think. I can see you cross the street and get hit by a bus, but you could decide at the last minute to turn left and be fine. I only see one version of events and there could be thousands, and they don't come when I want them. They just come."

"Then your visions are worthless then. Anything could happen," I snap, buckling under the anxiety.

"And in one of those coulds, *you* end up dead!"

He draws so close that his breath is warm on my face. "I can't let that happen, Collette. I just can't."

I think he's about to kiss me when a piercing tone like feedback fills the air and I wince. It takes a second for me to realize that the sound isn't coming from the speakers outside the room, but from inside my head. It gets louder, then louder, and then so loud that I double over in pain.

I look over at Matt for help, but he's fallen to the ground. The sound must have triggered another seizure because he's not breathing. His eyes have rolled back into his head and his feet are frozen at an odd angle.

"Matt!" I yell and crawl to his side. He doesn't respond. I'm willing him to breathe when in the next moment his feet begin to tap a horrible rhythm on the floor as every muscle in his body jerks.

I run to the door and fling it open to try and get help, but no one responds to my screams. No one even notices I'm there. They're all frozen in place, as if that horrible tone was the alarm that shut them off. I'm about to slap the nearest person out of this stupor when I hear a pop like a bursting balloon and the sound stops.

An eerie silence sweeps through the hall and Matt's jerking stops. I fall to his side to make sure he's started breathing again. He has, but it's shallow. I need to get him help.

I rise, eyes watering, and look to the hallway where everyone has started to mill about like before, but the music is gone. I can still feel the thump under my feet, but I don't hear it. Have I gone deaf?

She laughs.

Lilah. Lilah's laugh, inside my head.

# CHAPTER THIRTY-SEVEN

*You aren't the brightest bulb on the Christmas tree are you little witch?*

"Get out of my head!" I yell into the room.

A girl in a painted on red dress looks at me quizzically through the doorway as people start to move again.

Celeste.

I haven't seen her since gym class with Brianna. She doesn't recognize me.

*Who are you talking to? You're the only one who can hear me.*

I reach in my pocket and finger my cheat sheet willing myself to remember the words I've memorized for the stripping spell.

I can't think with her in my head.

*You should come outside. It's too hot in there, and I want to see your face when I finish this.*

I look at Matt. I can't leave him here. Think!

I roll him to his side and snatch a pillow from the bed to prop under his head.

"I'll be back soon," I whisper and hope that it's true as I close the door behind me.

I'm still invisible to the crowd and it takes me longer than it should to wade through. When I make it outside I find her at the head of the pool where she's fashioned a makeshift throne out of deck chairs. Tiki lamps cast shadow dancers onto the water.

The music stops for real this time and every mouth closes, a blank expression falling over all of them like ash.

"Oh, thank Christ. You just don't know how much energy it takes to speak telepathically." She pauses as if she expects me to respond.

"Well, well. You're here to vanquish me aren't you?"

I open my mouth to speak but she holds up a hand, and I struggle with the right words.

"Don't bother lying. I know who you are, and I know who he is. If I wanted him dead he would be. And just so you know that so called psychic ability he has is just a side effect, a funny little reaction to the blood vessel I broke in his brain when he decided to choose his girlfriend over me."

"And Tressa?" I croak.

"Her? Collateral damage of the sluttiest kind. I was lenient, though. That baby did enough damage to where no one will want her. Times don't change that much, sweetie."

There must be more than a hundred kids, all silent, all staring standing on the edge of the pool. The kaleidoscope of colors from their emotions swirls and disappears like fog after the sun comes up. There's nothing left.

"What kind of hold does she have on them?" I whisper to myself.

"Complete!" she cackles. Gone is the lyrically sweet tone she usually fakes.

"I'm really going to need you to speak up so I can hear your insults clearly. Okay?" she pleads as if this is all a game.

"Can we have some fun, Collette? I missed out on the fun with your dear mother. Fell on her sword and spirited you away. Clever bitch that one."

My fists clench at the slur.

"Single handedly wiped out my nest. We had just begun to settle in. Why are you looking at me like that? I don't think you understand." She pauses, brow furrowed.

"I have to make you understand. Let's play, then we'll talk." She takes a deep breath and straightens her spine. "Sweetie! Can you bring out our little mouse," she calls out into the silent night air.

No one moves. It takes a moment or two but then I hear it, the shuffling of feet and muffled screams.

Moving through the crowd, too far away for me to reach her is Summer, being dragged by Buck.

Her eyes are wild and she's fighting. Lord, she's fighting so hard.

"What are you doing?!" I yell.

"Ow!" Buck screams as Summer bites down on the hand covering her mouth.

"Let me go! Where the hell are you taking me?!" Summer screams.

Buck's hand returns to her mouth where her curses are smothered by the meat of his palm.

"She doesn't have anything to do with this. Let her go!" I scream, still rooted in my spot across the pool, still waiting for the best opportunity to strike.

"You still seem to think you have a chance so I have to show you."

She rolls her eyes at Summer, "Jeezus, shut up!"

Lilah uncrosses her legs and then her pupils go white as she sits up bone-straight in her chair and snaps her fingers. In the same second, Summer goes limp, eyes wide open, her breath puffing out in shallow wisps.

I run towards her.

"Stop right there!" Lilah shouts, but I don't listen.

"Stupid girl," she mumbles and snaps her fingers again. This time Summer winces in pain but doesn't wake and a tiny purple bruise blooms on her neck. I stop in my tracks.

"Now I told you what I did to Matt. Do you think it would be so hard to burst just the right vessel? Maybe the next one will blind her, paralyze her maybe?"

"I stopped alright! What do you want?"

"I want my sisters back!" she barks, jolting to the edge of her seat.

"I don't have anything to do with that!"

"The hell you don't, Willow!"

I don't know what to say to that. Am I really Willow? I have Willow blood, but I haven't really accepted it, not really, but I'll be damned if I give her the satisfaction of knowing she has the upper hand. I still have cards to play.

"I see you're still not getting the point. Any one of these fools would jump into that pool and drown themselves if I will it. In fact…"

The crowd parts and Celeste, pretty in her ditzy kind of way in a skin-tight white glittered dress and stiletto heels, walks slowly to the 9ft section of the pool. Her face is blank as the others part to allow her to make her way to the edge until she casually takes the last step that sends her careening into the deep end. I know it's just seconds, but it seems as if it is happening in slow motion. Whatever hope I had that she'd wake up from the cold of the water is dashed when I see her lock her feet and blow the air in her lungs out as she drops like a stone.

I don't think. I just jump in after her. I'm no champion swimmer myself, but I have to try.

"It's a waste of time!" I hear Lilah shout before her voice is drowned out by the water.

She's right. When I reach Celeste she flails and fights so hard that I can't get a grip on her arms. I can't even snatch a piece of fabric because the dress is so tight. I have to come back up for air three times and when I do Lilah's laughter is shrill and maniacal.

On the last dive there isn't any fight left. There isn't any life left. Her waist length extensions float around her head like a halo and her eyes look out into nothing as I pull her as best I can to the shallow end of the pool. I scream for someone to help, but no one hears me. I don't know if they even know what's happening.

Just as the realization that this girl is truly dead, and I am powerless to save her hits me; so does the realization that I've underestimated Lilah. No, I've overestimated myself. What am I doing here?

Lilah smiles through blood red lips, a severe bun atop her head pulling her eyes back in a fierce beauty. The guilt that I feel is short lived, and I have no time for self-pity. I look on the still body beside me and rage, fresh and hot as oven coals propels me forward. I launch myself at that pretty face intent on slapping the taste out of her mouth, maybe even ripping her head from her spine.

I don't even get within three feet of her before a hand reaches out and grabs me by the throat and I'm dangling above the pool.

"Until you showed up, I was enjoying a decades long post-victory vacation. Unfortunately, your arrival sent an energy beacon so high into the atmosphere that I'm surprised God himself hasn't come down to see what all the ruckus is. *You* have become my problem, Collette and I don't care for problems."

I can't breathe, and so I can't talk. I claw at the hands that hold me. I stare pleadingly into almond eyes. Chamberlain's eyes.

I reach out with my mind, trying desperately at the same trick Raphael and Lilah seem to have mastered. *Chamberlain, wake up!*

"Those eyes are moving wild. Are you trying to use telepathy?" Lilah howls. "That is so cute! He can't hear you!" she sings, "I tell you what. I'll give you a break."

He sets me down on the side of the pool, but doesn't completely let go of my throat. If I strain I can breathe, but I still can't speak.

*You don't know anything about me. You don't know anything about my mother.*

"Oh! I heard that! Just barely, but I got it. You are a quick study. Raphael give you a lesson? Good thing he's nowhere on this spiritual plane."

*You don't know where he is.*

"Doesn't matter. He's not here, so that means you're all alone."

My breaths are shallow and Chamberlain's grip is like rusted iron.

*What do you want from me?*

"Good! Negotiations have finally come around. I hate to admit this, but it seems that I can't kill you without getting all of that residual Willow energy all over me. This makes it very difficult to hide from people who don't care for beings like me. *And*, you can't kill me. Bonus. I'm hoping that's finally sinking in here. That means we're between a rock and a hard place, young one. So, I have a proposition for you."

"Join me."

*You must be joking.*

She laughs in that tinkling melody she affects. "No sweetie. I'm quite serious. I assume you know what I am."

*Succubus. Daughter of Lilith. Whore of the Unclean.*

"Haven't heard that last one in a while, but don't get cheeky. The air is changing. I'm tired of wandering alone, and I could use a sister for the War ahead. You're Willow, but not. Dead, and then not dead. You're human, but touched by the heavens. You have the ability to choose. You don't have to serve. You don't have to shrink under the weight of the Willow curse. Join me and men will kill themselves to serve you."

*And what do you get?*

"Now, now. Let me finish my pitch."

She raises her eyes in thought, and I take the moment to search around me for something that may help free me. Chamberlain's eyes are still dead as the others.

"Ah, yes 'kill themselves to serve you'," she mumbles and then raises her voice with a smile. "And you can have what you've always wanted. A family that loves you. Even children. In fact, he will be the most wonderful child that has ever walked the earth. All you have to do is what you want to do anyway. Fall in love with Matt."

*Matt? What does he have to do with anything?*

"Oh, he's the key Darling. He's the psychic. I couldn't find one in all these years. Believe me I've searched. So, I decided to make one. But the rules are clear. He has to love me by his own free will, and he doesn't love me. Fool. He loves you. To get what I want, I can make you like me and you two do the do and wham, bam, thank you ma'am. The new era begins!"

*Me? Like you? I'd be a demon.*

"You say it like it's a bad thing."

The devil is a liar, and I can't trust a word she says. I try to think of my options out of this. I can't speak any words of power because I can't speak. I can't move and even if I could I don't have enough strength to fight off every person here. I send a silent prayer for help up to Raphael, but don't expect much.

"My proposal is sound. What say you, little witch?"

*After careful thought, I must say,"* Hell, no!" I croak through Chamberlain's grip, my nails digging bloody fissures into his hands.

Lilah's face hardens and her lips purse. Once again she invades my mind.

*I take it you Willow Girls are fond of water and fire. Guess which one is my favorite.*

Before she can finish the sentence Chamberlain tosses me into the pool. When I try to come up for air, two hands grip my shoulders and hold me down so tight they threaten to break my collarbone.

*Screw it! I'll deal with the aftermath. Just do me a favor and die quickly so I can make my escape.*

Her words are drowned out by the rush of water and the beating of my own heart. I stop struggling, not because I've given up but because I need to conserve my strength and I need to think. I have maybe a minute, more if I focus before I run out of breath. I close my eyes and remember my meditations Miss Collins taught me. I reach down into myself. I crawl into the same small cavern that protected me when I was attacked at the Haunted House. In here, the flicker of flame that starts to warm my lungs from lack of air doesn't reach me.

I will not die today.

I look up from the well and see Chamberlain through a window of water, blind, possessed.

In my mind I reach up and finger the willow at my throat. I remember the pendant's twin at Mama's throat and soon I conjure her face smiling at me. The flame in my chest burns hotter, but smaller as I run out of time. Raphael's voice flickers like a ghost in my ears. "You are more powerful than you know."

I will not die today. There is a solution. I'm supposed to be the solution. I can see Mama's whole body now, sitting across from me in the pit inside myself.

Miss Collin's voice joins the chorus, "You can choose to be the solution."

I can only hold my breath so much longer. The flicker is almost out, but its white hot flame is radiating throughout my entire body. My blood starts to feel like lighter fluid. Mama, whose whole body I can see now, crawls over to sit next to me. She seems *so* real. My eyes reflect back to me in hers, and I'm asking the question with a mouth that doesn't move. How do I cast a spell if I can't speak? My purse is on the other side of the pool with the knife Ione gave me, still in its sheath. I am so stupid. Why did I lunge at her? I had a chance. A small one, but I had one and now it's gone.

I am so still that if I weren't being held down, I would float. Mama smiles and begins to sing, and then hum. At first I think she's here to help me pass to the next world, a sure sign I'm dying and then in the space of a long second as I fall into her smile I realize better. I know what to do.

Painfully, I come back to my body. Every muscle quivers violently and my heart pumps gasoline.

I am the solution. I remember the spell and though I have no voice I have a mind. I begin to recite the incantation in my head and I know Lilah hears me. My veins are filled with rocket fuel. Chamberlain's grip loosens, but doesn't let go.

I am the solution.

There is no shield. There is no pool. There is no self. The water begins to bubble. My throat is molten. I only have seconds left. This isn't working fast enough. Maybe I'm like Miss Collins and not a good caster. Maybe the spell is wrong. No, Miss Collins isn't the problem. I am not the problem.

Lilah is the *problem*. Mama's singing is louder, more beautiful than ever, and I get it. It clicks.

I am the solution. I stop reciting the incantation in my head and sing it. This time I hum the melody with my still closed mouth and the tiny bits of breath I have left. The humming is strained and slow at first and then in desperation it vibrates louder and louder until the water around me dances at its rhythm.

I am a supernova.

In a burst of steam, water explodes from the pool, knocking Lilah, Chamberlain and everyone on the edge of the pool flat on their backs.

I clamor to the side of the pool. I'm still gulping air when someone grabs me by the arm and drags me the rest of the way out, sending jolts of electricity down my spine that open my eyes and bring me completely back to the here and now.

Matt.

# CHAPTER THIRTY-EIGHT

Matt doesn't look so good. I don't know what to say, but before I can say anything Lilah grabs him by the back of the shirt and hurls him like a rag doll into the backyard fence.

"How did you do that?!" she yells as her nails dig into the sides of my cheeks. For someone so slight, she's as heavy as a grown man.

Everyone is waking up now. I hear a girl scream, and I know instinctively that they've found Celeste, dead.

"Lilah, what the hell are you doing?" Chamberlain asks. "How the f…What am I doing out here? What was in that punch, Lilah?"

She ignores him. Her face is still intent on me. So intent she doesn't see Matt come at her with a deck chair. The blow blindsides her, and I scramble to my feet. I stumble but Matt is there to catch me, and this time the current running between us is a comfort.

The chair may have slowed Lilah, but it hasn't stopped her. She's not human and to the kids who are looking, that is becoming abundantly clear as claws seem to be erupting from her fingers from bloody cuticles. Chamberlain rushes to her side, but she lands a kick to his chest that should crack bone.

"Don't touch me!" she wails. It sounds like nails on a chalkboard, high, keening and desperate.

Out of the corner of my eye, I can see my bag nearly ten feet away. I'm too far away to reach it. Lilah's steps are long and getting longer as her legs seem to stretch and grow like an insect's. Matt is on my side, and I look at him and then the bag. The hilt of the dagger is sticking out. It's so close and still so far.

Summer lies motionless next to it. While everyone else has woken, she remains entranced. If she could just wake up.

Matt rushes forward, but I catch him by the shirt.

The knife, I say without saying. My eyes flicker to my bag, but he has to know that if he goes for it Lilah will be directly in my path. I plead with my eyes. He has to go for it.

As soon as he dashes away, I'm lifted up in Lilah's claws, hovering high above her. Her gums have gone black and her once pale skin is deepening to pond water green.

Her mouth opens and a clicking sound erupts before she speaks. "You test my patience witch, and I will enjoy watching you die in pain." A second later a claw rips across my throat and bloods spills down my chest. I cry out in pain as she laughs and reaches back again for what I'm sure is the death blow. I'm hanging at a weird angle and I can't see anything but the sky above and in that moment I let go and become calm. I look down at Lilah who with lips drawn into an oval has begun sucking the life from me and smile.

She stops.

"You welcome death witch?" she growls.

I shake my head, catching Summer slowly pushing bag towards Matt with weak fingers. Quickly, I draw my attention back to Lilah, just as the realization hits her face.

"You forget I can see the future, bitch. You lose!" Matt says as he plunges the dagger into Lilah's side.

I drop heavily to the pavement and he stabs her again, twisting the knife for good measure. When he pulls it out, blood, whiter than milk, spills from the wound in great gusts so that he has to back up. He pulls me to him, and we both scuttle to the side to watch her die.

Fetid and sour rivers of blood spurt onto the cement while her body jerks to a beat of her slowing heart.

In under a minute, the only souls left on the deck are Matt, Chamberlain, Summer and I.

Celeste's body still lays lifeless and half-submerged in pool water and Lilah lays unmoving and half-transformed in a pool of her own filth just twenty feet away.

"It's over. Thank you Jesus, it's over. Are you okay?" Matt asks while looking over every part of me. He rips off his shirt to press against the ragged gash on my throat.

I nod, and he hugs me while my eyes remain pinned to Lilah.

"Matt, what did you see before? You said Lilah was going to kill me, but you told her that you saw her lose. Which one was it?"

I don't even look at him, afraid of what he'll say. He lied to one of us. Which one?

"I told you the truth. I saw you die."

With that, I hear something scratch and then thump wetly on the pavement.

We feverishly crawl back several feet as the scratch thump increases until a deafening crackle of bone sprays blood as the inside of her chest cavity opens and folds in on itself. First, a leg stretches out in a lean flesh-like copy of a house fly's, and her naked torso rises as her feet fold backwards, the weight resting on bulging ankles. Her arms shrink into themselves while her shoulders press backwards into bony spikes that sprout massive bat-like wings, the skin veiny, bluish and translucent. Finally, her head pops up as horns spring from her brow in curling bone-like spikes. Her tongue flickers like a snake and she hisses in our direction.

"You whore! Do you know how long it takes to fashion a human form like that? It was perfect and now it's ruined!"

I'm quaking with fear tinged with the slightest bit of anger at Thetis. What good is a knife that doesn't kill?

Lilah hacks out an ear-splitting cough. I'm running through scenarios when I hear the sirens.

"The police!" Chamberlain cries in relief.

She laughs humorlessly, "And what will they do? I gather as much as you have. Nothing. Nothing but PISS ME OFF!" she roars and scoops Summer into her claws and covers her mouth with hers. Summer's legs kick beneath her as she's lifted higher. With each moment that passes Lilah's sickly green skin begins to pale to its original color. Soon, the claws on her fingers begin to retract. Summer's life is giving her beauty.

"She's killing her!" I cry and Matt jumps to his feet. As if they both have the same idea, Matt and Chamberlain rush the creature and try to rip Summer out of her arms. Chamberlain tackles Summer, ripping her out of Lilah's grip while Matt kicks out with one leg, landing directly in Lilah's pelvis. She stumbles, and I jump to my feet.

With foolish confidence he tries for another blow and she catches his arm. This time I hear the wet snap long before his cries ring out. He crumples to the ground, and I rush forward before she roars. Hot, stinking breath flows out in my direction.

In a reflex-quick movement she grabs Matt by the collar and rises off the ground, wings flapping.

"I guess I have to kill him in order to kill you!" she cackles and rises higher, kissing him, sucking the life out of him as she rises.

Out of options I pick up the dagger, now covered in blood and fling it towards her, landing where it could do the most damage, her wings. As the hole opens up she's forced to drop Matt and there's nothing to break his fall when he comes crashing down, and when he hits the ground he doesn't make a sound.

The gash the knife made in Lilah's wings spreads like a cancer until there is nothing left but a skeletal frame, and when she crashes a second later she wastes no time in reaching for Matt.

"No!" I yell with everything in me, my hands outstretched towards him, the air crackles with the fire between us and the connection feels stronger than ever.

Her eyes dart toward me and then to Matt. "W-what are you doing to me?!" she screams through clenched teeth. Every muscle in her body is tensed and impossibly, she hovers at an angle that defies gravity.

"Let go of me you Bitch!" she wails. "Put me down."

"I haven't done anything," I huff.

"She can't move," Matt coughs from behind her and as soon as I take my eyes away she's rushing towards him again. Again I yell and throw my hand up and this time I scream louder than before, almost drowning out the sirens which have gotten even closer.

She's not just moving she's lifted higher. A scream erupts inside my brain and I cry out, loud and ragged, like a dying animal. My ears pop and bleed as Lilah is lifted higher and higher by the force in my outstretched hand. The world falls away and all there is is she and I as the lines of my friends and the form of the trees fall away and all that's left is color, color so bright and living it's like seeing for the first time. The stars rush forward and shine on everything and my body burns with their brilliance. Screaming, I feel my skin begin to loosen and my muscles begin to melt. By instinct I draw in the color around me and funnel it. Every light shines through me, and Lilah begins to wither. I am powerful for precious seconds and then I wither too.

"I told you, it's useless," she whispers and just as my eyes begin to close I see the crack. Thin as mending thread it opens and in a burst of sunlight Raphael appears as if he's walking through a door.

His breastplate gleams, but his sword shines ever brighter and with one strong swipe he swings, and I drop my hand as Lilah's lifeless body hits the ground and her decapitated head turns to ash.

# CHAPTER THIRTY-NINE

Matt won't let me go. The strange or maybe not so strange part is I don't want him to. The police arrest Chamberlain, because it's his house, but Officer John says they'll probably let him go in the morning. Everyone knew it was Lilah who spiked the punch and now that her hold on the Bells is broken, they are spilling all kinds of secrets, her weird initiation rites. How she'd hypnotized Tressa Thornton out of jealousy. Buck is arrested too, after Summer told them what he'd done to her. Every one of the missing girls had been to one of Lilah's parties and every one had been seen with Buck afterward. A fact the police never caught on to.

I won.

I touch the bandage on my neck, and the bruises along my shoulders and wince. I got off lucky.

"Do you want me to rub them for you?" Matt asks.

"No, I'm too sore. I just want to sit here." I know now that Matt didn't have anything to do with Tressa.

The house is a crime scene now. One by one everyone is being interviewed and released. Matt raises so much sand about my injuries, and my fragile mental state that he convinces the officers to interview us together. We're the last ones out.

"So, you two were the only ones who didn't drink the spiked punch?" Officer John asks.

"Lilah's parties get kind of wild. I got there kind of late and there were guys blocking the door. It took me a while to sneak around the back. That's when I saw Collette struggling to get out of the pool."

"Is that when the young lady attacked you and then fled?" the Officer says, enunciating every syllable in the most excruciating way possible.

"Yes."

The Officer stops the tape and pats Matt on the shoulder. I lean into his chest and inhale his scent, Old Spice and Ivory soap. I wrap it around myself like a blanket. I'm tired, and I've successfully convinced the Officer that I couldn't possibly give a statement until tomorrow.

Summer, Buck and Chamberlain are probably telling the truth somewhere in another tent, but Lilah's spiked punch storyline is convincing everyone that this is just a case of a drug party gone wrong. All that's left of Lilah is a pile of ash. Her body flaked away, just like her head minutes after we both crashed back to earth, a fact that I'll be keeping to myself.

When we walk out of the tent into the darkness we emerge just in time to see Celeste's body loaded into the back of the coroner's van. She was the sacrifice in the pool of holy water that allowed Lilah to be weakened enough for me to overcome. I crumple and Matt has to hold me up.

I failed that girl. Whatever I did to help wasn't enough to save her.

I can feel every muscle in his arm, every fingertip pressed into my flesh. I curl into him and turn away.

"Hey, let's get you home," he says tenderly, ignoring his own need to get his broken arm properly set.

"Not yet," I reply. "You need a cast and there's someone I have to see."

###

The crunch from the salt and brick dust wakes Miss Collins before I have a chance to. In fact, I'm surprised she can wake up at all.

"Hey!" she rasps, taking her oxygen mask off. "You won. You made it out okay."

"How did you know I won?"

She dips her head and smiles. "I felt a power shift late last night. The energy changed—for the better. I guess my vital signs picked up and they took me off the dope a few hours ago."

"She's dead. I didn't kill her," I say flatly.

"I didn't tell you to. It's probably better you didn't anyway. Death on your hands changes you."

She smiles at me, and I feel proud of myself for the first time that day. Given the circumstances, I feel like I got off light, like it was almost too easy.

"Look at you! What's this new smile? Proud of yourself?" she jokes.

"I guess, I don't know."

"No, that's not it, though you should be proud of yourself. Not even a full initiate and dealing out banishments like they're candy." She has to stop to catch her breath. She puts the mask back on. She takes a deep breath. "No, this is love on you. Did you see that boy again?"

I giggle nervously.

"Okay!" I announce. "I'm gon' go. I'm exhausted. I just wanted to check in on you. I'll be back tomorrow."

She laughs at me in the way you laugh at a child who put her shoes on the wrong feet.

"Okay child. Be sure you do. We have a lot to talk about. A great deal to do."

She leans back on to the pillows, and I tip toe as best I can out of the room.

As the door clicks shut I come face to face with a nurse. She's young, a little too young to be a nurse, and her smile is big and bright, even though her teeth are not.

"Oh, I'm just leaving," I say apologetically.

"Oh, you're fine honey. I'm just glad somebody visits. You know the ones with no family don't recover as fast," she says cheerfully.

"She's got family," I argue.

"Just 'cause you got family don't mean they treat you like family."

I nod silently and slide to the side so that she can get in the room. I decide to visit longer tomorrow and more often after that.

Matt's standing at the end of the hallway, as solid as an oak tree, offering relief. The stupid girl in me wants to run into his arms, but I don't. I have my self-respect.

And so, I just walk.

# CHAPTER FORTY

"Is that your story to the best of your knowledge," Officer John asks us. We both nod. It turns out that Matt is just as persuasive in real life as he is in my imagination and he convinces the police to let us interview together again the next morning.

"Alright. Let me get this written up. I'll let your Dad in."

"My Dad?" I ask disbelievingly.

He nods and sticks his head out of the office that's become the interrogation space. A second later a handsome older man with a salt and pepper beard walks in. No one else notices, but I can't be fooled. Raphael's divine light is almost blinding.

He holds out his hand to Matt and shakes it. He draws in a deep breath and smiles. "Good man! I can tell. Thank you for taking good care of my angel for me."

Matt stands up shakily, offering his left hand. The other is in a fresh new cast. "Thank you, sir. I mean, you're welcome, sir." He's doing his best to be respectful but nervousness is giving him a sickly snot-colored pallor.

"I'll take over from here," Raphael announces.

Matt nods and gives me a weak parent-appropriate hug before walking out of the room.

"Oooh, he's a good one. That energy must be intoxicating."

"You know what it is?" I ask.

He just smiles.

"He didn't tell them what he saw. He didn't tell them what I can do."

Raphael sighs and smiles again. "I suspect he won't. Unless he wants to tell them what he can do. It is quite amazing," he declares.

"I saw Mama," I announce.

"I know. She's always there when you need her. She's not bound by the same rules I am."

"I know. You're my guardian angel."

He sighs. "Yes, right now that is true. I can't put anything past you."

"So what's happening out there?" I ask and think immediately of Buck.

"Lots of human business. But of most concern to you is Lilah and Buck. Lilah used him to lure the girls, and then took his form as she fed. As long as they think she's still at large, he may come out okay."

"I levitated. I was like Mama. I lifted her up with my mind. What was that?"

"You are more powerful than your mother ever was, the once-in-a-generation Blessed Willow. It's why she bound your powers and kept you home. That ring," he sighs as he points to my finger," is the reason why you were able to call me from Heaven. Ione's ring stripped your mother's spell. It is old magic, almost as old as I am." He chuckles.

I twist the band around my finger.

"Is it over now?" I ask, suddenly impossibly weary.

"Oh dear one. You've done well and this chapter is done. A much longer, bloodier chapter has yet to be written."

"What do I do now?" I yawn.

"Well, first you should sleep and then do what you are blessed to do. Live."

# CHAPTER FORTY-ONE

"Well that's a nice touch," Miss Collins remarks as she peeks out of the window.

It only made sense that she would come to live with me once she got out of the hospital. Her family wasn't really willing to take her in, and I had no family at all. I'd had to convince her that it was only because I needed in depth teaching and not because she needed charity.

"What's that?" I ask.

"He's wearin' a jacket. Young men don't wear enough blazers these days. Oh, and he brought flowers," she sings.

I take a deep breath, but the butterflies are uncontrollable. Even 25 feet away and separated by a wood and a screen door (Miss Collin's addition), I can feel him near me. She says it may just be residual energy. His mother could have been Willow and passed down gifted genes. I'm taking it on faith that it's true, but something Raphael said makes me wonder.

"Calm down. Don't be so nervous. It's just a date."

"My first date," I whine. We both decided not to count the fair debacle. And I insisted we wait until we both had a chance to heal a bit from our injuries.

She smiles and crosses over to me and tucks a tendril of hair back into my bun. I smooth the lace down on my dress, a 1950's era red lace cocktail dress that Vikki had hidden in her special collection at the store.

274

"You look beautiful…and dangerous. Don't forget that."
She winks.

My cheeks get hot, and I can't look her in the face. She'll
never know how much it means to me that she's here with me.
I know now that being alone just won't work. It can't. What's
the point of life if you can't share it with someone? And
besides, I'll need her if my telekinesis flares up again. I've tried
to use it in my bedroom, when I'm alone, but no luck. Maybe it
was a fluke, something I can only access if my life is in danger.

"I'm really glad you're here," I say to her quietly, and I try
not to think of my mother. She would have loved to be here
right now.

"Oh, honey." She gives me a quick hug, and I'm filled with
the warm glow of love. The butterflies mellow out.

He knocks three times. I let Miss Collins answer.

"Evenin' Miss Collins," Matt says formally. He's playing
the part of the polite suitor. It suits him.

"Evenin' Matthew. Come on in," she says, enjoying the
pageantry. "Where y'all goin' tonight?" she asks.

"It's a surprise," he says answering her question but
locking eyes with me. "These are for you."

"Thank you," I say, taking the roses, yellow roses from
him.

"I'll put those in water for you," Miss Collins says as I
hand her the bouquet.

"You look…" we both say in unison and then giggle.

"Nice," I say.

"Breathtaking," he says, and I smile stupidly. "Ready?"

I nod, breath caught in the excitement.

Miss Collins calls for us to have fun as I slip into the front
seat. Before we pull off, I see her slide her hand around her
wrist reminding me of my bracelet. I try not to roll my eyes too
hard.

"Did I tell you that you looked beautiful?" he asks.

"I think you used the word 'breathtaking'," I reply.

"Ah, yes. Well, it's true. You do take my breath away."

I'm too embarrassed to tell him how he really makes me feel in all of its electrified glory, but I do reach over and awkwardly squeeze his free hand.

His face lights up.

It's a short drive before I notice we're on USC's campus. We're a little overdressed for any game activities I think before we pull into the empty parking lot of the Koger Center.

"Are we early?" I ask as he opens my door.

"Nope. Right on time. Trust me?"

"I trust you," I say, but I can't help but be a little nervous, as if I could manage more of the stuff.

We walk around the building to the rear entrance where a chair is propping a door open, spilling light out onto the snake berry bushes. By the time we climb the stairs and reach the balcony, the sound of the trumpets have me floating, and when I realize that there is dancing room in our box seats I'm almost flying. We're the only people in the audience.

He's set a candlelit table for two in our tiny section, tears prick my eyes, and I press my face into his chest, hoping my makeup doesn't ruin his shirt.

"I know you hate crowds, so I worked out a deal with my cousin. He's second chair in the jazz ensemble in the College of Music." He lifts his hand to wave to someone in the orchestra.

The music stops, and I blush at the few whistles and claps that I can hear.

"I can't believe you did all this," I marvel.

"Well, I can't take credit for everything. The orchestra is practicing for a big band concert. It just seemed right."

He wipes the few tears that I let fall from my eyes and presses his lips on my forehead. It's light and soft and the warmth from it makes me break out into a sweat.

The orchestra begins to play *Caravan* and before he lets me go, before I lose my nerve I push up to my tiptoes and kiss him. He tastes like cinnamon and hot peppers and for a second I'm blinded by orange light before the burning in my tailbone sends waves of current through my spine. Behind my eyelids, sparks erupt and dance like fireflies in time with the percussion. We separate with an audible sigh.

"What was that for?" he says breathlessly.

"It was me saying 'yes'." I say quietly into his chest. I can't meet his eyes.

"Wow! I think I had an out of body experience. It felt like I was floating for a second," he murmurs into my hair.

"Oddly, I know exactly what you mean."

CPSIA information can be obtained
at www.ICGtesting.com
Printed in the USA
BVOW03s1533290617
488030BV00002B/125/P